The Lucky Bastard Club

Letters to My Bride from the Left Seat

By

Roy R. Fisher, Jr.

with Susan Fisher Anderson

See more on our website:
www.luckybastardclub.com
or call Authorhouse at:
1-888-280-7715

© 2002 Susan Fisher Anderson. All rights reserved.

No part of this book may be reproduced, stored in a retrieval system, or transmitted by any means, electronic, mechanical, photocopying, recording, or otherwise, without written permission from the author.

ISBN: 1-4107-5646-7 (e-book)
ISBN: 1-4107-5645-9 (Paperback)
ISBN: 1-4107-5644-0 (Dust Jacket)

Library of Congress Control Number: 2003095022

This book is printed on acid free paper.

Printed in the United States of America
Bloomington, IN

1stBooks – rev. 09/24/03

Dedication

This book is gratefully dedicated to the crew of the
"Mission Belle"
without whose cooperation, enthusiasm and spirit
this story might have had a totally different outcome.

It is also dedicated to the memory of those who didn't make it back,
and who didn't have the opportunity
to have children and grandchildren
as we did.

Most important, it is dedicated to our children and grandchildren
so they may know what heroes their dads and granddads were.
A hero is someone who saved somebody's life,
often at the risk of his own.

We had a whole crew of heroes.
Thanks to you all.

Roy R. Fisher, Jr.,
First Pilot of the "Mission Belle"

Table of Contents

Prologue	*vii*
WAR	*1*
Training Begins	*5*
California	*11*
Learning to Fly	*15*
The Basics	*19*
FURLOUGH	*25*
Nine Guys and a Wedding	*29*
Headed for the E.T.O.	*39*
England	*45*
Home Base	*57*
Formation	*63*
Combat	*69*
Home Away from Home — London	*77*
Merseburg	*81*
Borrowed Time	*91*
Lead Crew	*97*
Back Home Again	*107*
Bad Weather, Worse Weather	*115*
Halfway Home	*125*
Almost Christmas	*133*
The Flak House	*147*
Back to the War	*155*
Belgium	*163*
Heading Down the Home Stretch	*165*
Thank You, Mr. Lundgren	*169*
Final Mission	*189*
Heading Home	*197*
Epilogue	*210*
Author/Editor's Note	*215*

Prologue

December 12, 1997

I sat quietly beside the metal hospital bed and held her limp left hand in mine. I had to hold her left, because on her right, the shoulder and chest were swathed in bandage and gauze. Out in the waiting room, the girls – six of our seven grown daughters – paced anxiously, also awaiting the surgeon's report. Her mastectomy was completed; it had gone well, except for a scare with the anesthesia, which had caused her blood pressure to plummet, threatening to take her from me. I gazed steadily at her still form; her breathing regular and slow, machines keeping count, measuring her vital signs. Her hair, still curly but slightly matted from the surgical cap, was now liberally sprinkled – but not completely – with gray, making her appear much younger than her 72 years.

The girls, who had flown in from Indiana, Wisconsin and Oklahoma, were worried as they watched her, their mother, aging, growing more frail; wrinkles appearing on her smooth skin. I didn't see the gray, the wrinkles nor the gradual sagging of flesh that had come with the bearing of eight children. I only saw what I had always seen. I saw my heart, my life and my wife of 53 years. Today, she had lost a breast to cancer. Unlike many husbands in my position, I couldn't have cared less about the breast. Me, I was more concerned about losing her – her laughter, her wit and her cold feet on my back at night.

As I searched her face for signs of awakening from the anesthesia, I thanked God for her. Though bandaged and hospital-gowned, all I could see was the bright face of my nineteen-year-old bride, dressed in the flowing white of her chiffon nightgown, the blue ribbons fluttering slightly as she moved towards me on our wedding night. White for purity, more scoffed at than celebrated these days; yet then, a sign of her virginity; her commitment to save herself for only me. And I, I had saved myself for her, only her. Her fingers moved as she struggled to wake up. Trying to focus on my face, disoriented, I could see them, the bright blue eyes which had captured my heart so many years ago.

Chapter One
WAR

I'm sure if you ask any man of my generation, he would be able to tell you exactly where he was when he heard the news. For me, we were sitting around after dinner at the Sigma Phi Epsilon fraternity house (Sig Ep to those who know) at Iowa State College, in Ames, in December 1941, when my story started. I was a freshman forestry student and considering pledging Sig Ep. We'd had a nice dinner, fried chicken, the way your mother makes it, mashed potatoes made from real potatoes—I could tell by the little flecks of brown skin scattered throughout, along with an occasional chunk of not-quite-mashed potato. And gravy, thick and light brown, made right in the pan after the chicken came out. Green beans, canned at the peak of summer with little chunks of bacon floating here and there, and homemade peach cobbler. It was so good I found myself glancing out the window to make sure it really was winter. The Sig EP's had one of the best cooks on fraternity row, which was a major consideration for a guy like me, away from home for the first time.

We guys were all just relaxing in the living room, letting dinner settle while listening to the radio — there wasn't such a thing as television back then. Suddenly, an emergency news bulletin interrupted the program. The next voice we heard was the familiar voice of our president, Franklin D. Roosevelt. President Roosevelt made a dreadful announcement: the Japanese had attacked Pearl Harbor in Hawaii. I didn't know where Pearl Harbor was, I barely knew where Hawaii was — somewhere out in the Pacific Ocean, where it had no effect on my life whatsoever. Until that wintry afternoon, that is.

Of course, we all knew about what Hitler had been up to in Europe; it had been on all our minds since the draft first started during my senior year of high school. It wasn't the kind of subject which made a great impact on a bunch of Iowa farm boys out in Ames, but it was never far from our minds, either. The war in Europe touched us, but not in a particularly personal way. Up until then, students were exempted from the draft, the intention of the draft being more precautionary than immediate. Suddenly, with that historic broadcast on a frosty, lazy Sunday afternoon, all our lives were changed forever. The war we had been talking about, thinking about, had found us. Found us all.

We were at war. There were mixed reactions. I'm sure most of us didn't really know what to think. War was something your dad did. And after all, we were just a scant 20 years past 'kicking the Kaiser's tail' in The War To End All Wars. In the past year and a half, "the war in Europe" had been a major topic of conversation all over the campus. Guys we all knew had gone to Canada to enlist in the Canadian Air Force to help out our buddies over there. Others had even gone to England to join the American Eagle Squadron of the Royal Air Force. It seemed that every other week, one of our classmates would do poorly on a test and suddenly decide he could do more good in the war, and off he would go to Canada. But with that famous announcement, that "day which will live in infamy," everything was different. What a few minutes earlier had been Europe's war, suddenly became our own. War meant soldiers, soldiers meant men; and that meant us.

Some guys began making plans to leave early in the morning to travel the thirty miles south to Des Moines, the state capital, to enlist. Some made immediate plans to get married — husbands were also exempt. Others decided to enlist in the Reserves in order to be able to say they were doing their part, while still being able to stay in school until graduation. Then we could go into the service with a commission — as officers, serve a couple of years and be done.

One thing was clear: unless you were married, blind or crippled, you were going to war. *I* was going to war — although I don't think that I really understood what that meant at that point in my life. For us young bucks, it was a chance to prove our manhood, join the team, play soldier. Fight for Uncle Sam.

The memories of "The Big War" were still pretty fresh in the minds of the nation. We'd seen photographs and newsreels about life in the trenches. We'd seen the rain and mud. Heard the horror stories about trenchfoot, etc. We'd seen the 'doughboys' in their flying saucer helmets and muddy knee boots trudging stoically through foreign battlefields. We knew what war was. And me, I was no stranger to soldiering. I had already spent three years in Infantry

R.O.T.C. in high school and was currently enrolled in the Horse-drawn Field Artillery at Iowa State.

I knew how to handle a rifle, of course I did. All us country boys could shoot. The Field Artillery was good exercise — freshmen groomed the horses — although we spent a good deal of our time playing polo, (officially, exercising the horses). It was a lot more fun than infantry, but still the images of muddy boots and wide-brim helmets stuck in my mind. I thought to myself that if I were to be drafted, that's probably where I'd end up. As a first-quarter freshman, eighteen years old, my hopes of being anything but "troops" were mighty dim.

However, times were changing and so was warfare. War was evolving just like the rest of the world. Besides that, my dad had been a pilot in the Signal Corps in WWI, and I had grown up listening to Pop's stories about flying. He had been one of the glamour boys — the barnstorming pilots of what had evolved into the Army Air Corps. Consequently, it didn't take much to convince me that the Air Corps was the place for me. That would be a great place to serve my country.

So the question became, How to get into the Air Corps? My plan quickly came together. First, enlist in the Army Air Corps Reserve, and then get a college degree so I could qualify for Flight School. It seemed like a good plan. And it was—for the next year.

America jumped into the war with both feet. Very quickly, the draft was no longer just precautionary. Now they needed soldiers, all kinds of soldiers. And quick. All over the country young men began to leave home as they were called up. The whole country began to knuckle down and get serious about this war thing. After all, war was still pretty vivid in the memories of the adult generation. And me, though I was involved in the reserves, the war still didn't touch me in a real personal way. I was still in college learning about trees, still had three squares — good ones — at the Sig Ep House, still could go home on an occasional weekend to visit the folks less than 200 miles away in Davenport. Life was still pretty normal for a college guy.

Then in December, 1942 the Selective Service began to run short of draftees. An order was issued to Reserve Units all over the country: Get your reserves in uniform and into training or they will be drafted. College students were no longer exempt from the draft. So much for my plan. Within a few weeks, I got my orders to report to Jefferson Barracks, Missouri, for induction. It was time to become a real soldier.

Chapter Two
Training Begins

BASIC TRAINING JEFFERSON BARRACKS
ST. LOUIS, MISSOURI   FEBRUARY 1943

It was mighty cold in St. Louis in February of 1943. Jefferson Barracks was up on a hill not far from the river. Not that we could really see the river, but we knew it was down there close by. We could feel the wind. The barracks were plank walls and windows with no insulation whatsoever. This was the army and soldiers didn't need all that fancy fluff. I guess it really wasn't that different than Iowa in February, except that this was real life now. Not college, not ROTC, where I'd been having a good time — working hard, but having a good time nevertheless — playing soldier with my buddies. Now we were really away from home. Not some cozy fraternity house, with house mother, meals and a warm bed. Nope, this was winter in the army. Cold reality — blustery cold. Yup, this was real, or perhaps I should say surreal.

It was at Jefferson Barracks where we were introduced to the real army. Even the uniform made me look like a buck private in the infantry, which would have been funny if it hadn't been so real. We had to send all our suitcases home, with all our regular clothes, and we received our introduction to the army way of life. Hurry up and wait. We spent most of our time the first week waiting for something to happen, we even waited in line for chow up to an hour some days. We got poked, prodded and stuck with needles. Some of the guys got real sick from the typhoid shots. I think I got a touch of typhoid myself. And we drilled. And drilled. For hours at a time up on jeep hill, the coldest place on earth, I think. We learned that, although we were part of the Air Corps, the Air Corps was part of the Army.

We also learned some valuable skills, like scrubbing floors on our hands and knees and waiting for inspection. And we learned the value of mail call. It was our only link with the real world and a nation which was itself, hunkering down for war.

Mom's letters were a point of contact, a connection to the life we had left behind. War is a terrifying thing, and there is nothing like the mundane things of home — crops going in, new puppies being born, even the old cow that died — to make a guy feel connected. Mom sent cookies and candy with her letters, and clean laundry. The goodies tasted so good. The guys all raved about them. I sent her my sugar ration book so we could have more. Most of the other guys in our platoon were city boys, or collegians, with a sincere desire to serve their country, to be sure; but in all practicality with little or no concept of what it meant to be a soldier. In that environment, my background in R.O.T.C. was quite obvious. I knew my right from my left; and had some aptitude and knowledge of the idea of marching in rows. I was made a platoon leader. Not commissioned, just giving commands, and trying to explain close order drill. We had to get to chow and had to get there in step. It was an amazing incentive.

Uniforms, drill, army chow, and a taste of the real army. Jefferson Barracks was also a basic training camp for regular army, and if we screwed up, that's where we'd wind up. It was a very short hike to the other side of the camp; one mistake, one misstep and you might never be heard from again. The 'regular army' would suck you in so deep, nobody would ever know what happened to you. That was another powerful incentive.

We were under the care, custody and control of Sergeant White. He was not at all convinced that College Boys could ever make soldiers, but he was determined to give it his best shot. Sergeant White had the biggest voice in the World. He could holler "where ya goin' BOY?" and from a block away you'd stop in your tracks. As for the poor fellows who didn't know their right from their left, Sgt. White gave them a rock to carry. And the more they forgot, the bigger the rock. In retrospect, he had a very difficult job: turn college boys into men in six weeks. Darn near impossible.

COLLEGE TRAINING DETACHMENT
DECATUR, ILLINOIS   MARCH 1943

After surviving basic training, we college boys were sent to colleges all over the country for CTD. CTD was like an accordion file for the Army. Because of the urgency of the war, they had a lot more recruits for pilot school than they had spaces to put them. Pilot training started a new class every month and there were a limited number of spots available. CTD is where they tested, sorted and culled the field of candidates to eliminate the ones who might not be able to cut it as pilots. Pilots were extremely valuable, both because of the job they would do in the war, and because of the extensive investment it took to train them. At CTD they would determine whether or not we were officer material.

We were all candidates for pilot training and math was the main criterion. Guys with good math skills could be trained as pilots, co-pilots, bombardiers and navigators. The other guys in the Air Force Reserve were destined for the more basic jobs, like gunners. We had to understand arithmetic because we would have to be our own navigators. A basic understanding of geometry was necessary in order to understand the concept of flying in a multi-dimensional environment; and to be able to grasp the concept of airspeed and wind velocity. I had already taken Statistics at Iowa State, so, in the math department, I went to the head of the list.

I was sent to James Millikin University in Decatur, Illinois. We let the town know we were there by a big parade down the main street, marching in formation and singing the Air Corps Song at the top of our lungs. Back then, it seemed as though Decatur had never seen soldiers up close before, and so we were treated royally. If we went to church on Sunday, we got invited to homes for home-cooked Sunday Dinner. If the household didn't have college-age girls, they invited some to come over and help cook or serve.

We were quartered in groups of fifty men, in barracks — which wasn't so good; but it was far better than the conditions we had endured at Jefferson Barracks. We were all thankful to have left there head first, rather than feet first. Alive, instead of dead. Basic Training can be hard on a guy.

CTD is where they separated the pilots from the infantry. Here is where they would school us in basic subjects, test our intelligence and choose the ones they wanted to invest in as pilots. The better you did, the quicker you might be assigned to Pre-Flight — the first step to becoming a pilot. They tested us in all the basic subjects: Math, physics, history, English and Geography. I passed out of most of them, so all I would have to take was Medical Aid, Civil Air Regulations and flying. I was especially excited about the flying part. As it turned out, I had to take some refresher courses in Math and History, more to have something to do than because I needed the study.

They made me a lieutenant and gave me a platoon to manage. All the drilling and direct discipline of the men was our responsibility as a cadet officer. It was a big responsibility, but good training, especially for me. At the beginning of our stay at Millikin, they fed us at restaurants or in the girls' dorm. Then our mess hall was completed and the quality of the chow began to deteriorate until it was low even for army standards. We all looked forward to Sundays. I wanted to get a weekend pass to go home, but it became more and more obvious that unless you were married, or had folks come to visit, that a pass wasn't going to happen. One weekend, just before my birthday, a bunch of folks from Davenport came down to visit their boy. Decatur was only a hundred miles or so from Davenport. It was great to have a real "Davenport Day" but I sure missed the folks, my folks.

Then, one Saturday morning, they called. They were going to try to come down. It really seemed impossible at the time, but they came, all of them, Pop and Mom and my two brothers — and they brought Joyce. That would be Joyce Day, my girlfriend from home. Perhaps now is a good time to tell you about Joyce. I had first met her in March 1940 at St. Johns Methodist Church. I was a junior and she was a sophomore at Davenport High School.

It was Epworth League night (Methodist Youth Fellowship). We met in the basement of the education wing. I was at the bottom of the long, wide, straight staircase, when this lovely girl started to descend the stairway. Man, she was pretty. About 5 feet tall, dark hair, plenty of curves in all the right places and the sparkliest blue eyes I think I'd ever seen. I'd never seen her before, and since I knew everyone, I figured she must be new in town.

Of course, I took on the job of making sure she felt welcome. That was a job I relished that night. Her family had just moved to Davenport from Burlington — a little town down the Mississippi River, about 90 miles from Davenport. I did the chivalrous thing and introduced her around, but I never quite let her go. I offered her a ride home that night — I often took girls home after the meeting. One of the other girls I took home that night was incensed that I took Joyce home last that night. It was sort of an indication of which gal I liked the best.

We chatted as I drove her home. I knew exactly which house. They had moved into the Melversled house at the top of Fulton Ave.

The Lucky Bastard Club

My dad was in real estate so I knew my way around town pretty well. She was the second of five children. Her older sister had stayed in Burlington to finish high school, so Joyce was the oldest at home. Her dad was in the insurance business, and eventually became a man of some influence in Davenport. She was sharp. I could tell, even from the little conversation we had that night, that this was no dumb girl. No, she was cute *and* smart and not afraid to reveal either. I don't know whether I believed in "love at first sight" or not, but that was the closest I ever came.

That night was the beginning of what would turn out to be the best thing that ever happened to me. Something in me didn't want to let her out of my sight. I took her home, last, all that year and the next — my senior year. I finally got up the nerve to kiss her sometime in December. I only took her on one date that I remember, to Easter Breakfast at High Y (the YMCA's high school fellowship group). After I graduated, we went on a couple of dates that summer, before I went off to college at Iowa State. I considered her "my girl," however; she didn't feel the same. She dated several boys during her senior year, while I was away.

The summer of '42 I was off to Forestry Camp in South Dakota. I guess I was rather incommunicado, because I received a postcard from Joyce. On the back was one word: Dead? I laughed out loud and quickly sent off a card to her, which also was only one word: Nope. Then I sent her a nice long letter. Fortunately, the letter arrived first or it would have been over right then and there. We spent some time together after camp, but when she went off to Cornell College in Mt. Vernon in the fall, she still considered herself a free agent.

Joyce was smart and beautiful, so she was a very popular coed at Cornell. But, thanks to Janie — a friend and fellow student at Iowa State (who, I think, would have liked to be more than my buddy) and who's father happened to be the postmaster in Mt. Vernon — I found out Joyce was dating, somewhat seriously. I quickly made plans to visit her in Mt. Vernon just before Thanksgiving. At the time she wasn't overjoyed to see me, but during the Christmas break we spent some time together and by then, I knew I was hooked, and — I hoped — so was she.

Roy R. Fisher, Jr. with Susan Fisher Anderson

For her 18th birthday, Feb. 7th, 1943, I asked Joyce to wear my fraternity pin. She accepted. The Sig Ep heart fit nicely with the Arrow pin she wore from her social group at Cornell. She was a freshman at Cornell and was wearing my pin, writing to me frequently and all, but still, with all the changes coming in my life, I didn't know what would happen to "us," Joyce and me. We hadn't talked seriously about marriage and I was far away. Guys were even then beginning to get the dreaded "Dear John" letters.

So, when Pop and Mom brought her with them that weekend in April, I was sure glad to see her. What a great weekend we had. It was the last one we would have together for a long time, so it was extra special. I hadn't realized just how much I really had missed them all. I felt like the luckiest guy in the world to have such swell folks and such a fine girl. I only hoped I could live up to everyone's expectations.

As the war loomed larger, it became more evident that I didn't want to spend my life without Joyce. It really got me thinking about the future — after the war. Sure, we had talked about our "future" together, but there's nothing like a war to bring things into sharp focus. I don't remember whether we talked about marriage that weekend or not, but a lifetime with Joyce was definitely on my mind, then and from then on. The war was still a far away, though, both physically — it was way over in Europe and across the Pacific Ocean — and mentally — we knew it was where we were eventually headed, if it continued, but we were still a long way, training-wise, from orders overseas. After all, we were just barely enlisted; we didn't even know how to fly yet. It was coming, though.

I passed all my courses at Millikin with flying colors, and when I got on the flight schedule, I loved it. We only got about 10 hours of dual instruction while in Decatur, but it was enough to help me know why Pop had loved it so much, and why it was where I wanted to spend the war. In the air.

Chapter Three
California

PREFLIGHT TRAINING
SANTA ANA, CALIFORNIA   MAY 1943

Six weeks restricted to base. How unfair was that? I had never in my life been to California. I would love to have seen some of the Pacific Ocean but restrictions prevented it. Our destination was secret, but we traveled by train from Decatur to Ft. Worth and on and on with nothing to do on the train but write letters or play bridge. When we arrived at Santa Ana Army Base, we were given a form letter to send home, I guess to insure that the boys would let their families know where to find them. The form letter was the CO's way of "letting you know where I am and that I am well." It arrived in Davenport in an official War Department envelope with the words GOOD NEWS prominently stamped on the front. I suppose that not all the mail from the War Department was Good News.

Before beginning pre-flight we had to endure classification. It consisted of more tests, more physical exams, more drills. The mental tests lasted all day and were like all your college finals in just one day. They were rugged. Just outside of Los Angeles, it was beautiful country, but it was a long way from home and we were restricted to the base. Fortunately we had too much to do to get homesick. Test, test, test, drill, drill, drill. I got used to my 'pattin leather shoes' — leather shoes <u>pattin'</u> on the ground. They made me the guidon bearer (the standard or flag for the squadron), mostly because I could pronounce the word correctly and also knew what it meant. When we mustered for parade, there were soldiers as far as I could see on both sides — with my peripheral vision, of course, since as the guidon bearer I couldn't turn my head. We were occupied from sun up to sun down, and busier than a toad under a harrow — that's busy.

Finally, I was classified as a <u>pilot,</u> and the folks got more GOOD NEWS. It would still be a few weeks until our transfer to pre-flight — still on the base at Santa Ana, so I tried to keep busy with other activities. The company commander gave me the job of getting some grass started around the barracks. I raked and watered and sowed, and finally got some grass to sprout. I guess you can take the boy out of Iowa, but you can't take the Iowa out of the boy.

We also had some time to bivouac up in the mountains, camping and hiking for a whole week. It was great for me, a forestry student and Eagle Scout, but was nearly the undoing of some of the city boys in our squadron. By the time we hiked the 15 miles back to the base, we all had a week's growth of beard and I was feeling better physically than when I first went to Jefferson Barracks. It was June and the country was gorgeous, but it was also Father's Day and I really got to thinking about my dad. I guess a fellow never realizes how much he has to be thankful for until he gets away from home and school and gets into competition with others. Anyway I didn't. Little lessons that were so hard to learn at the time — like doing the job right the first time — and doing it in spite of any obstacles, help a lot when you get in a place where they don't give you a second chance.

But, the most valuable thing Pop ever taught me was something that he and Mom did unconsciously and it meant more than anything else. They taught me how to live a life; how to have a good time doing things that don't cost any money. They taught me what a beautiful experience love is and how it is to be treated with the utmost respect and reverence. The little chats they each had with me helped, but in their everyday lives I could see it working and that's what it took to really convince a fellow like me. Then, when I met Joyce, I was thankful — as they said I would be — that I had never had any intimate experience with other girls. Joyce was such a sweet kid and her ideals for a home and family life were so marvelous that, were it not for such a swell background of my own, I could never have measured up to her standards.

Pop and Mom also helped me to make religion an active rather than a passive factor in my life. They led me to see God's presence in everyday things and especially in the out of doors. Perhaps that was one reason why I chose Forestry as a profession. As I reflected on my upbringing on that Father's Day, I remember hoping that Joyce and I could keep up the good work for another generation, for, after all is said and done, the family is the basis of all we believe and live and hope for.

It wasn't like that for other guys on our post. The cadet uniform really drew the women, and many of the guys used that to their full advantage. One night we went down the beach to Balboa where they were having a big dance. The idea seemed to be to get a woman and get her out on the beach as soon as possible. I couldn't take it. I went home and went to bed. The people out there were different than the down-home folks I was used to. Most of the coastal towns were in the business of keeping the servicemen happy and satisfied in more ways than one. It sure is lonesome out in California all by yourself. I finally broke down and spent five bucks to call Joyce in Mt. Vernon. It had been 13 weeks since I had talked to her. It was worth every penny to hear her voice. I sure missed her.

Pre-flight was where we took all our classes on aircraft identification. We had to know the name, designation and span for about 45-50 US and British planes. Where's your little brother when you need him? Ted, my kid brother, knew them all. He would have loved seeing all the planes, especially the P-38's diving, climbing and fighting. We also studied Radio code, learned to take it down. Also math — which was easy for me — and gunnery. I was a flight lieutenant and also the academic section leader — we got graded both for our conduct in class and in going to and from class.

The squadron party, celebrating our graduation from pre-flight, was dinner and dancing in the Blossom Room of the Roosevelt Hotel in Hollywood. I wished Joyce could have made it, but it was out of the question. I called a friend who was living in California, Twila, who picked me up and went as my date, instead. Twila was a schoolteacher, slightly older than I, who had lived in the upstairs apartment in our house during my high school years. We got to be quite good friends and she started dating my Scoutmaster, Doc Parker. Mom had kept me up to date with her doings. She and Doc were pretty serious and I was glad for her. Spending a little time with her was almost like seeing the folks, she was so much like family. Besides, as Pop always said, "Why would you take a girl to a show? You pay for two tickets and only see one show. A dance, however, is different — you can't dance with yourself." I was really glad she could come. It eased some of the loneliness I was feeling.

So, we graduated from preflight. Since our section had scored so well both academically and in other areas, we got to vote where to go for Primary. We voted for Hemet, not far from Santa Ana, and we got it. Now we could really get started. Finally, I might get to see the *inside* of an airplane for a change.

Roy R. Fisher, Jr. with Susan Fisher Anderson

Army Air Corps Cadet

Chapter Four
Learning to Fly

PRIMARY FLIGHT TRAINING
HEMET, CALIFORNIA   SEPTEMBER, 1943

Hemet was a very different animal from the other army posts I had visited. The school was run by civilians and was like a little community. Even the mess hall was air-conditioned. We were quartered in 12-man cottages — a sort of duplex arrangement with 2 baths and closets. Most of the area was in lawn or shrubs and flowers. It was really beautiful, especially since I was missing the flowers and gardens of home. Pop was famous for his roses. Our time was very full, but not so structured as before. Classes included Engines, Aircraft, Navigation, Japanese aircraft identification and stuff like that there. Our ships were fast little Ryans; low-winged, smooth-looking jobs. I couldn't wait to get into one.

My first flight instructor was Mr. Lundgren. He had been an Instructor in Canada, and was not only a good and patient instructor, he was also very familiar with winter flying conditions. I learned more than just how to keep from killing myself in a PT-22 (Ryan).

The PT-22 was a very forgiving aircraft. It had a special landing gear with an elbow, which allowed a drop in the landing without damaging the landing gear — very handy for new pilots who were notorious for rough landings. Most of those little, quick airplanes were so top-heavy and the stick was very sensitive. When landing, a little too much brake on one side or the other and the plane would spin around to that side, hitting the wingtip on the ground — sometimes even flipping over while spinning — and breaking the landing gear on that side. That was a ground loop, which was characteristic of many primary trainers, particularly the Steerman — nicknamed the "yellow peril." The Ryan PT-22 had a wide landing gear, which minimized the built-in ground loop.

During that early training, I began to have some doubts as to whether I really was pilot material, since every time we landed I had to run behind the plane and toss my cookies. Funny thing, though, after my first solo, I was OK. I never got airsick again. Our first days of flying were fraught with one accident or another near disaster. One day it seemed like everything went wrong. I made two landings against the flag and one in the take off strip, but that was mild compared to what some of the other fellows did. One of the boys stopped out in the runway and another ship ran into him. They waved all the rest of the ships off the field and gave them the red light — meaning "Do Not Land Here." <u>Nine</u> ships landed against the light <u>on the main mat</u> (the main runway). Those guys got confined to the post for the duration of their stay. We were lucky the accidents weren't worse.

After a few hours under my belt, I was beginning to catch on to flying. I wasn't so stiff at the controls, and I was beginning to remember to use my rudder. The PT-22 was a hot little ship, landing at about 70mph most of the time. Mr. Lundgren was the tail-chewing type, who griped from the time we took off till we landed, but he was a good instructor and a pretty nice guy. I figured out why I was getting airsick and started moving my eyes around more, looking at instruments and outside. The nausea really calmed down to where I was no longer afraid of getting sick upstairs. Flying was really marvelous. At six hours, we did spins and stalls, wing overs and lazy eights. And then, it was time to solo. I really wasn't expecting it that day either. There was no fanfare, no announcement, no preface, "Mr. Fisher, you've been doing a great job and I think it's time for you to go it alone." Nope. It wasn't like that at all. We were at an auxiliary field, ready for the next take-off when Mr. Lundgren got out of the plane and said, "Take it around the pattern". So I did. And it was an exhilarating feeling to know that you had taken off and landed safely, all by yourself. Maybe I was smart enough to be a pilot after all.

There's nothing like solo flight. Nothing but you and the airplane. You take the plane up by yourself and fly around, with beautiful puffy clouds to buzz through, and all that sky. Some clouds have hard centers, if another solo pilot has the same idea at the same time from the other side. No, there's nothing like your first solo. I guess it's kind of like when you were a little kid, learning to ride a bicycle. You flop back and forth from the right training wheel to the left one; right, left, right, left. Then, all of the sudden, you "get it." You finally understand the concept of motion and balance; and your dad lets go and you ride by yourself. What a thrill. Now the actual learning could begin.

So, we began to learn the things that would save our lives when we got to combat: stalls, steep turns, climbing & gliding turns, side stages — how to approach the runway from 90 degrees with another aircraft doing the same, opposite of you and land parallel, without hitting each other. Spins — how to get into one, and more importantly, how to get out of one. Here is where the foundations were laid. Although a PT-22 is a very different airplane from a B-17, the concepts are the same, like riding a bigger and bigger bike. Of course, there's more to do and keep track of when you have four engines instead of just one; and nine people on board, instead of just you. But the basic concepts are the same. The techniques may vary slightly, depending on the circumstances, but the goal is the same: take off, maintain level flight, land in one piece. Those concepts I can thank Mr. Lundgren for teaching me.

As the hours piled up, my flying continued to improve. I learned how to handle bumpy air and do all sorts of tricks. Slow rolls were hard for me, though. I was so small, I couldn't get the stick far enough forward while hanging from my safety belt. I tried it with three pillows behind me and it worked pretty well. We ate, drank, slept, thought and wrote flying. I loved it. Once I even did an over-the-top spin out of a steep turn and then a slow roll, since I had a lot of air speed. My weak stomach was a thing of the past. I had made up my mind that the sky was a pretty swell place to be. I was only sorry that I was learning to fly to kill. That was a pity, since flying in itself is such a clean, free feeling. None of us want to fight except when something we love is at stake; but then we'd stake our strength, ideals, lives if necessary to back up our ideas.

All I really wanted to do in this life was to settle down with Joyce and raise a family and try to make my home as happy and satisfactory as my folks had done. As long as I could do that, I didn't want to fight with nobody over nothing. But, when somebody stands up and says I can't do that; then that poor son of a gun has picked himself a fight and will probably find himself on the short end of the rope. I guess it's always good to remember why you're there.

And so we flew. Several hours at a time, seven days a week. Six hours turned into sixty very quickly. Mr. Lundgren taught us everything there was to know about flying, and some extra things as well. One day when the temperature at the flight line was well over

Roy R. Fisher, Jr. with Susan Fisher Anderson

100°, we gathered under the wing – the only shade in sight – for a few more of Mr. Lundgren's words of wisdom. In the shadow of that wing, in the autumn of 1943, Mr. Lundgren, our Canadian flight instructor, taught me the most valuable thing I learned in Pilot School: If you can't stop on snow or ice pull off the runway with power, use your rudder when you don't have brakes. It's the same concept as they now use in space with thrusters. That skill he taught me that hot day in California, later saved my life and the lives of my crew. Instructor Lundgren — a mighty force in my life — who taught me, "Keep your nose up, and your head out of the cockpit."

Chapter Five
The Basics

BASIC FLIGHT TRAINING
GARDNER, CALIFORNIA   NOVEMBER 1943

After the relative luxury and comfort of Hemet, Gardner Field was like a corner of Santa Ana — a G## d### army post again — except for the flight line. We slept in barracks and ate in a regular mess hall. The field was beautiful, though, with the buildings painted ivory and lots of grass and trees. Behind headquarters there was a big grassy square with a pen of pheasants at each corner. It made me homesick for the miles and miles of already-harvested cornfields of Iowa. No better place on earth to hunt pheasant.

Before we could fly we had to endure the customary orientation lectures on such interesting subjects as the Articles of War, "Military Discipline, Courtesies and Customs of the Service," and Sex Hygiene. I was bored stiff. Then there were some orientation tests in ground school before we could meet our instructors and start flying. It was November and the folks were talking about trying to come out for Christmas and bringing Joyce along. I doubted her father would allow her to come. Mr. Day wasn't anxious to lose their girl — I couldn't blame them, we all loved her. I really wanted to see them — and her. If not at Christmas, it might be graduation — three more months — before I would get a furlough long enough to come home.

Our Basic Aircraft was a Vultee BT-13. It also was a single-engine job, with a long, enclosed cockpit where the Instructor sat in the seat behind the student pilot — me. It was very different than the PT's we flew in Basic. This plane flew like a truck. The cockpit was like a great big greenhouse with room enough for seven other guys and a crap game. The seat was a big high chair overlooking the nose and most of the surrounding country. I spent most of my hour-long check ride just flying around and trying to get used to sitting so far up in the air. I must have done all right, though. The instructor, in the back seat, propped his feet up on the rail and went to sleep.

We began a grueling schedule of ground school, LINK (flight simulator) and flight time, trying to get finished with our flying while the weather was clear. Bad weather would only prolong the training.

We flew both day and night some days and I was getting dark circles under my eyes — getting less sleep than I had in college. We started learning to fly formation, a real change since up to now I had been spending most of my time trying to avoid other planes and now the idea was to fly among them without hitting them. What a job! But it was necessary for flying the big heavy bombers like B-17's. I had decided finally that those were what I wanted to fly, since I had a choice. I was a little concerned about my size to start with, then some WAAF's (Women's Army Air Forces) got picked up by a B-17-G with a girl for a copilot. I guessed that if she could fly it, I could.

The main purpose of the training at Gardner was to learn to fly instruments. It is absolutely imperative that a combat pilot learn to trust his instruments, and not just fly by "the seat of his pants." He must learn to control the aircraft without reference to anything outside the cockpit, because you can't always trust what you feel or see. And sometimes, you can't see anything. This training makes it possible to fly in clouds, fog, or at night, and keep the plane straight and level. In England, we would spend a lot of time in the clouds, and with lots of airplanes trying to share the same sky.

To learn the concept of flying by instruments, you train with a hood-like contraption which covers the inside of the cockpit and prevents you from seeing anything but the instrument panel. In the other seat, behind the student, the Instructor Pilot can see both inside and outside. Sounds easy, but it means constantly cross checking the instruments against each other, to be sure nothing is out of sync. As I was learning, I would focus on one instrument, while another would get out of line. I couldn't seem to keep track of all of them at once. My airspeed wasn't constant, I wasn't flying level, and I couldn't make a consistent steep turn. I found myself losing or gaining three to five hundred feet of altitude each time I tried. Finally the instructor got fed up.

"Mr. Fisher, you don't seem to be able to trust your instruments. Go down to 2500 feet. No, that's not low enough. Take it down to fifteen hundred feet."

Which shouldn't have been a problem except that the elevation of our field was 1,000 ft. Under the hood, I couldn't see anything but the instruments. Not the sky, not the ground, nothing but the instrument panel. As I watched the altimeter unwind, I was painfully conscious of the fact that in the past hour I had gained or lost 500 feet or more several times in one steep turn or another.

"Now do a steep turn."

I took a deep breath and put the ship into a 20° bank.

The IP said, "I said a steep turn."

Sitting behind me, he had his own stick. So, not satisfied with my timid 20°, he rolled it up to 60°.

"OK. Now do a steep turn."

I was only about 500 feet off the deck. And we did steep turns for two hours. I learned what instrument flying was meant to be that day. I don't know how many times that training saved my life over the next fourteen months. But, I know it was a lot. In fact, instrument training was probably the single most important factor in pilot survival as the war went on.

Christmas plans fell through as the time for the end of our training closed in. I was lonely, homesick and generally tired of the whole deal with no one to share my troubles with. Our Christmas pass ended up being only three days with a 200-300 mile radius limit on our travel. They had us and they weren't about to let us get too far away. I had several invitations to spend the holiday with fellows whose families were close and ended up spending it in Ventura with a lovely couple, the Finsters. They still send us a Christmas card every year.

When our leave was over, we came back to conversation about Marfa, our next stop. It sounded pretty rough, but I figured it couldn't be any worse than Jefferson Barracks. And Texas was a lot closer to home than California.

ADVANCED FLIGHT TRAINING
MARFA, TEXAS   JANUARY, 1944

All our training up to now had been in southern California. Now we were shipped to Marfa, Texas. Marfa is at the foot of the Davis Mountains in southwest Texas. This is the area where the Marfa Lights appear. We heard about them from the Advanced Class. They told us stories and assured us that if we said anything about seeing the Marfa Lights, we would get washed out. Needless to say I never saw the lights, or if I did, I never admitted it — and haven't admitted it yet. We were in the central time zone, but so far to the west side of it that it sort of threw the whole day out of joint.

We were quartered in regular barracks and I think, especially after our time in California, it was colder in Marfa than it had been at Jefferson Barracks. It wasn't just my imagination or perception. It was really cold. In fact, records set for cold temperatures in Texas during the late winter and early spring of 1944 still stand nearly 60 years later. Did I mention it was cold?

These barracks had concrete floors with two coal stoves for heat and separate latrines — with the hot water noticeable by its absence. But, the meals were marvelous — each meal a banquet. Almost as soon as we arrived on post, we were measured and fitted for our Officers' Uniforms. Upon graduation as officers, they would relieve us of our GI clothes so it was pretty important to get them ordered on time. We couldn't wear them until the big day, graduation, only about two months away.

The first order of business at a new training site is to get a DOLLAR RIDE. The Dollar Ride is an orientation flight, and a good method of showing the student pilots the local area, including restricted areas. It also included a brief overview of the new aircraft, and a chance for the Instructor Pilot to get in a few choice comments. My dollar ride in the AT-17, twin-engine trainer was only 35 minutes long, on January 15, 1944; just a short hop around the area — my first time out in a multi-engine aircraft — and the flaps stuck down.

One day shortly after my arrival in Marfa, I ran across Hubie Ruggles in the chow line. Hubie was a friend of Joyce's and mine — half of a pair of twins — who had briefly dated Joyce's older sister, Joanne. I had seen him back at Santa Ana but then lost track of him until Marfa. He was in Class 44B, the class ahead of me, and was set graduate and get his wings in about a month. We were Class 44C, set to graduate in March, 1944. The day before Class 44B graduated, a mid-air collision resulted in a tragedy. It hit us all pretty hard, especially me. Hubie Ruggles was in one of the aircraft involved. They were circling in upper traffic when the two planes collided. All four student pilots bailed out, but only three chutes blossomed. Hubie was blown out with his seat and by the time he could get his safety belt unfastened and his chute open, it was too late to break his fall. Hubie didn't make graduation.

It took longer for the hours to count up since for each hour of logged time, we had to fly two, one as pilot and another as passenger. Until we soloed and were checked out we always had three people in the airplane: two student pilots and an instructor. So, I had many opportunities to learn the ups and downs of multi-engine flying — the ups were easier than the downs. Cross country, night flying, night formation flying, instruments. All the same skills adapted to a different aircraft. Like riding a bike. I learned to turn away from a dead engine, and learned to use the radio compass. We did a lot of Beam Work, learning to fly the radio beam to let down onto the field. Since radar wasn't much in use yet — we didn't have any — most of our navigation was done by radio compass in addition to our regular compass.

Each field had a radio station broadcasting Morse Code signals from a point which lined up with the runway of that particular field. In each of the four compass quadrants, a different signal was broadcast so you would know where you were in relation to that station. The northwest and southeast quadrants broadcast the letter N (dash dot), while the opposite two quadrants (southwest and northeast) were broadcasting the letter A (dot dash). If you heard a steady tone, you were "on the beam" –on the compass point N, S, E, or W. The sound would get louder as you approached the station and weaker as you moved away. Directly over the station was the cone of silence — an area of no sound, which broadened as your altitude increased. When you hit the cone of silence, you knew you were directly over the station — in line with the runway–and it was time to get landing instructions from the tower.

So, if you were approaching a field from the southwest, you would hear the letter A repeated, and growing steadily louder. If you suddenly began to hear the N, you would know you had passed to the south of the field and were now southeast of it. It was a primitive system by today's standards, but it worked. Most of the time.

When we passed our check, we would be instrument-rated and qualified to fly in all sorts of soup. I was ready to solo in the AT-17 on January 20th and ten days later we started learning to fly in formation. We practiced formation flying a lot during those few weeks, not knowing how crucial that would be to our survival in combat. Over those two months, we learned a lot more.

Roy R. Fisher, Jr. with Susan Fisher Anderson

Graduation from Advanced Training was very special and we all looked pretty spiffy in our new officer's uniforms. Mom and Pop drove out from Davenport to attend the graduation, and Mom pinned on my wings. This was pretty special for Pop, also, seeing his first-born follow his footsteps into the wild blue yonder. I was now soldier # O-771366. No longer just a draftee, a reservist, nor even a cadet. I had made it. I was finally a pilot. A fly-boy, and an officer — we were commissioned as Second Lieutenants in the Army Air Corps (more GOOD NEWS). The United States of America didn't have an Air Force at that time. The Army Air Corps was a branch of the Army just like the Navy Air Force is still a branch of the Navy. The great responsibility associated with that rank didn't really hit me, though, until several months later when I was not only an officer, but the *Officer in Charge*. The Graduation message, delivered by a veteran combat pilot, included some wise words for us rookies, "When you get into combat, listen to the pilots who have already gone through the hell of dodging flak and enemy planes, because those men can teach you enough to save your life." It reminded me of an old adage about diplomacy, "Pray for peace, and prepare for war." We were almost ready.

After graduation we got our assignment to Transition, the next stop. We all had had a choice of whether we wanted to fly single-engine or multi-engine planes. I wasn't sure that my reactions were quick enough to fly Pursuit (fighters), and, after my experience with that female copilot at Gardner, I had chosen Multi-engine. I got orders for B-17 transition training at Hobbs, New Mexico. But first, furlough. It was a little crowded in the car leaving Marfa with my folks and a couple of buddies who needed a ride to Iowa, but I didn't mind. I was on my way to see Joyce for the first time in almost a year. I had a surprise for her.

Chapter Six
FURLOUGH

I went home to Davenport for furlough, and promptly got the flu. Isn't that the way it always goes. You push and push and finish the job, losing sleep, and then, when it's over and the pressure is off, your body shuts down. Joyce — in her sophomore year of college — was coming down from Mt. Vernon to see me. I had hoped to have some time to get re-acquainted. And I had the Flu. She hadn't seen me in almost a year, might be dating other guys at Cornell, and I had the flu. But, flu or not, I was not to be deterred from my goal.

While at Marfa, I had gotten into a crap game and got lucky. I used the proceeds to buy an engagement ring. So, sick as a dog, when Joyce came to visit me, I proposed as we sat on the lower bed of my bunk bed. I was thrilled when she accepted and we agreed that we would be smart and wait till I got back from overseas to tie the knot. Two weeks later, I shipped out to Hobbs, New Mexico for Transition.

B-17 TRANSITION
HOBBS, NEW MEXICO   MARCH, 1944

We quickly learned that the wind in Hobbs blew east on Monday, Wednesday and Friday; and west on Tuesday, Thursday, and Saturday. Sunday's wind was anybody's guess. Hobbs is the only place I'd ever been where the dust drifted on the *inside* of the window sill. We would learn to keep our air filters on all the way up to 10,000 feet, just because of the dust.

Upon our arrival at Hobbs, we got a Dollar Ride in a B-17. After a few of the ordinary instructions, the Instructor Pilot put us on oxygen, and took us to 20,000 feet. I happened to be the student in the cockpit at the time, and he had me take the stick.

With no further comment — or warning — the IP said, "Feather engine number four." This is what they call it when you angle the propeller blades so much that their edge is facing into the wind. This angle makes the prop quit turning, which stops the engine so you can turn the power off. The purpose of feathering it is to keep the engine from spinning out of control — a runaway prop — when it might fly off!

We went through the feathering procedure, and the outboard propeller stopped turning. The Number Four engine quit about two seconds later and I switched it off.

Then he said "Feather Number One."

I repeated the procedure, and the other outboard propeller stopped turning.

"Now feather number two."

All of us students looked at each other, but by this time we were pretty well used to following directions, so I feathered Number Two. Now we are at 20,000 feet, and three engines are feathered. Only one engine was still turning, Number Three — the one with the generator.

"Now check the rate of descent."

To my amazement, it was only about 50 feet a minute. At that rate of descent we could fly all afternoon. It was a comforting thought, to know that the airplane could stay in the air all day on fewer than four engines. The B-17 was an amazing airplane — well-designed and sturdy. It could hold a tremendous amount of weight and still be aerodynamically sound. We had a great time learning to fly that airplane, and it had a few interesting quirks. For instance, in a B-25, when you pull back on the stick to climb, the nose goes up and you climb. It's different in a B-17. In a B-17 when you pull back on the stick, the tail goes down until you achieve climbing attitude. Then you start to climb. A couple of my fellow student pilots learned this particular concept the hard way.

We were up on a night cross country, May 14th, with two pilots in each plane. The commanding officer of the base was up in the tower that night when we came back. When that particular crew called in to land, he recognized them and asked them to come over to the tower. After landing, the pilot taxied over and parked under the tower. The CO headed down from the tower and when he got to the plane the pilots were out and standing in front of their plane.

The old man asked, "Where you been flying, guys?"

"Well, we've been flying instruments at 10,000 ft over the desert, sir."

"Is that right?" He responded. "Come on back, I want you to look at the tail."

Well, the tail was riddled. Part of the horizontal tail is fabric, and that part of it was shredded. What had happened is this; there was a bunch of gals stationed over in Texas — Abilene, I think, which was not too far away from Hobbs; and who were in training to fly ferry command. That crew had gone down to buzz the gals. Well, they got a little low and when they tried to climb after buzzing the gals, they caught some treetops with their tail. They had been flying B-25's on Sub Patrol in the Caribbean and weren't used to the way a B-17's tail went down when you pulled back on the stick. During their return to Hobbs, the Old Man had gotten a call from Ferry Command. It wasn't too hard to figure out which crew had been cross-country to Texas. The evidence was right there on the tail. Needless to say, they didn't leave the base until we graduated from transition.

During transition we spent a lot of time on two and three engine landings and takeoffs. My Instructor was convinced that, at 5'6" and 125 lbs., I was too small to fly a B-17. He spent one three-hour session taking first one, and then another engine from me on a landing or a take-off to see how I would respond. I sure learned a lot about handling a four-engine airplane on fewer than four engines. That's what learning to fly a multi-engine plane is all about. We also did a lot of instrument, and formation flying, not that much different than we had learned before, except that there were more engines to keep track of.

I learned one other thing at Hobbs. I still had a lot of training to endure and if we were going to be assigned to places like Hobbs, I didn't want to be alone. Joyce and I were reconsidering our decision to wait to get married until I came back from overseas. It was hard trying to be responsible about our decision and be adult about the whole situation — me, barely 21 and Joyce, only 19.

Mom put it into perspective for us when she told Joyce one afternoon in passing, "I don't want to influence your decision, but no time in Jack's life will he need you any more than now." Thanks, Mom.

My next posting for training was to be Lincoln, Nebraska, to get assigned a crew. In our deliberations, we discovered that Joyce's Dad was going to be in Lincoln at the same time I was scheduled to check in. If one parent was there, why not get three more, and have a wedding? Sounded like a good plan to me.

Roy R. Fisher, Jr. with Susan Fisher Anderson

Chapter Seven
Nine Guys and a Wedding

TO CREW ASSIGNMENT
LINCOLN, NEBRASKA   JUNE, 1944

I flew my last training flight in Hobbs, New Mexico on June 1, 1944. The next three weeks were the most significant of my life. When I reported in Lincoln just a few days later, I found a small, white calling card on the desk. On it, printed with 8-pt type, were the words:

YOU ARE HEADED FOR COMBAT

It was startling news considering we were planning to have a wedding in a few days. We found out later about D Day, the Invasion of Normandy which occurred on June 6, 1944. I suppose the plan was, in case the invasion didn't go well, we were to go directly over to England with no time for crew training. There was really no way to tell in advance how severe the casualties of both men and aircraft would be, so they were keeping their options open. Fortunately, the invasion was successful, pilot casualties had been light because of the good weather; so the wedding was on for four days later, June 10, 1944.

It was not to be without complications, however. The State of Nebraska initially refused to recognize Joyce's blood test from Iowa and secondly, she had to have her dad, Newell, give his written permission for her to be married, since she was under 21. They arrived on Thursday to get it all straightened out, largely thanks to Newell's friend who was also in the insurance business and was able to help make things happen. All was not roses, though. Newell sat us down the night before and told us frankly, "I wish you wouldn't go through with this." It was not the first time her dad and I had butted heads. Fortunately, that night, Joyce was as determined as I was. We had decided we were going into this war together, as one; man and wife.

Roy R. Fisher, Jr. with Susan Fisher Anderson

June 10, 1944
Lincoln, Nebraska

The Lucky Bastard Club

Joyce and I were married in a little Chapel on the base at Lincoln — not the one where we were scheduled to have the ceremony, but at another on the other side of the base — changed at the last minute (at the convenience of the Army, of course). The wedding party was composed of Joyce's parents, Newell and Beatrice Day; her older sister, Joanne, who was the maid of honor and soloist; Roy and Eula Fisher, my parents; and my uncle, Rev. Carey Fisher, a Methodist Minister who assisted with the service. The base chaplain completed the party, since he could legally marry us. Joyce had somehow found the time, in those two weeks since we had decided to get married, to not only finish her final exams, but to make herself a white linen suit for the ceremony. She looked fabulous. The picture of her walking down the aisle towards me would comfort me during many a lonely night in the following months.

After the ceremony we had a "quick" dinner and reception at another hotel and then escaped, leaving all the guests to fend for themselves. I had previously registered at the Cornhusker Hotel and had the room key in my pocket. I had also made certain we were not listed on the register so we would not have to worry about being interrupted or delayed in registration.

Our next surprise occurred when we opened the hotel room door. Guess what! Twin beds! While the bell boy stood grinning like a Cheshire cat, I called the desk and got a room with a double bed. In the process of moving, however, we got listed on the room register, so about 10 o'clock that night, the phone rang. We didn't answer.

The message we got the next morning was from Newell. He just wanted to know if we needed any help. By the time we got the message he had already gone home, the last of the family to leave Lincoln. We were finally on our own — grown-ups, husband and wife, just like we had planned. We were ready to face the world — and the World War — together.

The last of the three significant things that happened in Lincoln was this, I met my crew for the first time. A very diverse bunch to be sure, but the next few months would weld us together for life. Allow me to introduce them.

STANLEY RUNDELL
CO-PILOT
My co-pilot, Stanley Rundell was a frustrated P-38 Pilot who would rather have been caught dead than in the right seat of a heavy bomber. About the same height as me, but five pounds lighter, he could fly better drunk than I could sober. (In Rapid City he had his mail sent to the Seventh Avenue Bar).

Stan's expertise and willingness to put up with me helped make us a fantastic team. Did I say he was a fantastic pilot? He was happy to let me run the crew and call him when it was his turn to fly, which, considering my light weight — and his, was every other 15 minutes when fully loaded and in formation. What a blessing he was.

ARTHUR (NMI) MILLER
NAVIGATOR
Miller was a California boy with a round face and long brown hair — that is, long for those days. He was about two inches taller and a little heavier than I, and sharp as a tack. He was a great guy and became a good friend. We called him Ott, who knows why. Ott's position in the airplane was just underneath my seat. He and the bombardier occupied the big plexiglass basement of the cockpit. As a navigator who truly learned the complexities of his trade, Ott was admired by not only our crew but by Group Staff. My toughest decision of the war was to keep all our crew together and not let the powers that be make Ott a Group Navigator. He was the reason we were even considered for lead crew, and the big guys weren't very happy with my decision. I don't regret it.

ROBERT MILLER
BOMBARDIER
Bob was truly a gentleman and a scholar. Outspoken and bright, he also had a background in real estate, so we spoke a common language. Bob was from Pennsylvania, tall and slender, with dark hair and sparkly eyes. His was a tough job, because he was trained to be a bombardier, and I forced him to become a second navigator. He and Ott — our search and destroy team — kept us constantly oriented, and enabled us to get home safely, even when we got separated from our

group. Since we were the officers, Bob, Ott and I spent a lot of time, both business and leisure, together.

SAM CARLINO
ENGINEER & CREW CHIEF

Sam was a make-it-work guy. An Italian from Baton Rouge, Louisiana and a shade taller and heavier than I, he could have been my twin — were it not for the drawl. Sam understood the B-17 like no one else. He worked closely with the ground crew chief to make sure we always got back safely. He was an expert at encouraging them to help him fix those minor irritants that made life smoother. In fact, he handled all the plane problems with the ground crew chief so well, I never even learned the guy's name. Every morning when it was time to fly, our ship was ready; with, I believe, only two exceptions during our whole tour. When we made an emergency landing on the continent, he patched things up so we could take off and get home.

Sam spent his time just behind the cockpit, with the calculating site and twin guns. From the time we hit enemy territory until we reached coast-out (crossing over the enemy coast on our way home), Sam stood with his head in the upper turret. He manned the twin 50 caliber machine guns and could shoot above, behind and to the sides, with special restrictive mechanisms to keep him from shooting our tail off.

More than anything else, Sam was the spokesman for the crew. If they had any problems, he and I talked them over and worked out a solution. If the crew had any physical problems, he listened and that's how I finally found out about Slim's nose.

JAMES HUME
RADIO-OPERATOR

He was always on the ball. His skill and attention to his job saved our lives before we ever got to our battle assignment. James was an easy-going, soft-spoken, blond fellow from Oklahoma. His station had a porthole above him so he could stand up and see the stars to get a celestial fix for our navigation. He could also poke a gun out of that hole if the situation warranted.

The radio operator had to constantly cross-check stations to get an accurate radio fix on our position. If necessary, he could get a confirmation from the command set — the radio the pilots had — which were stronger sets and able to pick up weaker signals. If we were still not sure of our location in relation to the field, a 360° turn would help us pinpoint our position.

James was very good at his job, and his skill saved our lives.

DAVID COLE
WAIST GUNNER

David was a big Texan, over six feet tall. He had worked as a roughneck and was tougher than a hog's nose. He was always ready and willing to take on any project. Manning the waist gun, in the middle of the fuselage, his job was to be one of the protectors of our REAR. With a background of self-preservation in the Texas oil fields he didn't get shook up easily and was always a calm voice on the intercom. He took special care of our ball turret gunner and saved Bob's life on more than one occasion.

JIM (or maybe John) RICHTER
WAIST GUNNER

He flew over with us and went on a few missions before he left the crew. He just wasn't meant to fly combat. Most of the crews flew with only nine men, instead of the 10 we started with. When Richter left, we flew with only one waist gunner, like most of the others. Some months after he left the crew he got back on flight status and flew a few more missions, not with us, but still as an official member of our crew. I think he went home when I finished, like the other enlisted men, but we lost track of him after the war. We didn't bond like the others with whom we spent so much time, and experienced so much danger.

ROBERT JACOBS
BALL TURRET GUNNER

A skinny little farm boy from Central Illinois, he was the only one who could fit in the ball turret, probably the most physically-challenging position on the ship. The ball turret was a 36" plexiglass sphere on the underside of the airplane, about midship. Lowered into position for combat, it had to be cranked up before landing or it would drag on the runway. It had its own oxygen supply in a tank mounted on the deck just beside the hatch. The gun could shoot every direction but up. He protected the underside of the aircraft from front to rear.

The ball was barely big enough for the gunner and his gun. It was not big enough for him to wear his parachute. Shorter than me, about 5'2", Bob was a good-looking fellow with dark wavy hair. He would fold himself in the ball turret with his knees touching his chin, and his hands on the controls over his head, then stay that way for the entire time we were over enemy territory. I don't know what the longest time was, but I'm sure it was nearly eight hours. What a job! He got a real good look at the war every mission.

STAN (SLIM) SCHANZE
TAIL GUNNER

Tall and lean, but still able to squeeze into the tail compartment, Slim constantly suffered from sinus infections, but wouldn't allow himself to be grounded. We finally had to ground him before our last three missions.

He stayed stretched out on his belly as long as we were over enemy territory. The combination of his alertness, our trust in each other, and the supernatural protection of Almighty God saved us time and again. Thank you, Lord! Slim lost weight during our tour and died a few years after the war. I think his death was service connected.

CREW TRAINING
RAPID CITY, SOUTH DAKOTA   JUNE, 1944

We didn't have to go to Europe as direct support of the invasion with no crew training, so after another week or so in Lincoln, it was off to Rapid City to begin learning to fly as a team. Most of the guys went by train, but Joyce and I decided to drive to Rapid City with another couple. I imagine they wondered why we sat in the back seat, under a blanket, in June.

Rapid City AAB was a great place for crew training. I had spent the summer in that general area two years earlier during forestry summer camp, so I knew a lot about the local area, and knew a lot of neat places to show my Bride.

We rented a one-room motel room and set up housekeeping. It was a really wonderful summer, except for a grueling flight schedule: night, afternoon, morning, then repeat. So after the early morning flight we were off till the following night. That gave us time to see the Black Hills, ride horseback, stay in bed, and have the crew over for dinner, two by two. Joyce got a chance to get to know each of them, preparing wonderful dinners, even Lemon Meringue Pie, on a stove-top oven and two little burners. Our experience with horseback riding convinced me we should have gone swimming.

Upon our arrival at Rapid City, our first trip was the Dollar Ride. Shortly after takeoff, I gave Stan the stick and went back to see how the rest of the crew was getting along. When I got back to the waist, they were all sacked out, sound asleep to a man. In gunnery school, the gunners had spent the time sleeping when they weren't on the gunnery range. I wanted them to know that we were all part of the crew, and a combat crew all depend on each other. When I got back up in the cockpit and took the yoke, I pulled the airplane up almost in a stall, and then dropped the nose suddenly. This maneuver rendered the rest of the crew completely weightless and I could hear them holler as they rattled around like popcorn. When we landed, a little extra effort was required to extract Slim's parachute from the tail, where it had gotten stuck during our dive. Not one of us ever mentioned the incident, but the message came across loud and clear. From then on everyone stayed at his post, and awake.

The navigator and bombardier learned to work as a team. Stan learned to fly a B-17, reluctantly, but well. Sam learned to keep that airplane flying, and Hume learned all about the radio. Slim managed to get over six feet of man in and out of the tail and we gradually learned to operate as one.

Even though we were very busy learning to fly as a crew, the posting at Rapid was a precious time for Joyce and me to get accustomed to living as husband and wife. They were wonderful times. I would reflect back on them many times later; even the not so wonderful times, like when Joyce got poison ivy so bad she couldn't move or sleep. She just laid in bed, furious, uncomfortable and covered with white ointment.

The Lucky Bastard Club

Midway through the summer I was able to swing a short furlough so we could go visit our folks back in Davenport. Before we left to return to base, Ted had a present for us. He had heard that many crews had a mascot, and he was determined our crew would have one as well. He had bought a cocker spaniel puppy from a breeder in Davenport, so "Red" (and he was) joined our crew. We made him an oxygen mask and he began to fly with us on every training mission.

On our last flight before leaving Rapid City, we flew a cross-country formation mission to Lincoln. During that flight we had three run-a-way props and two run-away turbos, which kept Stan and me more than busy — but we stayed in formation. All the throttle levers are together so the pilot can hold them in his hand as one. The goal is to get them all at a consistent speed so you hear one constant sound — all the engines running at the same level. If a prop or turbo runs away, its speed increases and you can hear the engine whine higher and higher as the rpms increase. Then, you have to back off on the throttle of that engine until it gets under control. You can't do that and fly in formation at the same time, so Stan had to manage the runaways while I flew with the other engines. It kept both Stan and me occupied during the whole flight, trying to manage our engines and stay in formation. Since we were used to flying in 15-minute shifts, we were really worn out by the time we landed. In fact, I don't think I've ever been so tired before or since.

At the end of the summer, early September, we were assigned to Lincoln for Staging, our last stop before shipping out. While the guys and I boarded a train for Lincoln — they weren't about to let us get out of their sight now that we were trained as a crew, Joyce and four other wives drove together to meet us in Nebraska. When they arrived and tried to check in to the hotel, each to a separate room, the desk clerk was very suspicious of those five young — and apparently single — women who wanted to stay in his reputable hotel. He relaxed a lot when they each signed the register as *Mrs.*

STAGING
LINCOLN, NEBRASKA   SEPTEMBER, 1944

This is where we were assigned a B-17 to ferry over to England. When we got off the train from Rapid City, Stan, my copilot, disappeared. We were scheduled to leave Lincoln at midnight

Roy R. Fisher, Jr. with Susan Fisher Anderson

Saturday night, September 16, 1944. When we took our ship up Thursday to check it out prior to acceptance, he still hadn't shown up. Friday afternoon, I kissed Joyce goodbye at the front gate of the post and sent her on her way to get on the train to return to Iowa, and to begin the fall semester at Cornell. The war was looming — larger and larger; and, although I don't know whether the reality of it had really sunk in, what I did know that night was that my arms felt awful without Joyce in them. My bed was lonely and I was dreading the months I would spend away from my wife, my life. For the next several months, perhaps longer, our only contact would be in writing. It would have to do.

Five p.m. Saturday came and still no Stan. Seven hours to takeoff and I had no copilot. At six he showed up. He'd been in the hospital all week with the "DT's". I was sure glad to see him. Another few minutes and I would have had to report him as A.W.O.L. (Absent Without Official Leave). Worse yet, I would have had to train another copilot on the fly — literally. So it was with much relief that we all took off, the ten of us, plus Red, and headed for Grenier, NH. It was a little unnerving, though. They had basically said, "Here, son, take this brand new 65,000 lb., half a million dollar airplane and deliver it to Scotland. Oh, and take these nine guys with you." We were finally on our way to the war. I was 21 years old.

Chapter Eight
Headed for the E.T.O.
(European Theatre of Operations)

On the way north, we flew over Davenport, and gave them a bit of a B-17 buzz job — flying low over the house so they could really experience the full effect of those four mighty engines, first hand. I even turned on my landing lights so I could find the house in the dark. My brother says we knocked him out of bed, but I don't know whether I really believe that. They knew we were on our way though; on our way to war. We didn't know for how long, maybe forever. Lots of guys didn't come back. We could only do our job, pray and write; and I would write nearly every day.

Sunday nite, (September 17)

My dearest wife,
Here we are — safe in New England. Our trip was awfully long and terribly boring — with perhaps one or two exceptions. I've been wondering if you were awake last night when I breezed by. Sure hope so.
Well — here it is only the second day since I've held you in my arms and my lonliness is about to overcome me. It is — however — very satisfying to remember that we are married and that we've been so close these past few months. Already I'm beginning to appreciate what a sense of calm is associated with those memories and I feel sure that it will be even more important as time goes.
Just sitting here thinking I fell sound asleep. As you can imagine I didn't get much sleep last night — not for the last week for that matter, But — believe me — I'm not griping. My only trouble at present is trying to make my jumbled thoughts mean something. I guess the only thing that I'm really sure of is that I love you — very, very muchly darling — more than anything else in the world. Here's a goodnight kiss from
Your husband,
Jack

Roy R. Fisher, Jr. with Susan Fisher Anderson

Our first stop was Goose Bay, Labrador. We had to gas up for the long trip across the North Atlantic. Goose Bay was a dismal place. I'm still amazed at how the men stationed there were able to tolerate the place.

Tuesday afternoon (September 19, 1944)

Hi Goodlookin'

What's on the fire? We're still enroute. Got here last night and they told us to hit the sack and stay there. Of course I'm not one to quibble about an order like that. Our ship is really a honey — I just wish we could keep it for combat. For some unknown reason nothing has gone wrong at all. Hope it stays like that.

We went to a show here on the base last night and boy what a poor one it was. It was a Columbia picture "Stars on Parade." If all the shows up here are that bad, I sure feel sorry for guys that have to stay here. Personally — I hope the weather gets real good and stays that way so we can get the he— out of here. But enough of this old stuff.

By now you're probably pretty well started in school. I hope you're nice and busy so you won't get too lonesome. Personally — I wish I was home — I don't like this solo sack time a little bit, but that's the way it goes. In spite of being so lonesome tho I have a tremendous feeling of contentment. Being married to you is the most wonderful thing which has ever happened to me. Even tho I'm a long way from home and from your arms I know that you're waiting for me — no one else and that when I get back we'll begin a real life together.

Till then, yours alone,
Jack

We were briefed for an eight hour flight from Goose Bay to Meeks Field, Iceland. We took off about midnight in fog so thick we could only see 200 ft. Stan flew visual, and I flew instruments from the ground. He kept it on the runway, and I flew it off. We were briefed to break out of the overcast at 5,000 ft. We went all the way to 12,000 ft. and never did break out, so we came back down to about 5,000 ft, which was our briefed altitude, where we picked up icing. Fortunately we remembered to climb quickly before the plane got too

The Lucky Bastard Club

heavy, and we finished the trip at about 8,000 ft., still in the clouds; we had never broken out. So much for the briefing. Iceland, as you know, is a little rock of an island country in the middle of the frigid North Atlantic Ocean. With the thick clouds, we would have to depend heavily on Hume and the radio compass to find it in the dark ocean.

After only approximately five hours in the air, about three hours before we were scheduled to arrive, our on-the-ball radio operator tuned in the Meeks Field beacon and said we already sounded real close to Iceland. I tuned in the Pilot's Command set, and we were indeed already almost over the station. We tuned in the radio range, and hit the cone of silence, and asked for landing instructions. We had picked up a powerful tailwind. Now we call them JET STREAMS. It added about 100 mph to our ground (ocean) speed. We were on the ground with a total flight time of five hours — having never seen the ground or clear sky till we broke out in our final approach to the runway at Meeks Field. Five hours, that's a long way from the 8 hours we were expecting. We kissed the ground and thanked the Lord.

Why were we so grateful to land? Let me show you the math. At our rate of speed, 150 mph airspeed plus 100 mph wind speed, our actual ground (ocean) speed was 250 mph.

150 mph (airspeed) + 100 mph = 250 mph (actual ground speed)
5 hours (total flight time)

Now, what if we had gone only an hour past our destination — still two full hours before we were scheduled to land. At that speed, we would have already been 250 miles past Meeks Field. If we had then turned around, we would have had a headwind of 100 mph to subtract from our airspeed of 150 mph, which would have resulted in a ground (ocean) speed of only 50 mph. It would have taken us five hours more to get back to Iceland.

150 mph – 100 mph (*head* wind) = 50 mph (actual ground speed)
250 miles (distance back to Meeks) @ 50 mph (actual ground speed) =
5 hours (flight time)
6 hours (elapsed time) + 5 hours (return time) = 11 hours (total flight time)

Oh, one other thing. Having been briefed for an 8-hour flight, we only had gas for about 10 hours flight time. Hume had tuned in Meeks Field three hours before our ETA (Estimated Time of Arrival) and saved our lives. Several ships overflew Iceland that day — we never were told how many — and were never heard from again.

(September 20, 1944)

Joyce Darling,

I am now somewhere in Iceland. Last night I was somewhere in Labrador. We really get around don't we. This was really quite a hop. Logged a lot of instrument time. And how!!!

Naturally no mail has reached us yet — so I'm quite the lonely little boy. Funny how much you miss a person after you've lived with them a few months. I really don't see why that is unless it is because that person becomes a part of yourself and the loss is proportionately great. My darling — I love you so very much. Living without you is so incomplete — please win this war in a hurry so I can come home to stay.

Now I must close and get to work. Sweetheart — I love you.
Jack

That night Marlene Dietrich entertained. Dietrich was a famous German actress who defected to our side at the beginning of the war. One of her more famous numbers was singing, "Go See What The Boys In The Backroom Will Have, And Tell Them I'm Having The Same," in a husky, gravelly voice. Most important though, she was most famous for her LEGS.

When she came on stage, dressed in a floor length gown, in front of two or three thousand GIs who had been in Iceland, some for two or three years, the boo's were deafening. They wanted to see her LEGS. She waved and smiled; then the stagehand brought out a chair and a saw, and a bow, and she sat down to play the saw. When she pulled up her skirt, so she could hold the saw securely between her knees, the place went wild. I don't know to this day whether she could play a tune on the saw or not. It didn't really make any difference. She was a hit.

The Lucky Bastard Club

Sunday nite
September 17

Joyce my dearest,

Still in Iceland. Nothing much to do today except catch up on a lot of sack time. I've slept eighteen out of the past twenty-four hours. Last night after I wrote you I went to a USO show at the theater. Marlene Deitrich and a pretty fair show. She didn't do much except stand around and look beautiful but the rest of the show was pretty good. Guess I'll drop over again tonight. One of the fellows was a tenor — boy could he sing:. "Lady of Spain" "Begin the Biegueen" "When Irish eyes are smiling" and a couple of others. They had a girl from Texas who played a harmonica and did a clever whistling act. They had a couple of vaudville comedians. You know — W.C. Fields stuff. The boys got a pretty good laugh tho.

It's really surprising to me to see these guys in such good spirits after being up here so long. I'm afraid I would go crazy around here. I haven't seen a tree since I've been here. Nothing but rock — with a little bit of mud thrown around here and there. What a barren spot.

We all went out to the ship this afternoon to pull an inspection. We couldn't wait for the truck so we just "borrowed" a jeep. Boy did we ever have fun tearing around the field.

We've still got "Red" with us. They may take him away from us but as yet we're still going strong. The ground crews here got a big kick out of him and Stan is having a good time showing him off to everyone. Stan has quit drinking — at the doctors request and he's really turned over a new leaf. I'm really awfully glad because down deep — he's a good boy. Ott is sitting here with me writing that little woman in Canada. He sure worked hard getting us over here. He really didn't have too many check points on that flight. But he never got worried and consequently neither did I. Sure is nice when you have a lot of faith in each other.

Roy R. Fisher, Jr. with Susan Fisher Anderson

Don Current just stopped by and said to send you his love. While I'm about I'll send you a little of my own. Did I say little? I mean a lot — In fact all of it. You don't mind if I love you more than anything else in the world do you? Well — I do darling — whether you like it or not — I'm just built that way I guess.

Now I must sign off for now,
Goodnight darling,
Jack

Friday nite
September 22, 1944

Hello Darling,

How's the most wonderful wife in the world this evening? Fine I hope cause I'm feeling bad enough for both of us. This is sure a hole. We almost got out today but the weather looked pretty foul. We're scheduled to leave tonight and I spose we will. Sure glad I got some sleep this afternoon. I was on guard out at the ship and went to sleep in one of those little sleeping bags they gave us.

Ott and I played a few hands of double sol this p.m. at the plane, and naturally I couldn't help but remember all the games we played together back in Rapid City. Guess that just sorta started me thinking about that wonderful three months. You know — darling — as I look back over it I can't hardly believe it was reality and not just a wonderful dream. Even now it seems too marvelous but I know that you are really mine and believe my dear — I'm yours alone forever. Now — much more than ever before. And the most wonderful thing about being married is that when I come back we can start in right where we left off & build a wonderful life together. I guess I just say the same things over & over in my letters but those are the things I feel daily. I do love you so very much and I'm so thankful that you're my wife.

Your loving husband,
Jack

Chapter Nine
England

After a three-day wait on weather, we went on to Valley, Scotland, and completed the delivery of the plane. We had to put our dog, Red, into quarantine. On the total flight over the North Atlantic, I logged nine hours of Actual Instruments for a total of 9:25 hours of AI time and a total of 533:10 total Hours when I reported for Combat Duty at the Replacement Depot — Reeple Deeple for short. I got a dollar ride, got checked out on instruments, and had a day checkout with Squadron Commander, all within my first 14 hours in England. They were serious about this war thing.

(Sunday September 24, 1944)
Dearest wife,
Here we are — somewhere in England. We got here yesterday. So far the weather has just been wet. I know now why people have so much trouble keeping warm around here. The cold seems to go right thru everything.

Sunday nite — the 24th of September — just seven nights since we've been together and yet it seems like an eternity. Funny isn't it — how very much you miss someone you love when they are away — even for a short time.

I got to thinking about little things that we did together last night before I went to sleep. The one thing that I remember most clearly is the way you used to meet me when I came home at night. You were always so glad to have me home it was a real experience to come home to you. Your face would light up like an angel's and you'd tell me how glad you were to have me home and no matter how rough the day had been — the whole world seemed brighter. Gosh, darling, it's so marvelous to love you and be married to you.

Goodnight my own,
Jack

Roy R. Fisher, Jr. with Susan Fisher Anderson

(Monday, September 25)

Hello darling,
    Here's that man again. Just dropped in for a little chat. How's the loveliest woman in the world this evening. Yours truly is curled up on the sack, Stan is here writing and the other boys, Ott & Bob, have gone to the show. It's raining a little and just generally nasty. A perfect night to just stay home and wish I was with you. There are so many things we could do on a night such as this. It really isn't good for much except loving. But — what a wonderful night to hold you close to me and tell you how much I love you. I'd sure like that – would you? Silly question #7,641,092.
    I sent you a cable today — hoping that it would reach you before this mail does. I just wanted you to know I'm well & as happy as is possible considering the fact that I'm a million miles — more or less — from my heart.
    They put "Red" in quarantine when we landed and unless we send him home — he'll stay there for six months. I wrote the folks today and told them I might send him home. Heaven knows what they'll do with another dog.
    I'll tell you a secret — I know a guy who loves you muchly
    Guess who — Jack

(September 26, 1944)
Tuesday afternoon

My dearest wife,
    Today has been an extremely dull day with one or two exceptions. We got up at 7:00 & went to breakfast and then took some pressing over to the tailors. Ott picked up the laundry we did yesterday afternoon & brought it home while I sweat out the line. Oh — yes — we do quite a bit of our own laundry. That's the only way to get it done. After I finally got to the place and turned my stuff in I went over to the censoring rooms. That's the only kind of deal we pull here. We have to censor mail. I'd sure hate to do it all the time. It is terribly dull. That job lasted all morning and tho dull we did get a few good laughs.
    I just had a nice shower & I shaved and really feel like a new man. The shower is in a bathtub and I thought about the times we had so much fun taking bubble baths together. Just doing ordinary —

everyday things is always so much more fun when I do them with you. Living with you was the most marvelous experience I've ever had.

This morning when the alarm went off I was dreaming about you and that room in the Capitol Hotel. I reached over to grab the alarm clock and banged my fist against the wall. You see — this room is built the other way and the dresser is at the foot of my bed. That way I can look at you the last thing before I go to sleep.

That's a kind of a habit I got into and I still like it very much only I wish I had you instead of just your picture to say goodnight to. You were always so sweet and loving to your husband. I've often wondered if your dreams of married life were as happily & fully realized as mine were. Being married to you has been a complete and marvelous realization of all the dreams & plans which we built together before we said those marriage vows. I only hope that you have been as satisfied as I have and if not I wish you would say so. Actually, we have an excellent opportunity for not only strengthening our marriage — but also improving it by this separation. We have the opportunity to examine married life from a distance and then to see what — if anything — needs to be done to make our life more warm and full and loving than it has been thus far.

With these thoughts, darling, I'll leave you for now.
All my love — forever,
Jack

Sept. 27 — Wed nite.

Dearest wife,

Still no news from the home front but I'm sure that it will catch up with us before long. Gosh I sure hope so. I'm getting restless and lonesome for the most wonderful wife a man ever had. That's a funny thing — I guess every man thinks that his wife is the best in the world. And yet I can't imagine how any of the girls that I have known all thru these years could possibly be as kind and considerate and loving as you are to me. I was talking to Ronnie Dierks — a forester from Ames — he is a bombardier on a B-26. He told me that he was married and when we got to comparing dates, We've been married just about 1 hour longer than he has. He and Don Current are very good friends. Don has left — by the way for his unit and I don't know where he's going. Don always was pretty eager.

Roy R. Fisher, Jr. with Susan Fisher Anderson

 I also met a fellow from school who used to live in the same house I did when I lived at that rooming house. Bob Halferty is his name. He's that fellow that was such a good singer. Remember? He's a P-51 pilot and we had a pretty good discussion of B-1-7's v.s. P 51's. I think I came out on top of the discussion but I suppose he thought he won too. Those boys are sure the old HP's (Hot Pilots). Personally I wonder just what would happen to them if they ever got into any weather. Perhaps I'm just envious but I don't think so. I'm really much happier where I am. I don't think I could stand the nervous strain of a fighter anyway.

 Speaking of nervous tension. I had a little luck in a game tonight. I'm going to send you your $20 with interest. They paid us our per diem today and that was just about 4 lbs I hadn't figured on so I figured I'd invest it in a little game. I came out about 40 lbs ahead. One lbs or pound is equal to 4$ in our money. Not bad eh honey, I'm sorry I couldn't keep out of the game altogether but there just hasn't been a thing to do and with no war and all I've just been biting my nails for something to do. I hope you'll understand. Last night I got a six hour pass and went into town to see what these limey's are like in their own environment.

 It was really quite interesting. Little or nothing except a sign or two would indicate that you were on the main street of town. Although there are a few streetlights, the windows are all curtained & black. However — nearly every other door is a pub and there the townsfolk gather to drink a glass of bitters & pass the time of day. It is really very interesting but I don't think I'll care to spend too much time in the towns because you can't get anything to drink except bitters & it is certainly correctly named. We have no transportation to town either so the walk was even more pleasurable.

 Well — I could probably ramble all night but I really should go to bed and get some sleep. It's always about this time of night that I miss you the most. It's 10 p.m. here and 6 p.m. there. You're just sitting down to supper. How I wish I were there with you, sitting down to one of my wife's famous dinners. But now I'm feeling sorry for myself and that's not good. Goodnight my own sweet wife,

 I love you,
Jack

The Lucky Bastard Club

(September 28)
Thursday nite

Joyce darling,

I finally got some mail today. Just one letter from Mom but she said they'd heard me buzz over. I'm glad because it was so dark I wasn't sure that I was directly over the house. Also I was afraid to go much lower because I couldn't count on my altitude.

Mom said she had a nice visit with you before you went up to school. I'm glad you got to get home for even that short stay. Perhaps it helped to quiet any harshness caused by my visit.

Probably I'll get a letter from you tomorrow then I'll know all the news. Gosh, dear, I sure hope so. I'm sure getting anxious to hear from you. I was all set to go to town tonight but we had an inspection this morning and I was promptly red lined from the pass list. Ott & Bob & Stan were still in bed & I had just gotten up when he came thru. Butts all over the floor — everything strewn around in general — it's no wonder he wasn't happy. Now — we're on censorship detail again tomorrow. Maybe I'll get to town tomorrow night but I'm not really very anxious about it. I sure wish we'd get the heck out of here. Time's awasting & we could be getting in a lot of missions instead of sitting around on our fannies.

The post is really a beautiful place in spite of the weather. There are several flower gardens. One pansy bed over by the finance office is particularly lovely. The weather seems almost too cold for the flowers to survive and still they bloom. It must be all the rain that makes them bloom so well.

As you see — I'm enclosing a money order for $50. Please let me know when you get it. Also I would like to know our account numbers so it will be easier to send money home. I'm also sending a money order to the bank for $100.00 and it will require a letter of explanation so that they get it into the right account. I think I might as well put it in the checking account & then if you want to switch it you may. Just in case you may need a little spare cash now.

This is really very poor stationary. I'll admit, but I lost the other box and this is all I could hustle together. Actually — I guess the kind of stationary doesn't really matter — so long as there are letters on something or other.

Roy R. Fisher, Jr. with Susan Fisher Anderson

 I haven't seen the moon since night before last but it must be nearly full by now. Seems funny that — although we're a couple thousand miles apart the full moon that I look at is the same as the one over your head. I can just see you tottering on the edge of the roof — Don't hurt yourself when you fall. I just wish I could be there so you wouldn't feel so lonely. Remember anyway darling — I love you very, very much. When this mess is finished we'll be able to begin again where we left off and build a love that is even stronger & more beautiful than the one which holds us together now. Yes — darling — I'm sure that it holds us together. As often as we have become not two but one person our lives cannot help but be one in purpose & ideals — if not in fact. And it is one of those times I think when I'm particularly lonely or blue. It seems that the knowledge that you are always with me is a tremendous power which overcomes always any lonliness. Now darling, I must close for tonight.
 Your husband loves ya — but you'll have to sit on your hands,
Always,
Jack

(Sept. 30)
Sat. morn 9:15

Dearest wife,
 Here it is Saturday and still no mail from the states. I guess that one sack of mail must have come by plane and the rest of it by a slow convoy. I'm sure getting lonesome for a letter from my wife. I sure hope some mail comes thru today. I know you're writing — it isn't that — it's just that I'm so gosh darned far from home.
 Right now we're sweating out a big inspection by the commanding officer. This is just like cadet days. We got up and made our beds very carefully & swept & mopped the floor — dusted & put everything that wasn't nailed down into drawers or closets. The only thing I didn't do was shine my shoes and since I've only got one pair and I have them on — I didn't worry about that. I just hope the major likes our barracks. If he does we will be able to get passes for Sunday afternoon. I would really enjoy taking a nice long hike around the countryside in the daytime. So far most of our free hours have been after dark. I'd like to go around & visit some of these beautiful gardens. The farms here are certainly a lot different from ours. The

fields are all very small. One or 1 1/2 acres at the very outside. All have a stone or hedge fence around them and usually there is a stile instead of a gate. It really isn't very hard to tell that we're in a foreign country.

I got another six hour pass last night and went into another town near here. The one where we went last night was quite a lot larger than that first town I told you about. There was a big public dance and so I went to it. First we had some coffee & cake at the Red Cross. Roy Shoaf, Martone, Re d (LA.) Smith and I went together. I guess the dance was OK but you know how I feel about public dances. They're more like a public sale and I'm just not in the market for what they've got for sale.

This morning is just another day. The sun is shining but the clouds are so low that at times we're in a sort of fog & then the sun comes out again. Boy — if the weather is always like this I can certainly see why we've had so much instrument training.

Gosh I'm hungry. I'm afraid I'm going to have to start getting up for breakfast. No more work than I'm doing it would seem that 2 meals per day should be plenty but I guess you spoiled me for breakfast. Why wouldn't a man like to eat breakfast when he has a lovely wife to prepare it & sit across the table from him while he eats. Yes — you've spoiled me all right. Not that I mind having the most wonderful wife in the world — you understand.

Gosh, darling — I love you so very much. I better go see if the inspecting officer dropped in to see us. See ya' later.
    Your own husband,
    Jack

                              Saturday nite
Darling,
   Here it is Saturday night in England. I'm sitting here writing the most wonderful wife in the world a letter. This is an anniversary letter darling. The way I figure — this is our eleventh week anniversary. It is also the third Saturday night since I've held you in my arms. Gosh, darling, it seems like ages ago that I kissed you goodbye at the gate in Lincoln. Seems funny that our living together should start and end for a while at the same place.

Roy R. Fisher, Jr. with Susan Fisher Anderson

Yes — here it is — Saturday night. There is an overcast which hides the moon, but I'm quite sure — and I'll bet you are too — that the old moon is quite full and round. Quite a calendar we have — isn't it.

Today has been rather dull. Little or nothing to do. Our inspection was very satisfactory and so the whole barracks is going to get the afternoon off tomorrow. We really surprised ourselves. We didn't think we could do it.

I took a nap this afternoon and shined my shoes. They really take a beating around here with all this wet weather.

Well — isn't it a nice nite out at all — so lets just stay home and go to bed. I'm kinda tired oh — not too tired. Whoops — almost forgot.

What'll it be — blue lollipops tonight? Well — that's the way it goes. Hope you don't mind if I go right on loving you. That's a funny thing about being a husband. You love your wife regardless of the calendar. My darling, I wish I could make you see that a few hundred miles of ocean can't possible ever change the way I feel about you. I'm sure that was the case before we were married and now that we've lived together & loved together and started a truly marvelous life together that feeling is so much more powerful than before that it becomes a refuge in itself. It becomes a strength when I'm lonely or depressed. Just knowing that regardless of time or space or countries or wars or anything on earth — our spirits have been united by the holy vows of matrimony and that, with God's help, the vows so made will stand inviolate. You see, darling, before we were married we believed that to sacrifice our purity would be sacrilege. That is still as true as ever before and now with the beautiful experiences which we have known together we can realize even more fully the value of guarding that purity. I say purity because I feel that — to me — you will always be as you were when I first knew you. It's because I know you are mine and mine alone. With that feeling comes a sense of peace and security that — God willing — you shall always have. For I'm sure that you must feel the same strength that I do.

Perhaps you'll think this an unusual anniversary letter, but I can think of no better time than this to renew my vows to you. You see darling, I want you to know that being married means just as much to

me as I know it does to you. With this thought I'll close for tonight.
Happy anniversary Joyce
    I love you
    Jack

Oct 1. (Sunday)

Dearest Joyce,
    I received two lovely letters from you — also the first since we've been married. One was dated the 19th & the other the 22. That really isn't bad at all. Eight or nine days for airmail and V-mail is one day slower in most cases.
    You sure are correct about the things you said about that first letter. I can see how, to you especially, our life together could seem more like a dream than a reality and yet when you get verification in written form it makes everything seem more real and more wonderful than ever.
    It rained all afternoon and so I didn't go out even tho I did have a pass. I may venture into town tonight but I doubt it. We played bridge all afternoon & Renning & I beat Sharp by 30 points. That's pretty close bidding.
    I got a small letter from your Dad today — He told me all about his speaking tour and what a marvelous reception he got. He's sure going to town — isn't he.
    Well — darling I guess I'll quit for now —
    Your loving husband,
    Jack

Monday Oct 2

Joyce my own,
    Those two sweet letters I got from you yesterday have brought me many hours of comfort and pleasure—they really help a great deal. I only wish the mail service were a little more regular. We put in another morning of censoring today and I resolved that hereafter I would endeavor to make my writing as legible as possible. Ordinarily my mail will not be censored beyond my signature but just in case it is I don't want anyone else to have as much trouble as I did this morning. Believe me — some of these guys don't even try to write. I've often thought that my letters were anything but model writing but

some fellows are even worse than I. To begin with I'm going to buy some decent stationary as soon as the opportunity presents itself and then I'll avoid the use of V-mail except when I want you to get some news in a particular hurry. I think that I'll write the folks on V-mail cause I can put forth the pertinent poop in a very limited space & save both time and patience.

    But — my first wife — you shall receive long — yea endless — letters sent by airmail. Sounds like a will doesn't it. I've been reading Mr. Pinkerton goes to Scotland Yard. Nothing but murders & wills & more murders.
    Today was payday and after all deductions and allotments I still got nearly $150. None of the enlisted men got paid so I'm going to hang on to most of it. I think when we get to our next post we'll get them paid & then I'll send some more home.
    Well honey chile it is just about chow time and so I had better get my clothes on and go get my face fed.
    So long for now darling — be back tomorrow for a short visit a hug and a kiss from
    Your loving husband,
    Jack

Tues. Oct 3
8:20 pm

Dearest darling wife,
    Here's that man again. Persistent ain't I? Just dropped in to say a few words tonight. Principally and primarily I'm lonesome — gosh what a masterpiece of understatement that is. Nevertheless — lonely I am and as a sort of refuge I'll turn to the sweetest wife a fellow ever had. I have one thing tonight to look forward to — we are going to leave this post & I hope go to our unit. In spite of the fact that this is a nice safe place I see no percentage in spinning my wheels any longer. We're over here to do a job and we won't be home until we're finished so I'm in favor of getting started as soon as is humanly possible. Personally — all I want is to go back home to my sweet little wife. Perhaps that isn't a very patriotic viewpoint but I can't help it. Guess it's just because my love for you is so overpowering it just doesn't leave to much room for other thoughts.

Today has been one of those days. I swear I don't know whether or not I'll ever be warm again. I've had that feeling ever since I landed here but today has been especially miserable. If only there were some place to get warm once or twice a day it wouldn't be quite so bad. But there I go — getting bitter again. It really doesn't help so I'll quit. I'm sitting here in the officer's club writing. The radio is playing — not noticibly — just playing. There is the eternal crap game in the other room. I see no reason why I should get in it. Stan's up in the sack at the barracks but I think he'll be down after a while. I guess I'll stick around and try to get some coffee and donuts at 10 — We have to get up at 5:30 in the morning and you know how hard that is. Particularly when it is cold out. Sure wish I had you here to keep me nice and warm.

Gosh darling, I sure miss you terribly. I think — so often — about those months we spent together and try to relive them again. Those memories are priceless darling and I shall always cherish them regardless of what the future holds for us because you were so very kind and understanding. Your cheerful smile and sparkling eyes made each homecoming a joy and a real morale builder. You made that little shack where we lived together the most marvelous mansion in the world — just because you were always there waiting for me and telling me how glad you were to have me home. Gosh, honey I love you so very much. I just hope that the next homecoming isn't too far off. Remember darling that no matter how far I am from you — I will never belong to anyone else — I'm yours dearest — alone — forever.

Your loving husband,
Jack

Roy R. Fisher, Jr. with Susan Fisher Anderson

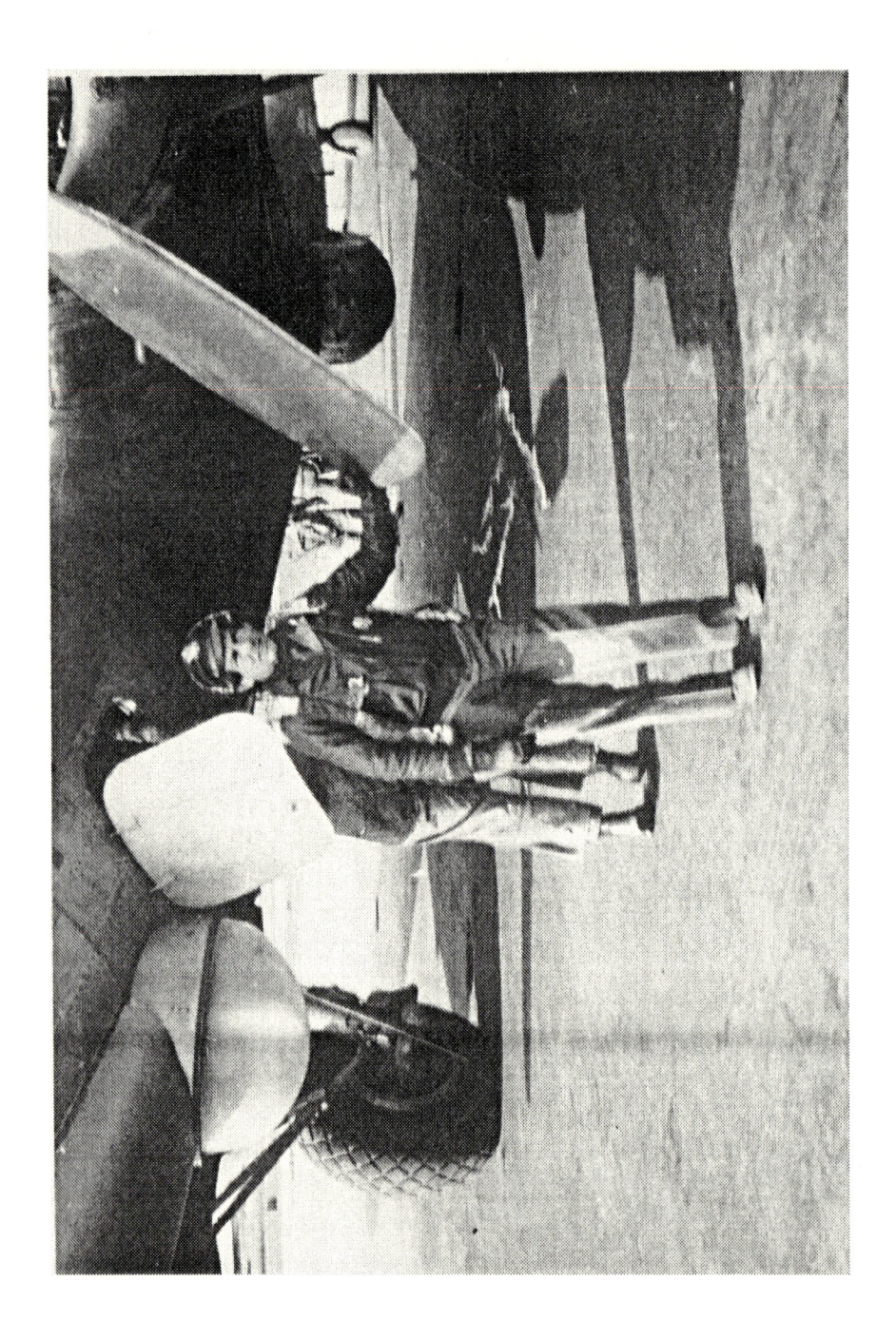

Chapter Ten
Home Base

94TH BOMB GROUP, 331ST BOMB SQUADRON
BURY ST. EDMONDS, ENGLAND   OCTOBER 1944

We reported to Station 463 at Bury St. Edmonds, England. When we reported to the Quonset hut which was to be our home, there were 12 of sixteen beds empty. They had had heavy losses in the 331st squadron of the 94th Bomb Group. We were their replacements. The reception we received was cool, to say the least.

New crews are dangerous. They don't know how to fly formation, They don't know the rules; they aren't properly trained; they can't fly instruments, and they replace crews which are either MIAs, or dead. Three crews bunks were empty (four officers in the crew).

When we arrived, three of the four officers in the barracks were playing bridge. Their welcoming comment was,

"I suppose none of you know how to play bridge, EITHER".

I said I'd played a little bridge. (At the Sig Ep House we played bridge all the time.) So I joined the game and picked up the first hand. It was unbelievable. I needed only one ace for a Grand Slam. Laydown. I opened with four no-trump. My partner responded with five diamonds, and I bid and made SEVEN NO-TRUMP. From then on the atmosphere warmed up considerably.

Oct 6 — late

Joyce Darling,

Well, here we are in the 94th. I told you I had a notion we'd be on the move before long & sure enough the next day we loaded up and went for a ride in a choo-choo train.

This seems like a nice base. It is spread all over the countryside but that is a good deal in some ways tho quite a contrast to the row on row of barracks back in the states.

We fly a practice gunnery mission tomorrow and I will do a lot of the same kind of training we've done before — lots of ground school etc. — also there's just a slight possibility that we may see some action. Am I kidding?

Roy R. Fisher, Jr. with Susan Fisher Anderson

The only means of transportation around here is by bicycle and so I bought one today. Second hand for about 9 lbs. That seems expensive but it's more or less rental until we leave & sell to someone else. Nearly all the boys in the crew got one today and so now we can really make some time. I sure get tired of walking.

We haven't gotten any more mail & from what I hear we won't get any for some time so I guess I'll just resign myself to the fact.

Nite sweetheart — I love you,
Jack

Sat. afternoon
Joyce Dearest,

I've got a few minutes before we go to school so I'll start this & finish it tonight. We have classes from 8 am till 9 pm so you see we're pretty busy. Yesterday we flew a camera gunnery mission. Same old stuff. I took my crew and the gunners from Aherns crew. I had an instructor pilot for c.p. & boy was he ever nervous. I'm sure glad I was flying instead of him. I made a poor landing but a safe one. The kind that hits hard but stays.

Last night we rode our bikes into town. Nice little place but we didn't stay long. Had a beautiful ride home in the moonlight. There were a lot of ships flying around and it was really beautiful. The ride was all uphill but it was fun anyway.

Well — we haven't become operational as yet and I'm not too eager to begin. These boys over here play for keeps and I'm not too eager for that old stuff.

I'm going to try to get the enlisted men paid their per diem this afternoon as soon as the finance department gets back from lunch so I better quit for now. Bye sweet — I love you.

Oh my darling — the sun just came into my life all of a sudden. I went off to class and the class was cancelled. In fact all of them are cancelled for this afternoon. We didn't expect any mail for several more days but when I went to the box there was — not one but two of the most marvelous letters from you darling. One was written a week ago last Thurs & the other a week ago Saturday.

From what you said the mail situation on your end of the line hasn't been too sharp either. I can't figure that out, because we mailed letters from everywhere we stopped. You'll probably get them all at <u>onct.</u> I've already sent you my A.P.O. but in case this gets there first it's:

94th Bomb Group 331 Bomb sqd.
APO 559 c/o Pm N.Y. N.Y.

Judging from the way your letters get mixed up when they come in you may get this letter before you do the V-mail.

I just got back from class darling and I'll add another note or two before I go to sleep.

Your two lovely letters have made you seem more near than at any time since I kissed you goodbye. I've had the same trouble that you have trying to feel the nearness, thru letters, that we have known together. Now — tho it seems that you are right with me all the time. That feeling has been much stronger than before we were married but there seemed to be a vacant space when I sit down to write. Now that void seems non-existant.

It would seem that Cornell was getting a football team. Now all we have to worry about is the Iowa State team. I'm still afraid they won't be so lucky.

Gosh darling, I got so lonely for you when you started talking about how we would <u>ruther</u> stood in bed than get up & play tennis. I'm sorry you got mad when I razzed Cornell. You should know that in spite of my remarks I wouldn't want you to go there if I didn't think it was a good school.

Say, honey, what's the deal on this bad cold? Looks like you need your daddy around to tell you when to wear your rubbers. Oh my darling — please take good care of yourself. You mean so very much to me.

I just wish I could make you see the loneliness that is in my heart tonight. Things have been a little rough the past few days. I know that you share my feelings, tho darling, so I guess you understand. How I long for the touch of your lips on mine. I'm getting sedimental so maybe I better quit.

Nite my darling I love you,
Your loving husband,
Jack

Roy R. Fisher, Jr. with Susan Fisher Anderson

Sunday night

Dearest wife,

How's the most wonderful wife in the world tonight?

We had ground school all day again today. I never saw such a poor excuse for a ground school. We had ten one hour classes scheduled and we had about 5 hours of class. The rest of the time we sat around waiting for things to start. The idea of ground school is something new around here and they can't figure it out. The Colonel is sure that he should keep us busy but the organization is very weak.

After class tonight I went to a U.S.O. show. They only had five people on the cast but they really put on a good show and I got some good laughs.

Yesterday afternoon I did my washing and I'm still waiting for the clothes to get dry. We had nice sunny days for a while and I thought they might last. No such luck. Sure wish the sun would come out so I would have a clean pair of shorts.

Tonight we have a big blackjack game going in the barracks. Spencer's crew is here and they're making quite a bit of racket.

This afternoon after dinner and while we were waiting between classes I just devoted all my thoughts to you. I closed my eyes and just thought about us and all the fun we've had together. Remember that one bed in Rapid City that made such a noise. And how we had to go clear downstairs to brush our teeth.

It's funny how things like that are so much fun to do together and are just routine tasks when you do it solo. Like sack time fer instance. Oh well — it can't last forever — that's one consolation. Gosh darling — the ache in my heart gets worse every day. I love you so very much darling. This being so far away from one you love so dearly is really no joke is it? But here I go again. I wish I had something to write about so I wouldn't get started thinking about how long it might be till I hold you in my arms again.

I was awfully interested in what you said about that new course you're taking about child development. That is an experience which is almost too marvelous to believe. That's why I want to be there with you when we have ours and then, darling, we'll spend the rest of our lives building our home and family.

Now darling I must hit the sack. All my love — always
Your loving husband,
Jack

The Lucky Bastard Club

Mon afternoon
Oct 9

Joyce my darling,

Another sweet letter from you today. My darling that helps so very much. Even tho I know it was a week ago last Thurs that you wrote it, nevertheless it brings you so much closer to me.

Questions & answers —
Your letters are not censored & mine will be only in exceptional cases so you may say anything you wish darling and I'll do the same.
So far I've gotten five letters from you — on three different days. That I think is about the way it will be. I surely hope so because I'd much rather get a letter every day than two every other day. As for the boys' home addresses I'll have them write to you & send that info.

So you want me to walk around the campus with you — that's OK by me. The stacks sound romantic. Wheeee.
Darling it makes me feel so good inside when you tell me that you're glad I'm your husband. I really can't imagine belonging to anyone else either darling. Being your husband seems so natural and right, I'm sure it could never be that way with anyone else. When I hold you in my arms and you snuggle up against me it just makes me certain that you — only — forever — can ever be the one for me.
Honey — remember the night at Rapid when we were hurrying to get ready to go out and you dropped that bottle of lotion. Yes – you dropped it — course I won't say I didn't have anything at all to do with it. Well dear it is chow time so I'll quit for now.
All thru with classes for tonight sweet. Nothing to do now but drop a few more lines to my wife and then hit the sack and dream.
I walked home with Spence tonight and we had a good time talking about our respective families. He's really convinced that fatherhood is the finest thing in the world. Dear — we have so very much in store for us. Actually it seems to me that no one could possible be any happier than we've been together. It is inconceivable to me that there is a breadth and depth to our love that we have no idea of. And yet — in the few months we spent together our love

increased to a point which was far beyond our dreams before we were married. I'm so glad darling that our life together has been as sweet and happy as it has. We know now that all it takes is a little consideration and unselfishness and a lot of love to make two people live in a little world all their own.

Those nights when I climb in the sack all cold & lonesome I think about when you were with me. I never needed to worry about being cold when you were there. I just hope that when I come back I won't have such hard work to do during the day so I won't be as sleepy at night. I can see how it might be pretty tough to not have a husband all day & then have him so tired he goes right to sleep. Someday darling —

Now, Mommie, if you'll just hold my head on your breast for a few minutes I'll be asleep before you know it.

Nite darling,
Jack

Oct 10, evening

Hello dear,

Pretty rough day today. We had ground school all morning and flew formation all afternoon and then had a class tonight. This place is worse than Rapid City. I just hope we become operational before long. All this messing around isn't bringing you any closer to me. And anything that doesn't bring me home to you is a lot of bunk as I look at it.

Got another letter from you today and one from home. The one I got from you was dated the 26th when you were just trying to get out of the hospital. I hope you're all better by now.

Dinna Shore is singing — no love — no nothing — and that's a promise I'll keep — no love — no sir — no nothing till my baby comes home. My eyes are getting so heavy darling I can't stay awake. As you see I really don't have a thing to write about except that I love you — oh so muchly —

Goodnight my only —
Jack

Chapter Eleven
Formation

We learned to fly a tight formation. Here's how it went: An "ELEMENT" is three planes — a lead ship and two wingmen. It is important to learn that tight formation means that the wingmen are so close that the nose of the wingman is ahead of the tail of the lead ship, with his wing overlapping the wing of the lead ship. Above and just behind the lead element is another element who fly so close that a fighter cannot slip between the lead ship of the high element and the lead element. These six ships are called a "FLIGHT". Another flight flys below the lead flight. They were designated as the low element and the low low element. These two flights make a squadron and three squadrons make a group — thirty-six ships. Typically the squadrons are identified as High Squadron, Lead Squadron, and Low squadron — which often had an extra plane in the low low element, Tail End Charlie.

The High squadron usually flew to the right of the lead squadron when the pilot of the High Squadron was flying the lead ship, so he could look down and out of his window and see the Lead Squadron. When the co-pilot was flying, positions were reversed. As the winds aloft usually increased with altitude, the High squadron usually had to zigzag a bit to stay behind the Lead squadron. We still didn't know about the jet stream, we just knew there had to be adjustments made as the altitude increased.

The opposite problem occurred in the Low Squadron. They had a tendency to lag behind, and straggle a little. That made the Low Squadron an inviting target for fighters. The Fighters could attack the Low Squadron and peel off with less exposure to the guns of the other ships in the Group. When under attack the Group tightened up the formation so all the guns were at their best.

The climbing speed of a B-17 was 130 mph and the fully loaded aircraft had most of the throttles at full speed during a climb. Consequently, if you fell behind — pilots don't like the word fell — *lagged* behind, the only way to catch up was to cut off the ship ahead on turns.

Roy R. Fisher, Jr. with Susan Fisher Anderson

Formation flying was the key to the reason we had to fly 35 missions for a full tour instead of 20 or 25 like the guys a few years before us. During those first few years of the war — while I was in college and then in training, the life expectancy of a B-17 pilot was considerably shorter, his chances of being shot down much greater. As the crews became better trained and able to maintain a tighter formation, the opportunities to protect each other from enemy fighters greatly improved. Another reason for the decrease in casualties — and increase in crew survival — was because of the fighter escorts, P-51's, which were a part of the team when I got overseas — a part which had been lacking in the first couple years of the war. However, no matter what fighter pilots tell you, only a portion of the changes in crew survival rates could be attributed to fighter escort, since their range was considerably less than ours, and they usually had to turn back to their base — often long before we reached our target. No, most of the difference was formation flying. I was determined to learn it well — as if my life depended upon it — which it did.

Oct 11 — Wed

Dearest wife,
Another day — another week — just that much closer to the end of this mess and to the day when I'll come home to you.
I'm plumb wore out again tonight. Today was a lot like yesterday. We had ground school this morning and flew this afternoon. One of these days I reckon I'll get to the place where I can stand this old stuff but as yet — it's a lot of hard work. I think you know what I mean. We were scheduled for ground school again tonight but I just can't see going out on such a rainy miserable night. Just about the time we went to chow it rained cats & dogs and I almost got soaked. Fortunately that raincoat I bought is long enough to keep me dry — even on a bicycle. I sure don't like this idea of flying & then coming down & going to ground school. These— — <u>feet</u>. All they know is that there is a lot of blocks on a wall chart that has to be filled up. I just wish they had to do some work once in a while.
The boys are all sitting around in a big bridge game now. I played awhile before supper & we made about 4,000 points in less than 2 rubbers. Bid & made a slam etc. Now they're arguing about why they made a slam & only bid 4 diamonds. That's the way it goes.

On that bid that we made — my partner opened with a spade & I bid 4 spades. He came back in Blackwood & I bid 5 no. As it happened I only had one king but it was the one he needed so we made a grand out of it. Sure is fun to bid a hand like that. Would you get scared if I gave you a triple jump like that? I had a pretty good hand — 4 aces — king J of spades couple small ones, lotsa queens & jacks — no losers. What a hand —

The rain on the roof this evening brought back so many memories of the nights at Rapid when we could lie there in each other's arms and listen to the rain on the roof til we went to sleep. Little everyday things that happen seem to bring back such sweet memories. It's like you said in one of your letters. I used to miss you most at night but now the time of day makes very little difference — I just miss you all the time. That lonely ache is helped somewhat by all the beautiful pictures that keep flashing thru my mind. Pictures of your face when I hold you close to me & you look into my eyes and say "Darling I love you so" — your eyes always told me darling that you were mine and could never belong to anyone else. I hope that you could read my eyes as well dearest because they were telling you the same thing. That I was yours first and will be yours alone always. That is a feeling which — now that we're apart — makes the experience we shared so full and complete and beautiful that I know I could never spoil it by knowing another. I've rambled a lot in this letter tonight but I hope you won't be too bored. It's awfully hard to write with as many interruptions as there are around here.

As I sit here and look at your picture I just think — Gosh — I'm sure a lucky guy to be married to such a wonderful woman. My darling — I love you so —

So very muchly —
Nite sweetheart
Jack, your everloving husband

At the flight line, there were a bunch of officers who didn't fly. Some of them had finished their missions, and others weren't even pilots. They were in charge of filling the group — assigning planes to elements and squadrons, weather briefings, etc. They taught ground school and tried to fill our lives with as much misery as possible, or so we assumed. Much of the time, it seemed as if they really had no idea of what we had to endure as pilots. We didn't have much respect for them in general and lovingly — though not to their faces — referred to them as "paddlefeet" or just "feet" for short. A few had extra responsibility and authority, though not necessarily higher rank. They were the "wheels."

Thurs nite
Oct 12

Joyce Darling,
It is already way past bed time but I do want to drop you a line. I just got home from seeing "Mutiny on the Bounty." I can't remember having seen it before and I enjoyed it immensely.

Your letter today said that you had received several of mine. Perhaps from now on our correspondence will be a little more satisfactory and not so irregular. You know a letter from you makes the whole day all right or the lack of one makes it dead. I took a shower in cold water today and even that wasn't too bad because you say such sweet things that I can think of little else. You're very right darling — we mustn't feel sorry for ourselves because we really do have so much to be thankful for. Our months together made me realize that life is so big and wonderful that is impossible for you to comprehend it without sharing with someone else. Just had an air raid in town — and about five minutes later a buzz bomb went over. Gosh those things make a noise. Fortunately they never land near here — I hope. Sorta makes you wonder — I always thought we were fighting a gentleman's war but I guess they want to play for keeps.

Well — don't worry about me. We've got the best crew in the airforce. Now all we need is a little luck.

Must close for tonight sweetheart.
See you in my dreams — cause I love you so —
Jack

The Lucky Bastard Club

Oct 14

My darling wife,

At last the letter I looked forward to for so long landed in England. The one where you told about going to the hospital to see all the new babies. Those two letters the one you wrote before you went & the one I got today were just about 5 days apart. I received three letters from you — 1 V-mail and 2 from the folks today. And — a lovely letter from Grandma & Grandpa and — an awfully nice letter from Jo. So you see today was quite a day. On top of that I flew three different times today & now I'm checked out. Well — that's what I came over here for and the quicker — the sooner.

Well my sweetheart — it's 10 o'clock now and I've got to hit the sack cause I'm gonna really get up early tomorrow — How I wish I could tell you the thoughts that are in my heart tonight but it is just as well perhaps because they are not all pleasant.

The main theme tho overshadows the rest because it is the most important thing in my life. That my sweet — is my love for you. A love which has become so strong that I feel your presence with me tonight even tho you are many hundreds of miles away. I know that your thoughts & prayers are with me as mine are with you and in the knowledge there is strength. A strength which helps me to do my job when my own resources are exhausted.

And now I must say Goodnight my Beloved Wife — I love you so
Your husband
Jack

Roy R. Fisher, Jr. with Susan Fisher Anderson

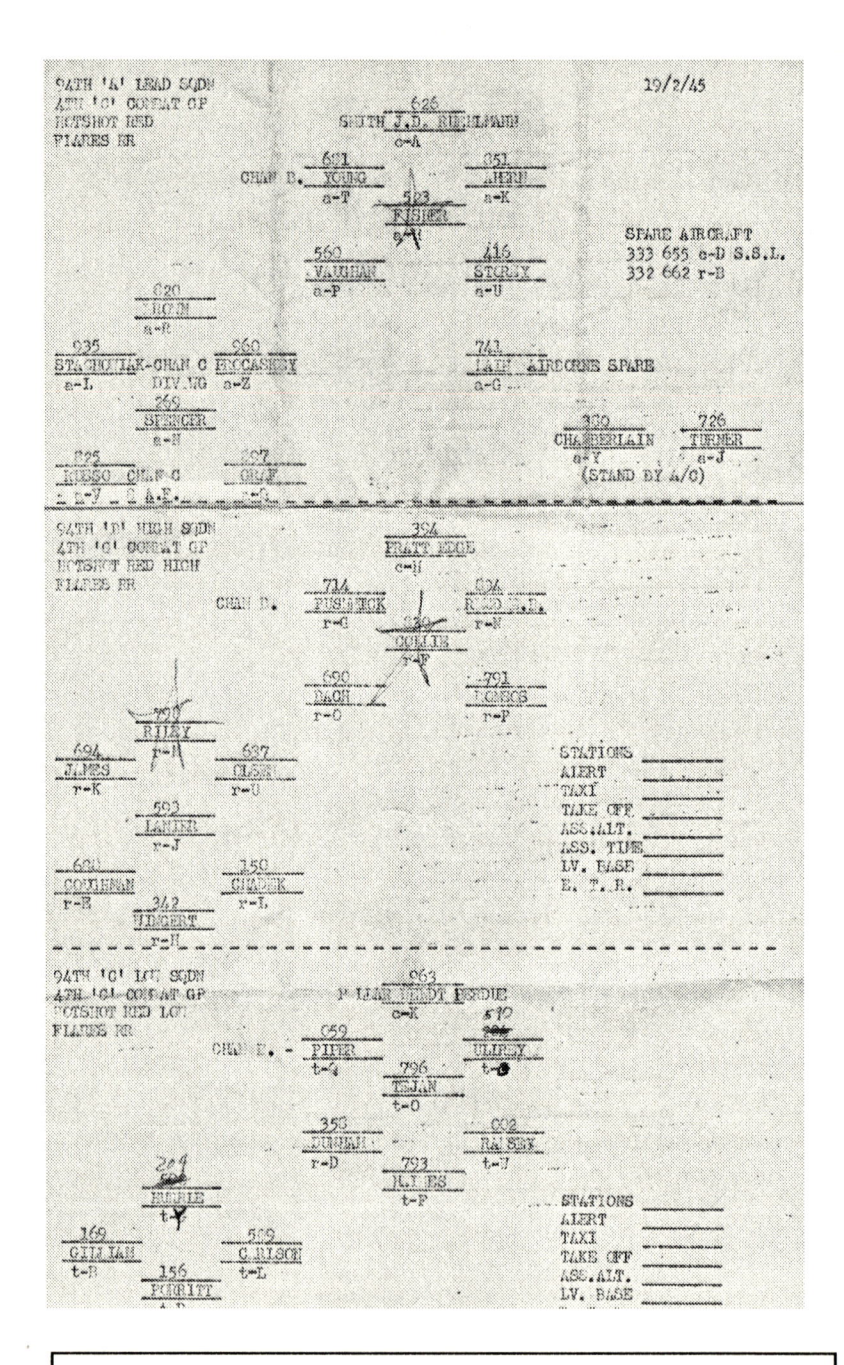

Mission Briefing sheet. You don't know the players without a program.

Chapter Twelve
Combat

MISSION # 1   OCTOBER 15, 1944
COLOGNE = 7:00 HRS

A new pilot always flew at least three, sometimes many more, missions as Co-Pilot with an experienced crew before taking up his own crew. Trained crews were expensive, and they wanted to be sure the pilot wouldn't crack under the pressure of both being in command and being shot at. So, sitting in the right seat of a B-17, I flew my first combat mission as we took off before dawn to join the strike force.

A strike force was a series of Groups headed for the same target on the same day. On any given day there might be three or four strike forces of six to twenty Groups. Each strike force would have Fighter Support, consisting of pursuit aircraft — P-51's and P-47's, to fly along their route and protect the Bombers from Enemy Fighters. Unfortunately, though, the fighters had considerably less fuel capacity, and thus, a much shorter range. We often lost them long before we reached the target area, and long before we encountered enemy fighter patrols, itching to shoot down heavy bombers.

A "maximum effort" might include over 2000 Heavy Bombers: two Divisions of B-17's and one Division of B-24s. In addition there were many squadrons of Light Bombers B-25s, B-26s, and A-20s.

As each strike force left the coast of England, they would head in different directions to encourage the German Fighters to spread out to defend against the different strike forces. It was just one big chess game. The whole idea was to divide the enemy so the main strike force would have no more than their share of fighters.

Well, today was number one and boy I was tired, surprised, and a believer. They can send me home any time now.

Roy R. Fisher, Jr. with Susan Fisher Anderson

Oct 15 – Sunday

Darling — my own,

Went on a mission today. Where or when is of course secret but at last I've started my tour. From here on each flight brings me closer to you.

I'm a little tired but otherwise I feel fine so you really don't have a thing to worry about.

Last night I was so tired I didn't feel much like writing so if that letter was incoherent just think nothing of it. I didn't get to tell you all about the nice letter I got from Grandma and Grandpa Smith. She told me all about the farm and what they were doing. I was so glad to hear from them and I'll try to answer it tonight.

Jo wrote me an awfully nice letter too — she told me all about her work and what she was doing. She writes a very interesting letter doesn't she.

Today didn't seem at all like Sunday for some reason. Just once, I'd like to get to a base where they recognized that the Sabbath should be observed. I haven't been to church for such a long time I'm ashamed of myself. The only way I know today was Sunday was that we had chicken. Fried — no I guess it was stewed — but anyway it was awfully good. I hurried over and beat some of the "feet" into line so I got some white meat & a leg. We also had some ice cream — chocolate — no less. The civilians haven't seen ice cream in several years.

Well — darling — it is getting awfully late and I'm very tired to perhaps I should hit the sack. Perhaps one of these days I'll be able to write a good letter but at present my thoughts are rather scattered.

But — I loves ya — honey —
deed I do —
Jack

Oct 16 Mon

Dearest wife,

The "feet" slipped up today and didn't wake us up till noon so I really caught up on the sleep I'd been missing the past few nights. Then we went up and flew formation all afternoon but the weather feet screwed up the forcast so we spent a lot of time trying to find a clear spot and so the formation didn't last too long. I'm beginning to *catch on to formation flying again now too and so today wasn't rough at all. Stan flew quite a bit & we held it reet in there.*

Tonight we had a poop session with the Old man and I never saw such an outright farce. No matter what subject we brought up — he avoided any issue on any matter. I got told a couple of times so I finally just shut up.

We had some hot water tonight so the kid took a shower and even washed my fair hair. I got to thinking about all the times we used to take our showers together. We sure have had fun haven't we. I should get a lot of sleep tonight I feel so nice & calm. That is really something out of the ordinary over here.

It rained all morning and every time I woke up I could hear the rain of the roof and go back to sleep & dream of you. Then when I got up the sun was out and the woods were beautiful. There are a lot of trees around here and they are all changing color now. Looks a lot like home.

There are a lot of oaks & Maples with a few evergreens sprinkled in here & there to add variety. It is just the time of year when it would be so much fun to walk thru the woods with you. Wouldja like that? Huh? I sure would. It won't be long dear —

Now must say goodnight & sweet dreams. Gosh darling — I miss you so very much.

Your loving husband,
Jack

MISSION # 2   OCTOBER 17, 1944
COLOGNE = 6:15 HRS

Funny how little it takes to make a man uneager. Just a minute or five minutes when someone is shooting at you seems like an eternity and yet it is all over in practically no time at all. Pop didn't miss much. My footlocker still hadn't caught up with me, and I was running out of clean underwear.

MISSION # 3   OCTOBER 18, 1944
KASSELL = 8:00 HRS

Two more missions in the right seat (copilot). Since I was such a little guy, I could only handle the stick for about 15 minutes at a time. The temperature also decreased with altitude (about two degrees centigrade for each thousand feet of altitude). Thus if you take off at freezing (0 degrees C), at twenty thousand feet the temperature is 40 degrees below zero. That's why we had heated suits (if they worked, which they did most of the time). We were tolerably warm, except of course for the tail gunner, who huddled in that small space with only a thin metal skin between him and the frigid atmosphere. It was impossible to get heat back there, let alone keep him anywhere warm since he had to stay in his position the whole time we were over enemy territory.

Oct 18

Joyce — my own sweet wife,

I got my anniversary card today and also the nicest letter so in spite of a rough flight I'm in excellent spirits.

I've got three missions now. They will begin to count up after a while I guess but as yet it's a pretty small pile. I just wish I were a little larger because we both get tired too quickly. Of course — you know just how formation tires me out. Right now I'm in my own little sack logging a little time. I'm so tired I can't hardly keep my eyes open so I may quit in the middle of a sentence but if that happens — you'll understand.

I was so thrilled by your letter today, darling, the things you said about my homecoming to your open arms made me feel warm and happy all over. You've no idea how much it meant to get home tired and dirty to find such a marvelous letter from you. Joyce — you're so wonderful. I find it hard to believe that I am actually married to such a marvelous woman. I'm so supremely happy to be your husband, and you know darling that I'll be home to your waiting arms as soon as possible.

Now I'll cap my pen & close my eyes & dream of you —
I love you
Jack

MISSION # 4   OCTOBER 19, 1944
MANNHEIM = 7:00 HRS

The BIG ONE. Our first mission as a crew. Finally — after all the training, all the classes, all the practice — we are all together, in our own plane. It really is quite a daunting realization for a man just 21 to think that the lives of ten men depended on my every thought and action. Yes, they all were adults — when do you really begin to feel like an adult — they all had their own jobs to do, but I was the pilot. I was in charge. Five foot six inches, one hundred twenty-five pounds and I was in charge of that huge aircraft and the lives of those nine other men.

When we left Bury St. Edmonds that day, everything was fine. In fact, it was exhilarating — just me, the guys and the great, big sky — well, there were also several hundred other huge aircraft in the immediate vicinity. We were on our way to Mannheim, on October 19, to wreak some havoc on the Furher's territory. We almost never got there.

The Enemy had installed extensive anti-aircraft defenses along the coast; that we knew. They were some of the best in the Reich. As our strike force approached they would begin shooting those huge guns, adjusting the altitude and aim as we approached. As each shell exploded at its pre-determined altitude, shards of metal went flying in all directions, to the detriment of any aircraft in the vicinity. The ships in the lower positions could see the bursts of flak as they tracked our route. On that day, we were flying low, low element in the low squadron, and we were the target for the day. As we flew over the Friesian Islands — off the coast of Denmark, suddenly the ball turret gunner, Bob, called on the intercom,

"We've got tracking flak, PULL HIGH AND RIGHT".

I asked no questions; I just pulled back on the yoke and cranked it to the right. We sailed out of the formation, and the next burst of flak was right in our spot. But, we weren't there. Bob's warning — and our training, saved our ship from a direct flak burst, right in the bomb bay — on our first mission. The other two ships in our element got some big holes; we just got a few small ones, some dents and a good dose of adrenaline to get us to our target.

That day was also our first experience with contrails. Under certain conditions of temperature, altitude and humidity; a cloud called a "contrail" forms behind each engine. They are beautiful to see from the ground, but no fun to fly in when you're trying to stay in formation. With thirty-six ships in the group — each with four engines, we made some serious contrails. As group after group pass through the contrail altitude, the contrails remain as thin clouds which make it still more difficult for the later groups to maintain formation. Once in a while a ship got lost or, worse still, there was a collision.

Anyway, that's one for the crew. Now the enlisted men only had thirty-one missions to go. They only flew when I flew, and finished when I did. Officers had to do the full thirty-five.

Oct. 19 Thurs.

My darling wife,
I'm pretty much mixed up on time and dates but I checked with the rest of the boys and I'm pretty sure the date is right.

I got <u>four</u> letters from you today sweetheart. Dated Oct 2, 6, 7 &9. As yesterday — I was really awfully glad to get them. It just makes all the difference in the world to have you tell me you love me and that everything is really all right. Of course I really know all the time that you always love me but when the days are rough there is nothing like a little moral support from the light of my life to put me back on top again.

I've got four (4) now and the wish you expressed in one of your letters that the first five were already history almost came true. They just about are. So far I still feel perfectly OK with perhaps a tired feeling in my back that needs a couple days of rest to clear it up. I use the rudders a lot more now than I did before and it sure shows up in a hurry. I thought my back would never get tired but I'm wrong again. Stan has two missions now and he is pretty tired too. More so perhaps than I because he makes it so hard the first little while.

Our flight today was beautiful. Of course I can't tell you where we went but I believe I can tell you about the beauty of it all. We flew quite high and there were contrails behind each ship for 200 or 300 yards. We were high enough so we could see other formations below us. They looked like little water bugs swimming on very clear water and leaving a lot of foam in their wake. Once a formation passed directly in front of us a few hundred feet higher in almost perfect formation and the white clouds behind them were just as perfect. Then every once in a while some fighters would zoom past and it was a really grand feeling to know that those boys were around for protection. The crew is sure working together as a perfect team. I'm so glad that we were so conciencious about our training. You certainly helped a lot to mold them into a crew. There's something about the way you treated the boys when they came to visit us that really made an impression. But why wouldn't you? Gosh darling — I love you so. I just can't see how anyone could ever fail to be impressed.

So you got your hair cut again. Well well what do you know about that? I think you look awfully nice with short hair darling. You never need worry about whether or not I'll like the way your hair looks. It always looks beautiful to me.

And — darling — please don't think I could ever get impatient with you because you show me you love me. Please don't ever stop — I love it. That's one thing I'll never tire of. I want you to be proud of me — just as I am of you. When we walk down the street — I want you to take my arm so everyone will know that I belong to you — and you to me — now & always

Yours
Jack

Friday nite, Oct 20
Joyce Darling,

Here's your lovin' hubsband just droppin in for a chat. How does that suit you?

I haven't done much of anything today. We had a couple of lectures this morning by our C.O. and he told us that he wasn't happy — Hell — we knew that. He's going to make an example of someone. That's nothing new. We're all going to get up at 7:00 — yes 0700 every morning until we get on the ball. This is sure getting to be a rough damn war.

We got assigned a ship today. The "Mission Belle" by name. She's a beautiful ship and the boys are all thrilled to have a ship of their own.

Of course that means that all the boys will be able to take care of one set of guns and then they can be sure they'll work. Our crew chief is an on-the-ball man too — he even had ashtrays in the ship so we wouldn't throw butts on the floor. He even had a couple pieces of armor plate under the seat. Good man!

This clipping came out of "Stars and Stripes" ~~yesterd~~ or rather today about noon. For once I beat the paddlefeet to the chow line & got a paper.

Roy R. Fisher, Jr. with Susan Fisher Anderson

We had a big bridge game again tonight and I got trimmed slightly. That's the way it goes.

Well darling — I've got to get some sleep tonight — if you see what I mean. Dearest I love you so — nite Joyce

Your own Jack.

Chapter Thirteen
Home Away from Home — London

(American Red Cross Stationary)

Sat nite Oct 21

Joyce Darling,

As you will probably be able to tell — tonight I'm in London on my first 48-hour pass. As you can also see — I neglected to bring along my own pen and so I'm scratching this out with a very poor excuse for a hotel pen.

We left the base early this evening and arrived here about 11. We are located at the Red Cross — "Dutchess Club" which is all the Red Cross is at home with a hotel to boot. Ott & Bob went downtown but I decided to stick around here & go to bed. I wandered into the library which is where I am now and found a beautiful grand piano. Also found a book of Spirituals and so I spent the better part of an hour picking out the various tunes by the hunt & peck system I'm really glad no one else is ~~about~~ (damn limeys) around so I could disturb no one with my poundings.

We had some "cheezeburgers" and a cup of coffee tonight but they didn't measure up by quite a bit to the ones that my wife makes. In fact they were quite bad but you can't expect much — after all.

Tomorrow promises to be a big day. I want to get up early enough to go to one of the beautiful churches for the service and then will spend the rest of the day — sightseeing. I'll let you know all about it tomorrow nite. How'll that be. Perhaps for once I'll be able to write about my day's doings without being afraid of violating regulations.

Now my dearest I really must go to bed. Gosh how I wish you could be here with me — I miss you soo very much, my life —

Goodnight Joyce — I love you
Jack.

Oct 24 – Tuesday

Joyce Darling,

Here I am — back at the base — after a quite enjoyable 48 hour pass. I really wanted to write you Sunday night but I was so tired I just tumbled into bed.

Roy R. Fisher, Jr. with Susan Fisher Anderson

The first thing we did Sunday morning was to go to church. We went down to Westminister Abbey and saw an Episcopal service. In a lot of ways it is just like a Catholic service except that everything was in English instead of Latin. The sermon was pretty good but I could hardly hear him. Gosh — that is a tremendous church. After the service we went around and looked at all the memorials and tomb stones. There are all sorts of memorials dating way back to the 16th century. It seems more like a museum than a church. After church we wandered around the Thames and saw some of the sights in the local area. In the afternoon we went to the Officers PX and picked up some stuff. I bought another pair of pinks and some more wool socks. Our foot lockers haven't come yet and so I'm still trying to catch up on my laundry. I really should do some today but I'm 'fraid we're going to have a practice mission this afternoon. But to get back to my itinerary. Sunday night we — Bob — Ott — and I went to the Tracodero for dinner. They did their best to entertain us but every time the band played anything it reminded me of you and I got so lonesome. Monday morning I got up bright and early with every intention of watching them "Change the Guards at Buckingham Palace" but the Red Cross gave us a bum steer and we were just one day late. Stan came in Sunday nite & so I went up to the PX with him. We didn't buy much the place was awfully crowded. I bought a pair of bars for my raincoat. I got picked up by an MP in Picadilly Circus for not having any pretty gold bars on my raincoat. This place is worse than the 2nd A.F.(in the states) We went thru St. James park on the way to the PX and saw three big beds of Dahlias that I've ever seen. I took a picture of them so you can see them too. There are so many beautiful sights over here darling that I'd like to share with you.

We came back last night on the 6:25 train and got in here about 11:25. Five hours and only about 90 miles. Whata ride. We met a Lt. from the infantry who was coming up to visit his brother so we took him under our wing. When we looked up his brother — he had gone down Oct 5 over Big B. That was pretty rough to take. We kept him here with us last night and helped him get squared away today & I think he feels a little better.

Now — I must go to chow — we do have a practice mission this pm. — Damn —

The Lucky Bastard Club

Just came back from the line. Stan had his fingers crossed and for the first time it worked. He was afraid that he was out of his sphere of influence but it seems that things are going better now. These practice missions are sure tiresome and I'm tired anyway so I'm glad to be back.

Oh yes — I almost forgot. Yesterday afternoon I bought you a Christmas present. Another one of those times when I couldn't find anything for just you so I got something for both of us. I really wanted to get you something nice to wear but with the rationing system over here it is almost impossible to find anything except Blackmarket and I haven't located one of those yet. Gosh, dear, I hope I get a letter from you today. I haven't heard a word for nearly five days.

I bought a few Christmas cards the other day. Just a few — nuff for the folks and Danny Fischer and one or two others. As for the rest of our mutual friends I think I'll just leave that in your capable hands and let you decide to whom we ought to send cards. Oh yes — Christmas presents — I think it would be a whole lot better for you to get just some little remembrance for all the folks and make it from us rather than for me to try to find anything over here. Well, my own — I've said all that I had on my mind now it's high time my heart had a word to say. I'm really afraid to let it get started because I don't know how to stop it once it starts telling you just how much I miss you all the time. Each time morning rolls around I dread getting up because I know that I'll just get thru another lonesome day without you near me. "Our" days used to be so much different. Each new day was full to overflowing with love and hope and happiness. From the time I opened one eye and kissed you goodmorning the whole world seemed right. Even when I got up at 4:00 to fly it was still OK because you would get up with me and get my breakfast. Gosh what a lucky guy I am to have such a sweet wife.

Things like that mean so much to me darling. It just proves to me — over & over — that you love me as much as I love you. And I do love you darling. Always — only you.
Now bye pretty baby —
Your hubsband,
Jack

Roy R. Fisher, Jr. with Susan Fisher Anderson

Chapter Fourteen
Merseburg

MISSION # 5   OCTOBER 25, 1944
MERSEBURG = 7:25 HRS

On October 25th, we made our first of five trips to MERSEBURG. Merseburg was in the Poleisti area of oil refineries. As the war progressed and oil became very critical, Merseburg was increasingly and heavily defended with anti-aircraft (Flak) guns. That first time, we didn't know why the others moaned and groaned when the target was announced. We would learn quickly.

As we began our bombing run, the flak was so thick that we couldn't see anything but big black puffs with red centers and they were all so close that it felt like we were riding propwash. One of the boys right ahead of us in formation blew up–he got a direct hit in the right wing root and before I could write about it, he had exploded and the pieces flew back through our formation. Over the target a piece of flak shot into the upper turret — Sam Carlino's position — just behind my head. It was so hot we could smell it even with our oxygen masks on. As it spun around the waist like a bee, Sam pressed down the mike button and prayed aloud in a low, slightly shaky (especially for Sam) voice, "Hail Mary Full Of Grace, Blessed Art Thou among Women, And Blessed Is The Fruit Of Thy Womb, JESUS". That is a Catholic Prayer, but there was nothing denominational about that prayer that day. He was praying for all of us.

When we left the target, we peeled off so fast that I'll never know why there weren't more collisions. We missed one ship by less than two feet. He got in propwash and skidded into us. It took all Stan and I had and all the help the Good Lord could give us to miss him. He was trying to miss the pieces of one that blew up in front of him. It was only that the Lord was willing and the devil had no objection that we got through.

After that first scary trip, whenever Merseburg was mentioned it started the "Sweat that didn't stop" till we had completed the mission. I've still got that piece of flak. There were times I was pretty well convinced that it was a rough darn war. The only good thing is that the time goes so fast, I can't for the life of me figure out where it went.

Wed. Oct 25

Darling,
   Just a few lines cause I'm so tired I can't see or sit up. I'm lying in my sack now writing this before I drop off to sleep.
   We have five missions now and as I said before — I'm tired. I'm just about convinced that it would be better if I weighed about 200 lbs. It would make for more endurance.
   Darling — you seemed so near me all day long today. It seemed that many times my mind would wander or completely ignore the business at hand and dwell on a much more pleasant subject — you. I thought all about you and how much I love you. I thought of how sweet your hair is and how your eyes sparkle and I longed to rest my head on your breast and have you tell me that you love me. That's the way you are with me darling and without you I'm sure I could never make it. Because with you — there is something to fight for. Something to live for — Someone to love.
   I hope you can see just how much these things mean dearest. I do so want you to know how marvelous it is to love and be loved by you.
   Forever —
   Jack

I think our first trip to Merseburg was when the reality of war really started to settle in. I think this was when I made a conscious decision to not share with Joyce the reality of what we were up against. Of course, the threat of censorship of my letters was always present. But, more than that, I had seen the way worry cast a dark shadow across her crystal blue eyes, and I guess I couldn't bear to think I would be the cause of that shadow taking residence in her sparkling eyes for the duration of my tour. Perhaps it was selfish on my part. I really needed the picture of those eyes, sparkling the way they did, to lift me up when I was down or so bone-tired I couldn't lift the pen to write. I decided to censor myself, to protect my sweet wife from the horrible things I had to see and do. "Keep the love-light shining in her eyes, so blue." My sweetheart. So, I decided to leave out the frightening details of our missions. Why burden her with them, when there was nothing she could do to help? Instead, I filled my letters with newsy, mundane details of our life at the base. Then, I could retreat to the safety of her love for me, knowing that it was pure and undefiled by the horrors of war. I could remember the way she looked when I last saw her, and not have to imagine how she would look as she read my letters filled with fear and near-death experiences. So, my double life began. I would share my fatigue, but not my fear. We both would be better off than if she really knew the whole truth.

Loving Joyce became my escape. Not from reality, but to it. I often wrote her how I would escape to thoughts of her, her face, her voice. I don't know whether she realized how true it was. She was my lifeline, my security, my certainty that the war was only temporary and that the true reality was not England, not Germany, but Iowa. Reality was a beautiful blue-eyed brunette going to Cornell College and searching the mailbox every day for a word from me. Reality was a sparkly-eyed coed with a ring on her finger — a ring which declared to all the world that she belonged to me, and I to her.

Thurs nite Oct 26

Joyce my own,

Tonight for a change I'm not tired at all — In fact I really feel in good shape tonight. How's about a big night tonight. We could go out somewhere for supper and a show — first. Does that sound OK to you? Personally I'm getting awfully lonesome for a certain little wife — for whom I have a very deep love. Funny isn't it? Don't suppose you feel that way — much.

I didn't do much today. Had link this morning and AFCE for an hour this afternoon. The rest of the time I just sat around and read. This afternoon I went over to the enlisted men's tent. They've got it fixed awfully nice now. Heater — electric lights, — radio and everything. They all got promoted to Sgt yesterday. That is — excepting Richter. They only fly 9 men and so I dropped him. It helped the crew I think but it sure is tough on him. The rest of the boys are pretty happy about the whole war. I don't think they expected to be promoted for a while so it came as a sort of surprise. Then too — they were the first in that group we came with to get it so they really can lord it over the other boys for a few days.

Roy R. Fisher, Jr. with Susan Fisher Anderson

 Aside from these little details the war is still going pretty much the same so I'll cap this pen & say good night. It's been awfully nice being with you sweetheart — I love you.
 Jack

Friday nite
Oct. 27

My dearest wife,
 Five — yes (5) letters today from my own today. Darling they helped so very much. You asked what you could do to help me release nervous energy. Your letters help as much as any one thing.
 Perhaps before I do anything else I'll tip you off on some of those rumors you got. Yes — we are offered a shot of Scotch after missions but I've not acquired a sudden desire to forget all my ideas about drinking and smoking. Stan usually takes care of my Scotch and I can always get rid of cigarettes. Once in a while I do smoke a cigar but not much more often than before. It is quite true that I do become sexually overstimulated at times because of the nervous tension but I never need to worry about that as long as I can relieve that pressure periodically with a strong right arm. Perhaps that isn't the wisest solution to the problem but I'm convinced that it is the only logical answer. Does that answer your question? As for the rumor that we haven't got anything left to bomb — He's crazy as Hell. Perhaps the targets aren't the same as they have been but never-the-less — as long as there's a war on over here — the 8th will be here too. I really wouldn't get too excited about me getting home before my tour is over. Well — that just about takes care of rumors. Huh hon. The moon is about three days from full over here and it is really beautiful. Most of the leaves are off the trees now and the moon was shining through the trees just like autumn back home. The chestnuts are falling and the funny thing is that there are no squirrels to chatter at you when you raid their stores.
 This afternoon Slim & Sam and Hume and I went out to the ship and while Slim sketched the words I painted the names of our women under our windows. So now your name is right outside my window so folks can tell to whom I belong and I do darling — body and soul — always and always; I love you so —
 nite Joyce —
 Jack

The Lucky Bastard Club

Sunday night
Oct 29

Joyce dearest,

I just got back from church and I've a few minutes to let you know I love you very, very, dearly.

I flew a practice mission this afternoon with Clare — that Redheaded fellow from Rapid City — you met his wife. He's in the 333rd sqd. And I was checking him out on formation. While we were flying at 20 thous or so we lost contact with the lower ball and they messed around several minutes before they let us know and when they did I dove out of formation and down to ten thousand feet so he would come to. He recovered quickly at the lower altitude and happily suffered no ill effects but it was close enough so he nor I nor any of the crew will easily forget it. For that reason it was a successful mission. They or rather we learned a lot.

As I said before — I'm surely glad I trained my crew before I got over here. You don't realize just what a good crew means until you ride with a poor one and see how they fail miserably in the most simple practice missions. They may have a little trouble with the real thing.

(Time out for Charlie McCarthy) He was good and now Judy Garland is singing "I'm glad there is you." Gosh darling – am I ever.

Ott is strutting around in his new battle jacket tonight. He bought a blouse in London and had it cut down into a beautiful jacket. I've been debating about having one made out of my blouse. I sure like the looks of them but I'd like to have your opinion on the matter. Funny thing darling — I never like to do anything unless I find out how you feel about it and whether or not you agree with me. That's just another of the wonderful things about being married to you. There are so many nice things about being your husband. Each day that goes by makes me more conscious that the woman I left behind and who is waiting for me is the most wonderful woman in the world and the finest wife a man ever had. Truly darling — there could never be a finer companion for a man than you have been to me.

Soon we'll be together
for always —
Jack

Roy R. Fisher, Jr. with Susan Fisher Anderson

MISSION # 6   OCTOBER 30, 1944
MERSEBURG = 5:55 HRS

When Merseburg was on the briefing map, we started sweating and that continued till we were back on the ground. This time we groaned with the others. We knew it would be a dangerous mission, and some of us wouldn't come back. Who? We were flying in formation over the target when Stan slapped my arm and pointed out his window. The lead ship of our element had taken a direct hit and its port engine was headed straight for us. We both pulled back on the yoke as hard as we could. The engine missed us by inches. We would live to fly another day.

Monday nite
Oct 30

My darling wife,

Number six today. Gradually they seem to pile up in spite of the fact that at times there is apparently no movement of time. Actually I guess I shouldn't say that because time passes so very quickly that I am amazed when each Monday comes. It hardly seems more than a couple days — and here's another week gone.

The moon tonight is so full and beautiful. As we came back from chow we could see him peeking over a bank of fog and from between the tops of the pine trees. It was lovely darling and as I watched I remembered that night at Rapid when we climbed the hill behind our little cabin to watch the moon and the lovely lights. Remember? How could you forget. Then — I remember the times you used to show me the moon out of your window. 'Member how I had to get way over on your side of the bed to see out the window.

Darling — we've had so much and there's so very much more ahead of us. Someday —

Now my own precious wife — I'm so tired I simply must hit the sack.

Nite honey,
Jack

The Lucky Bastard Club

Halloween nite
31

Joyce my dearest,
    Just got home from an excellent show — "Two girls and a sailor" with Harry James Xaviar Cugal, Lena Horn and lotsa others. I enjoyed it so very much. I haven't been out much this past week and so it was really welcome. It was the sort of picture that made me miss you terribly but you seemed so very near. So much of the time I'm so busy that my thoughts are otherwise occupied and I don't like it. I just wish I could spend every day thinking about you but I'm 'fraid that's impossible.
    We got up real early this morning but it all come to naught. We went back out to the ship about 10:00 to swing the compass and finish our painting but I taxied off the runway and the left wheel sank in to

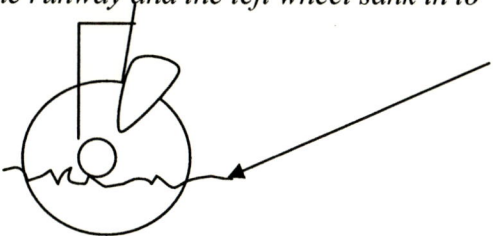

there
so it took them the rest of the morning to pull it out so we gave up. They took our ship up on a practice mission this afternoon so we can't seem to make a nickel. This afternoon I had an hour of Link — practiced making autopilot landings — I'm going to try that some one of these days. Just practicing of course.
    Well — we promoted our little dog "ammo" to major yesterday so now he's still the ranking officer in the barracks. I guess I never told you about Judah Madenski — he's the squadron navigator & he lives here with us. As you could guess he's Jewish and a hell of a good guy. He got promoted to Captain just the other day. He's been sweating it out for several months. That's why we had to promote "ammo."
    Just got in a big long discussion on "The merits & demerits of Jefferson Barracks." More fun —. This place is getting loud again and so I might just as well quit trying to write. When they get started it goes on & on.
    See you tomorrow night my dearest —
    Darling — I love you so
    Your husband
    Jack

Roy R. Fisher, Jr. with Susan Fisher Anderson

MISSION # 7   NOVEMBER 1, 1944
RUDESHEIM = 7:01 HRS

This was not a particularly long haul, but boy was I tired. Our ships did not have hydraulic assistance. It was all manual. Rudders, throttles, yoke, brakes. Wrestling that 36 tons. of metal, fabric and men — not to mention several thousand pounds of ordnance — really took a toll on us little guys. Some days were worse than others.

Nov. 1ˢᵗ
<u>already</u>

My beloved,

Four wonderful letters from the swellest wife a guy ever had and boy did they help. I was awfully tired tonight but I really feel better now. Had a pretty rough day. Not such a long haul but a heavy one and it wore me out. That makes #7. Gosh how I wish it were over and I could be with you again. Your letters are so refreshing darling because they help me to think a little. I'm 'fraid our thinking is rather limited and we have none of the thought provoking oportunities that you are experiencing, Rather — it is to our advantage to do as little thinking as possible because it only disturbs our peace of mind.

Stan just discovered that "ammo" wags his tail up and down instead of back & forth. That is a sage observation and is typical of the trend of thought. We're all so tired we can't think rationally.

So my darling I'll close with the thought that is always foremost in my mind. My love for you — the greatest thing which has ever happened to me. My own wife — I love you so very much & always will —

Jack

The Lucky Bastard Club

Roy R. Fisher, Jr. with Susan Fisher Anderson

The strain of combat and command is starting to show.

Chapter Fifteen
Borrowed Time

MISSION # 8   NOVEMBER 2, 1944
MERSEBURG = 7:45 HRS

Today, when the target was announced, our blood turned to ice water. As we were approaching the bombing area, we saw a cloud of black smoke at our altitude and several miles off to our left. It appeared to be several miles long, and 4,000 to 5,000 feet thick. As we got closer we could see aircraft flying through the cloud in the opposite direction to our course. As we got even closer, we could see an occasional ship blow up from a direct hit from the flak bursts, which were creating the smoke. I remember thinking to myself, "Boy! Those poor bastards are really catching hell."

Then our group made a 90° left turn, and then another 90° left turn, to arrive at the starting point of our bomb run. Now it was our turn to be the "poor bastards" as we flew through the most concentrated flak barrage of my entire flying experience. Fortunately, we were able to complete our bomb run with no serious holes and no Purple Hearts (no injuries to crew). (Thank you, God, for your protection.)

We will, however, remember November 2nd forever. From then on our memories were designated as before or after November 2nd. If Hell could be described, perhaps it would be similar to that day over Merseburg.

Thursday Nov. 2

My dearest,

After today I won't even be able to write a letter but perhaps a note will keep you from worrying. Having survived the raid today we're now on borrowed time so to speak. It was really rough. Not much more I can say except that it was number 8.

We've been talking over the flight and it is just one of those things that gets worse with the telling. The more you talk about something as rough as that the worse it makes you feel. Telling you won't make me feel any better and it will make you worry so I'll just skip it. It'll be a lot brighter tomorrow. It's just that tonight it looks pretty bad.

Roy R. Fisher, Jr. with Susan Fisher Anderson

    Boy — the B-17 is sure a marvelous airplane.
    Today — I thought a lot about you darling and how much I love you. That thought and a prayer were the foremost thoughts in my mind. I've prayed more sincerely if not more prolifically the last few weeks than ever before in my life. Darling — I want so very much to come back to you and hold you in my arms again. And after today — I'm sure the Good Lord has His Hand on me.
    Now sweet — I must hit the sack — Darling my own
Goodnight —
Your loving husband
Jack

Friday Nove 3

Joyce, my own,
    Such a sweet letter today. The first I've gotten which was addressed to this new A.P.O. That warm glow which I feel all over when I read your letters isn't nearly as nice as actually having you here but under the circumstances it is all I can ask for. Just to know that you are waiting for me and planning for the day that I come home helps me to forget that this is a rough war. It helps so much to get my eyes on those clouds way up in the sky — on the dreams that we've always dreamed together. I know darling — it hits with quite a jar once in a while when we know it may still be quite some time till we're together and yet we have to hope and pray that it won't be too long. And even if it does take longer than we want it to — Darling we have so much to be thankful for. Just to know that we have become one person in ideals & purpose as well as in mind and body is the most wonderful experience that life has to offer. We're so very fortunate to be able to look at our life together and know that it has been pure and beautiful in every sense and — as you say — the love which we knew has already grown in our hearts by our separation and has made us both more conscious of just what we have been blessed with.
    Now dearest — it's time to quit for tonight. I'll dream of you I hope —
    Nite hon,
Jack

The Lucky Bastard Club

MISSION # 9 NOVEMBER 4, 1944
HAMBURG = 7:45 HRS

This trip to Hamburg I made with a new pilot riding instead of Stan. He was having trouble with formation flying. Well, more than trouble. Pop would have said he couldn't fly for sour apples. When the group came home from a mission, the squadrons would enter into the landing pattern stacked at various altitudes but all flying the same pattern, a great big square, each leg determined by the direction of the wind. Since we would land into the wind, our first leg was upwind; then we made a 90° turn and flew across the wind direction. Next we made another 90° turn, flew with the wind, the downwind leg; then another 90° turn for the base leg, across the wind again. The base leg was followed by another 90° turn to get the plane headed upwind again for our final approach.

Every pilot knew the pattern, we learned it in our first week of flying. In Basic we had even learned *side stages* — so they could get a lot of ships on the ground — and off — in a hurry. We had two runways, parallel, with the stage house in the middle of them. Groups of ships would stack up in opposite patterns on either side of the field; one side flying clockwise, the other counterclockwise. On final approach the ship in the left group would make a 90° left turn to final approach while the ship in the right group would make a 90° right turn to land beside and parallel to the other plane — with the stagehouse between them. They did that at Basic so we could all practice, practice, practice landing and taking off in the pattern. I could do it in my sleep — and often did (in my dreams, of course). Upwind, crosswind, downwind, baseleg, final approach. Everybody knew the pattern.

Here, in the E.T.O. the rules were the same. Ships returning from a mission would align themselves in the pattern in squadron order, by flights: low element, high element, lead—at their assigned altitude and would gradually descend as the ships below them landed. You stayed in position, waited your turn, and everybody got home safely. And you stayed in order, generally, except that ships with battle damage or wounded men aboard went to the head of the line to be the first to land. My copilot that day still didn't understand the pattern. Earlier in the week he had peeled off third and landed first, who knows how he did that. He was more than incompetent. He was dangerous. His flight refused to fly with him again, so they sent him to fly with me.

It was a very grueling mission, and a very hard day. Since the new guy was totally incompetent in formation, I had to fly most of the mission, which wore me out. Then, the lead ship that day was very erratic and hard to follow. It was one of my most exhausting missions. Needless to say, I didn't OK the new pilot. He might get somebody killed up there, and I didn't want to be responsible for turning him loose in the air.

Saturday Nov 4

My darling wife,

Three letters today from my sweetheart. Gosh I'm sorry that you had so much trouble with the mail department. I'm sure that — by now — you've had lots of letters because I've been writing every single day darling.

We had another one today. That makes nine sweetheart. We are still going strong. Another first Pilot rode with me as copilot today instead of Stan. We also took his waist gunner instead of Cole. The Command Pilot wouldn't fly autopilot today so we went up & down all day. It was so much more work than it would have been if he'd not been so bullheaded. Today was one of those days too.

I enjoyed that picnic so much when I read about it dear. Funny how just thinking about doing things with you gives me a thrill. So you want to get burried in leaves, huh — Well — I know I'll never forget that day or rather that night when you were a Freshman. I couldn't quite understand whether you were just being coy or whether you really didn't like me. I've never known you to by coy so it had me worried. But that's all water under the bridge. Now I know that you do love me and that's all that will ever matter. All your theories on how our family should be managed interests me considerably. Naturally I want to be as good a Father as I know you will be a Mother and for the time being it is up to you to keep me up on all the newest theories. One thing I'm very sure of darling and that is that our children should never suffer from neglect. They will always feel that they are wanted because the one thing we both want more than anything else is a child. That is a feeling which cannot be accounted for by any other reason than the fact that our love for each other is just too big to be so confined. It needs room to grow and there is no finer way than through the building of a home & family.

Now beloved I must go to bed — all my love always & always
Husband
Jack

MISSION # 10 NOVEMBER 5, 1944
LUDWIGSHAVEN = 6: 01 HRS

Up at 2:00 am. Take off in the dark. Assembly at 10,000 ft., just at dawn. This was the major difference between the American and the English Air Force. While the Brits preferred to "carpet bomb" (hitting anything and everything in the area) at night, the U.S. strategy was precision bombing in the daylight. We were thereby able to bomb specific targets: factories, railroads, ammo dumps, etc. to cripple the Reich's war effort by destroying militarily strategic targets. Unfortunately, since we could see our targets better in the daylight, so also could *they* see *theirs* — us.

Once we got in formation, the rest wasn't too bad. Today however, we were the 12th ship to take off. The one behind us, number thirteen, didn't make it. They crashed and burned at the end of the runway. Its pilot was the guy I had refused to approve. He went down and took nine guys with him — and right at the end of the runway where we could see it and think about it all the way to Germany and back. What do you do when a B-17 catches fire? Let it burn. And it's a huge bonfire. The Texas Aggies have no idea what a bonfire is until they've seen a B-17 burn. It made a hell of a fire. With the runway blocked, no more 94th ships took off, so our squadron had to join another group for the mission.

Sunday nite
Nov. 5, 1944

Hello Sweetheart,

How's my honeychile tonight. Just fine I hope. Today I got the letter which you wrote a week ago Friday. That really isn't bad at all — is it? So Homecoming has come and gone. Gee — it sure is getting along towards Thanksgiving. I have absolutely no conception of the passage of time. When we get up to go fly it is dark — usually about 2 or 3 & by the time we eat & brief & get everything ready to go — it's

Roy R. Fisher, Jr. with Susan Fisher Anderson

still dark. Often we take off in the dark and dawn meets us about 10,000 ft. It is just like climbing into a different world. We usually climb thru an overcast and then of course we can't see the ground at all and we are just ourselves with no relation to the ground except that there is a powerful force down there below those white clouds somewhere that resists the climb of a heavily loaded ship and wants to pull us down to the world which we have left. All day long we fly in formation and for a while people — or at least they tell us that they are people — shoot at us with big angry puffs of smoke. When we come home we're all so tired we eat, clean up, write a letter & go to bed again. It really isn't any wonder that time flies so quickly. You see I flew #10 today and you know when I started so you can tell how busy I've been.

Well — I've got to take a shower & shave before I go to sleep tonight and so I really better get started.

I know you're anxious to begin our family darling — but it still may be some time before we get started. In the meantime you can just spend your time being my mommie. I'll be such a good boy with such a sweet mommie.

Now — nite mommie — gotta sleep.
Jack

Chapter Sixteen
Lead Crew

MISSION # 11   NOVEMBER 6, 1944
DUISBURG = 5 HRS

The mission was a breeze, but it left me wondering. We had flown six missions in eight days. Was this a test? Yes, and we had passed. With flying colors. I wish we had failed.

Monday Nov. 6

Joyce Darling,

Tonight I have a story to tell you about what happened today. We have accepted our lot with mingled emotions and as I tell you all about it you will understand what I mean.

When I came down from the mission today (# 11) I was greeted with an order transferring me to the 333rd Bomb Sqd. On the face of it that means very little except a process of moving. That irks me considerably but actually there is a lot more behind it. Actually what it means is that we are to be trained as a lead crew. This training may be quite extensive — lasting perhaps over a period of six or eight weeks. During that time we will not be flying any operational missions. In other words — after such a swell start — we are shelved — so to speak — for several weeks. At the end of this period we will begin to lead missions and will probably not fly nearly as often as we do now — with the result that our tour would be longer than ordinary.

Of course — as in everything — it does have its good points. First of all — we're only required to complete 30 instead of 35 missions. Secondly — if we do a good job, there is a good chance that I'll get my captaincy. They made me a "first lieutenant" yesterday, so now I'm wearing those silver bars. I was already in my sack last night when Captain Modensky called from operations, but I didn't even get up. I just rolled over when Stan came in all thrilled and tickled and thrust a couple of silver bars into my hand. Then I rolled right over and went to sleep again. It really was quite a surprise but I just couldn't seem to get much enthused after having so little sleep.

Roy R. Fisher, Jr. with Susan Fisher Anderson

Now I outrank POP — he was only a second Lt., and he never went to combat.

    Well — now that you've heard my little problem — you see what I'm up against. It really is an opportunity to do a good job tho and now that we've got it — we're all going to work hard to do it up brown. It may be late winter or spring before I get home to you darling but we've got the job to do and the only way to finish is to do our job to the best of our ability. I know you wouldn't want it otherwise. Just remember, darling, that — no matter how long I'm away — nor how grey the days become — I love you more & more each day that goes by and the longer we're separated the more I realize just how much I have to come home to, and now — goodnight my love —
    Hubby
    Jack

                                                            Wed Nov. 8

Hello dearest,
    I'm awfully tired tonight. We just got back from London. As I told you — we wangled a pass on the strength of our transfer to another squadron. After we got everything finished here — we were too late to get in London that night so we waited till Tues morning. We got in for lunch and then went up to the P.X. to get some more sox & underwear. Our duffle bags still haven't arrived so we're still short on some of those things. I got some nice soft cotton undies — sorta like lollipop pants — only longer. They sure feel nice & warm. It's getting awfully cold over here now and none of the buildings have what we would consider a permanent heating system. Most of them are heated by very small coke stoves which are very poor.
    This morning I got up early and went to see the changing of the guard but I was on the wrong day again. Sometime I'll get there at the right time — just wait and see. Failing in that I wandered up to the Tower of London — Stan was going to go with me but he got lost on the subway — so I went on by myself. My trip through the Tower was extremely interesting. The tower is really a sort of medieval castle with a moat between the river & outer walls. There are several towers — each with its own particular history. Then there are two old chapels — one was part of the original castle — built in the 13th

century or so. The guide took us up to the museum of all kinds of armour. Some of them were used as a basis for designing our flak suits. He also showed us the spot where they used to have the scaffold and the official execution block. He went into detail about the different people who were imprisoned and executed. I wasn't particularly hungry by dinner time.

We came home on the two o'clock train so we could be back on time. This squadron isn't too liberal about getting back late from pass. So here we are, back at the old grind again.

Well, dearest — as I told you a few pages ago — I'm awfully sleepy tonight so I better call this to a halt.

Darling — I miss you so — but I'd best not get started on that. See you tomorrow —

Your loving husband,
Jack

Thurs nite
Nov. 9

Joyce my own,

Here's your lovin boy for a little chat. I got your "red letter" letter today. I'm so glad you finally got some mail. You see — sweet — I have been writing — it's just this postal system over here.

You sure are having fun with all those babies aren't you darling. I'm sure that you're enjoying that course much more now that we're married and yours aren't so very far away. Sure I know it seems a long ways away at times but as long as we both want it so very much — it surely will come darling — a real family — one we can be proud of. And when we do become proud parents, it will be worth every minute of anxious waiting. Our life will be complete and the boundless love which we share will be enlarged to encompass our little ones.

We had a practice mission today. The first of many before we will become operational again. I got quite a bit of instrument practice — the idea being to smooth out my flying after all that formation I discovered that I was really awfully rough. It will be quite a while before my flying is smooth enough for lead. We're all just about resigned to our fate now — that is all but Stan and he still hates the idea of being a tail gunner. He can't quite get used to the idea of

Roy R. Fisher, Jr. with Susan Fisher Anderson

going from the front seat to the back seat and not being able to do any flying.

Gosh was it ever cold up there today. We were only up for about three hours but I really got froze — Then to make matters worse, all the windows iced up when we came down. Couldn't see a dogone thing out of my windows and there was a formation trying to land at the same time. Mr. Anthony — have I got troubles.

We were all set to see "For Whom the Bells Toll" tonight but it didn't come and so we stayed home. I'm going to hit the sack early tonight. I wish that we were together tonight. My sack is always so cold — but it wouldn't be if you were here. Don't spose your sack is very warm either is it —

Now sweet I must close —
Nite my love
Your hubby,
Jack

Friday nite
Nov — 10

Joyce — my own,

Well — well — whatcha know an anniversary. Just think darling — we've been married five whole months. Or rather three whole months and two very incomplete ones. For time cannot be whole when you're not with me darling — I'm just living half a life — or less. But there is the consolation that when we are together again we'll be able to make up for all these empty months when we're so very lonely and unhappy. Just to be together again will be enough to make us forget that we were ever apart. Just to hold you close to me and make you my very own will make these lonely nights fade like a bad dream.

I'm lying on my sack now just reminiscing. It's so much fun to think back to the day we were married, and the night before.

Remember what a lot of worries we had that night, and how worried you were about the moon. Well — I may have worried a little too — yep — may have! But — all our worries were for naught.

Then — that lovely week in Lincoln — sure was hard to get up every morning at six. I always waked up on the bus and couldn't figure how I'd gotten that far. Then our honeymoon trip to the Black Hills and that lovely hotel in Alliance and — O — that nice big room

at the Hearney Hotel. A bed for each of us. Couldn't quite see it — huh — Such good times we've had together. Just thinking it all over makes me very happy and a lot less lonely. You see — I'm quite sure that tonight you'll be thinking the same thoughts that I'm thinking now — and my dreams will be with you and you will be with me. We'll always be one in our ideas and dreams darling and that makes us so very close. Joyce — my dearest — your love means everything in the world to me and I'll do everything within my power to always be worthy of that faith & love — Now goodnight dear.
   Your husband
   Jack

(Clipping Enclosed) Nov 11
Saturday night

My beloved wife,
   Another week gone and I'm just that much closer to you than I was at this time last week. Two awfully nice letters from you today darling. I just read them cause I've been away from the shack all day and one of the boys brought my mail to me. They were postmarked the 1st and 2nd of Nov. and so that is really good service. The one was where you started a sermon and then apologized for sermonizing. I don't like sermons — that's true but I do need to be reminded that the things I'm doing aren't just funny ideas that need to be changed. Of course darling, there really isn't much chance that my ideas and philosophies are going to undergo a complete metamorphosis but nevertheless it helps to keep me on the beam. I need all the help you can give me darling because the longer this lasts the worse it will be. Right now — the feeling that is about to overcome me is the futility of this whole mess. Just about the time I had gotten to the place where seeing pictures like this didn't bother me too much we are put back in training again. I'm sending you this picture because I want you to save it. I want you to put it away in a scrap book somewhere so we can look at it sometime and thank God for letting us get thru a wall of

Roy R. Fisher, Jr. with Susan Fisher Anderson

They Carved Their Epitaph in the Clouds

U.S. Army Air Force Photo

This remarkable shot of a shattered Flying Fortress plummeting to earth shows the grim risks of aerial combat. The plane was brought down as the Eighth Air Force raided a synthetic-oil plant at Merseburg, Germany, on Nov. 2. Enemy fire tore off the entire nose section of the Fort, with the pilot, co-pilot, bombardier and navigator inside. One engine was wrenched off as the plane plunged amid flame, smoke and debris.

flak without getting hit. It's really a marvelous picture darling and the whole picture is there and gone in the blink of an eye.

We had a big practice bombing mission today. Took up ten blues to drop from 14,500 but the stuff was down at 3400 so we bombed at 3500 — just barely in the stuff. Finally we got tired of flying instruments and came home & landed.

We had a couple minutes to spare coming home and we had a good time skidding & slipping & doing everything but snap rolls than we came over the field by ourselves & peeled off for a landing. We really got a kick out of just flying for a change. We had a couple of poor classes this afternoon & then I got my haircut. High time. Got enough cut off the top so It doesn't hang in my eyes. (if this seems a little disconcerted it's this 50 to 0 over Notre Dame that did it.)

We went to see "Cover Girl" again tonight. Mighty fine picture but I enjoyed it more the first time.

Now — here I am at home again — My day — hasn't been so hot either.

Perhaps if I just go to bed and dream of you darling — the rest of my day will be complete. Just to dream that you're in my arms again will make life complete. Goodnight my own —
hubsband Jack

Sunday — Nov 12
9:00 pm —

Hi Sweetheart,
Here's that man again. Just dropped in for a little chat. Nothing out of the ordinary today.

We took a new ship up this morning for an acceptance check and had more fun than I've had in weeks. There was an overcast about 6,000 or so and they were cumulo-bumpus clouds only weren't very bumpus so we buzzed them. First Stan would peel off & dive at them & then pull out — then I would & we really had ourselves a time. We climbed up to 20 thous & ran the racks thru a couple times & then got cold. It was about noon and I wanted to get down so I just sorta let her go & we came down so fast that all the windows iced up. That quite often happens but today the flaps froze too and so I made a no-flap landing. We came in pretty hot but I couldn't see going around because the windows were icing up worse all the time. As it was tho

Roy R. Fisher, Jr. with Susan Fisher Anderson

we were on the ground before 12:30 and so that wasn't bad at all. From 20, thous to ground in less than 30 minutes.

This afternoon I went to Link and that just about took up my time. After supper tonight I went over to the Chapel for the 7:30 service and enjoyed it very much. After the service we had a communion service. The Chaplin is a Methodist and so the service was very familiar. It really made me feel good all over. I've been needing a real "Mountain Top experience" — as he expressed it and it meant a lot. I just wish you could have been here to enjoy it with me.

Now — sweetheart I'm fraid I'll close for tonight because my eyes won't stay open. Goodnight my darling I love you — so very very much —
Your very own husband
Jack

Monday nite
Nove — 13

Joyce darling,

I'm the luckiest man in the world! Why — cause I'm married to the most wonderful wife — any man in the world ever had. I got your blue ribbon letter today sweetheart and I've already read it three times. It's that morale building sort of a letter that makes my whole world seem brighter.

You're certainly right about that little blue ribbon darling. I knew what it was when I first saw it in the letter. And the memories it brought darling. I remember so well just how you looked that night in your bra & panties — my mind just photographed a picture of you because that was the first time —. You know darling as I think back to that night it seems more beautiful with each recalling. As I remember what you must have gone through it helps me to realize just how great a thing your love for me is. At times I wonder if I can be worthy of such a love darling but then I read a letter such as the one you wrote today or — rather that I got today and I can see that by living the life that we both believe in as fully and truly as it is within my power to do — I can — perhaps — be worthy of your love. Darling — I wish I could tell you how much your letter today meant to me. It's true I'm awfully lonesome but when I know you are there waiting for me and that you're as lonesome as I am it helps to ease the pain a little.

That picnic in the cornfield sounded wonderful. Especially that walk home and then lying in bed listening to the rain. We like to lie in bed & listen don't we dear. Those little things mean so much when you do them with someone you love so much. And I do love you darling — very — very much. Now goodnight my darling — yours alone —

Jack

Tues — Nov. 14

Dearest wife,

How's my honey tonight? I got awfully fed up with the setup this afternoon and so I got a pass & breezed into town. Had dinner at the Red Cross & just visited with some fellows from various other stations herabouts. Even went uptown to the dance for a few minutes but it was so cold & nasty out that I just went back to the club & then came out here. It satisfied that pent-up feeling and so I really feel better now. (I can't figure out what's the matter with this damn pen). I get that pent up feeling awfully easily when there isn't anything to do but sit around the shack.

We've sure had crazy weather lately — Just after I wrote to you last night and climbed down into my sack the rains came. Just a nice soft drizzly sort of rain. Did all last night. It cleared up a little today and then tonight it snowed — that wet nasty sort of snow which turns to water just as soon as it hits — So the nasty night. Now it's settled down to a plain rain again. Nice to sit inside & listen to but awful to be out in.

We're sure getting a good rest these days. Still haven't started training for Lead & so we're just doing "busy" work & very little of that. Yesterday for example we took a 15 minute flight to another field to ferry a new ship back.

When I hit the sack last night darling you seemed so very near. Perhaps it was that sweet letter I got yesterday, perhaps it was just because I was so very lonely & blue but I felt like I was really talking to you — I wonder if you felt it too. It was such a remarkable feeling that I'm sure you must have felt it too. Perhaps before too long darling — you will actually be in my arms and those empty dreams will become realities. I want so very much to have you put your head

on my shoulder again — you're sure right about that. We were made for each other darling — for no one else.
   Yours, Jack

   Now we have ... the rest of the story. In considering our transfer to lead crew there were some very specific factors to consider. Here is where the pressure of command really takes shape. As captain, I had to consider the ramifications of the decision and how it might affect my men. For instance, with the Lead Crew the Command Pilot of the Squadron flew co-pilot, and Stan would have had to fly in the tail gunner position as FORMATION CONTROL OFFICER. As much as Stan wanted to be a pursuit pilot, I was afraid that having to fly as tail gunner would trigger a relapse for him, after he had worked so hard to get and stay sober; so I started the procedure to get transferred off lead crew status. That did not make the Brass happy.

   I explained as well as I could and said we just wanted to fly our missions as a crew, and finish up. Finally after ten days we were transferred back to the 331st and put on the board. Now maybe we could get on with the War, and finish up. I now realize that our selection for lead crew was a very high compliment for the entire crew, but especially for the navigator, bombardier and pilots. Oh well.

   After returning to our unit, we could finish our missions much more quickly. Occasionally, we would fly as Deputy Lead. This was a well-trained crew; which would be assigned to take over leading the air force if something should happen to the lead ship.

   We were so assigned on the day General Castle flew his first mission as a general. He lost an engine just as we hit the coast and we took over as Lead of Air Corps. We moved up to the lead squadron as he slipped back to join the low squadron for protection. As we got along side the lead group, the low squadron got hit by fighters. The German ME 109's hit them hard, knocking down 11 of the 12 planes of the low squadron. General Castle's plane was also destroyed. Twelve ships went down, 108 men died – including General Castle.

Chapter Seventeen
Back Home Again

MISSION # 12   NOVEMBER 16, 1944
DUREN = 8:00 HRS

It felt like a really long mission, but was otherwise uneventful. Just a reminder of what we had on our plate; but it's good to be back on active status. That's the only way we can finish up.

Sat nite
November 18

My poor lonesome wife,

I'm sorry I've neglected you the past few days but I'll let you know all about it.

First and foremost — we've been transferred back to the 331st so as you can easily see we're back on operational status. We were transferred on Wednesday afternoon and Thurs we flew a mission. Wed afternoon I went to another base with Bob to see his cousin and we got the train schedule screwed up & didn't get back till 2:30 am. He went right down for pre-briefing and I hit the sack but I hadn't even gotten to sleep when they called me too —. So I got up and flew with no sleep at all — oh well — When we got back that afternoon — the field was socked in so we were diverted. We landed at a limey field & they fed us and then we went to another place for billeting. So there we were, many miles from our own field with no razor — soap — towels, writing paper or anything. Well we stayed there till this noon before we could get off the ground and get back home. Then when we did get back to our ships we had a flat tire & so we were 'fraid we'd have to stay over another night but we got it pumped up and it held till we got home. I called the base when I came in & told them I might have a flat tire when I landed & after I'd taxied to my area a jeep pulled up and some of the "wheels" wanted to know where my flat tire was. I think by gad they were disappointed that we hadn't made a crash landing. Sldkfjl;a feet.

Roy R. Fisher, Jr. with Susan Fisher Anderson

Well — anyway — here we are, back at our own base after a nice long rest.

When we got here today I had six letters. Two from Mom and four from my sweet wife. One even had a picture in it. A picture of the most beautiful girl in the whole wide world. I'm going to reread them all again now so I can answer all of your questions.

First — about the other boys I came over with. Spence & Staff are here with me but I haven't seen the rest of the boys at all. Oh, yes I did see Ben Rolfe in London but I haven't seen anyone else. A little item in one of your letters interested me very — very much. The one thing I've thought about more than anything else during the past few days is what to do when I get home and we have 30 days together to do as we like. Your suggestion that we get a cabin up in the woods somewhere is just about what I was thinking about. If that is impractical I would like to get an apartment somewhere away from home where we could just live and love and be content for a couple of weeks. Just any place darling where we can be together and where we won't have anyone to bother us. Just think how marvelous it will be to never have a schedule to meet or early flying or formation to get me so tired I can't do anything but go right to sleep.

Actually — darling — ours was a pretty rough honeymoon from that standpoint. And yet it was the most wonderful experience I could ever imagine darling. Just to love and be loved by you. Even when you're so very far from me physically your love permeates the very atmosphere in which I live. That sweet picture you sent makes me realize even more than your words just how much little babies mean to you. Of course I want you to be my mommie darling — I want that more than anything else in the world and I want very much to be the kind of father who really deserves the name. I want to have just as big a part in raising our children as you do. You see darling — I'm convinced that although a woman can — by herself — raise a lovely family — she can with the help of a husband do a much better job. In other words — cooperation is the whole idea in married life and without that close cooperation no family life can be complete.

And now my dearest — you've got a little better idea, I hope, of the ideas that have been running thru my mind the past few days. I hope that you're not quite as lonesome as I know you have been. Remember Joyce that I love you — and you alone — always with all my heart and soul. Now sweetheart I must close for tonight and hit the old solo sack — you bet your life — I don't like it any better than you do.

Goodnight my beloved wife —
Your loving husband
Jack

Sunday nite
Nov. 19

Hello my darling,

Here's that man again. Just got back from chow. I wore my new battle jacket to chow tonight. It fits swell — and I'm sure you'll like it. It looks like a regular mess jacket except that it's O.D. or rather green instead of white.

We had chicken for supper as is usually true on Sunday night. I hurried home so I could write you before I hit the road for church. Then when I come home I'll be able to hop right into the sack.

We got up early this morning but it was just a waste of time. Spent all morning trying to get this hut warmed up but couldn't seem to manage. Coke is rationed so we've been poaching on the Kings timber — it doesn't burn worth a damn.

We finally got our compass swung this afternoon. We did it on the ground and it was a lot easier than up in the air — but not nearly as much fun. We had to do it a couple of times before we got it right — but we finally made it.

That about takes care of all the news darling — things really haven't happened very fast around here today. Just the old stuff, work like mad all day to keep out of doing work.

So with those words of wisdom (?) I'll just say — Goodnight Sweetheart till we meet tomorrow —

Your best beau
Jack

Roy R. Fisher, Jr. with Susan Fisher Anderson

Monday nite
Nov 20, 1944

Dearest Joyce,

Toldja I'd be back tonight & here I am. We almost made one today but had to come back on accounta weather — which same was socked in up to about 35,000 or so. They don't count up very fast that way.

Last night I went to church after I wrote you. It was an awfully nice service. The sermon was on "Prayer." He brought out the angle that Jesus told his disciples about the son who asks his father for bread "Would you give him a stone" etc. & pointed out that if we — with all our faults would never refuse a request — surely The Heavenly Father with all His wisdom would not refuse our request. He suggested we pray for assurance and he's got something there. Any way it was pretty good.

They're going to have a Christmas choir to sing a few carols and I told them I'd like to get in it — so you see — things are beginning to roll again. I'm glad that we're going to do something a little special for Christmas because it would come and go around here & never even be noticed.

I thought about you so much today. We are flying deputy lead now — number two spot & so I usually have a lot of time to think.

Got to thinking about that time in Lincoln when we went swimming. That was so much fun. I even remember how impatiently I waited for you to come out of the dressing room — and how proud I was when you did come out — all dressed up in your new swimming suit. I'm so very proud of you darling — proud to be your husband. And I know I always will be — You're so sweet and kind and understanding and I love you so very much. I've often wondered if — when we walk down the street together — people can tell how much we love each other. I don't see how they could miss that loving glow in your eyes and I wouldn't be a bit surprised if I might have one too.

That's cause I love you so very, very much Joyce my own.
Now Gnite — darling
Forever your loving husband,
Jack

The Lucky Bastard Club

MISSION # 13   NOVEMBER 21, 1944
WETZLER = 5:15 HRS

One more mission completed. We went on the mission with very little sleep, having just gotten back from London. We really sweat out number THIRTEEN. We were superstitious about everything. We wore the same clothes and went through the same routine so nothing would be changed. Our flight clothes would get pretty foul by the end of our tour.

London Thurs.
Nov 23 or so

Dearest wife,
Just at the end of a most remarkable three days in London. We came in day before yesterday in the afternoon and in the hours since I have been about as low and about as high as it has ever been my experience to be. The first two days were awful. It rained and I went to see a poor stage show and got my feet wet (it rained) and ate poor food and caught a nice cold (it rained) and missed the changing of the guard cause it rained & they called it off.
But —
Things were different today. This morning I got out of the sack in time to go to the big Thanksgiving day service in Westminster Abbey. I've not seen as many Americans in one place since I left home. There were all manner & sizes of people there with ranks from pvt. to general with generals predominating. The service was marvelous. I'll enclose a programe which will speak for itself. After the service was all finished the dignitaries paraded by and it looked like the county fair on Saturday afternoon.
After church I came back here to the Duchess Club & had a lovely Turkey dinner — on the

<u>House</u>
===

Perhaps it wasn't as much as I would have gotten at home, But the spirit was there and I enjoyed myself immensely.
Then — I went to a most remarkable stage review called "Happy & Glorious." And perhaps you have guessed that as the reason for this letter. I've not seen such a remarkable show in a good long time

and it really gave me a thrill. The star Tommy Trinder is the English Bob Hope and he is a scream. He has a good time with the audience and so everyone has a good time. The singer Elizabeth Welch is a negress who rivals Lena Horne.

I had such a good time and I hope that this letter can convey some of my enjoyment to you.

It is nearly time to return to base now darling and I must catch a bite to eat first. Lots & lots of love from your
devoted husband
Jack

It's amazing what a little laughter can do to change a man's state of mind. I still remember that show and how much we laughed. At the beginning, just as Tommy Trinder was starting his act, a whole bunch of sailors trooped in and made their way to the front rows.

We Army guys roared when Trinder commented, "We always have to wait on the Navy, 'cause the Navy has to wait on the tide."

Friday nite
Nov 24

Hello darling,

Nothing much to say tonight — just one of those days when I couldn't make a nickel. I got your letter in which you asked for a lecture on why you shouldn't use profanity. I said under the circumstances I'm hardly the one to lecture on that particular subject to anyone. And yet if I do just give you my ideas on the subject it might help us both.

In the first place I don't like it. I don't like to hear women use profanity at all. A lot of women over here seem to think that it's smart or cute or something and in my opinion it is neither. Further — it merely shows a lack of an adequate vocabulary because if you can use the right words it isn't necessary to swear. Besides — darling — it's your job to transform me back into the kind of fellow who will make a good father and that will mean breaking some of my bad habits. "So — you see — it's all up to you — you can be better than you are — We could be swinging on a star."

Darling — please be the same sweet girl I left behind me —
Your devoted husband
Jack

The Lucky Bastard Club

MISSION # 14 NOVEMBER 25, 1944
MERSEBURG = 8:45 HRS

Merseburg again. Sweat that won't stop. Nothing but flak today. They really try to protect this target. German Fighters on the way in, a whole line of them, wing to wing — A Company Front. There must have been 40 or 50 of them but they made only one pass. They left when we got to the flak. I don't know which is worse.

We found out later that this area of Germany was where they made synthetic oil and gas for tanks, planes and anything that moved. Without fuel nothing moves, so this was where we really hurt them and they were doing all they could to stop us. Stan wasn't feeling well so I flew most of the time. That really wears a little guy like me out.

Saturday nite
Nov. 25

Hello my dearest,

Just a short note tonight. Today was an awfully rough one and I'm so dead I can't see. Stan was off the ball & so I flew a lot of the time myself & so I'm pretty well worn out. Having gotten thru today tho I consider myself awfully lucky. It was one of those kind. Nothing but flak but oh so much ———

My sack is awfully inviting — I just shaved and washed and it sure looks enticing. I got two sheets yesterday at the traveling P.X. also a couple of pillow cases. It surely is a treat after sleeping between GI blankets for all these weeks.

I'm afraid my writing is sorta scattered tonight darling — I'm so tired but I do love you so much. I want you to know dearest that I'm so very proud and happy to be your husband.

Your package with the cookies & candy came yesterday darling and I was so glad to get it. The cookies were still moist & fresh & not broken at all. I guess that's because the popcorn sorta padded them. We're all enjoying them so much. You're such a good cook darling. And besides that I love you — D'ja no that.

Well — I do — lots & lots —
Nite sweetheart —
Jack

Roy R. Fisher, Jr. with Susan Fisher Anderson

Sunday nite — again —
Nov. 26

Joyce Darling,
I just got back from church. We had an awfully nice song service tonight and a fellow from another base near here sang a solo which was very good.

After the service I met a Capt. Schutz — base adjulant — who lives in Burlington. He used to sell cars or something there & knows my father-in-law — Doesn't know my wife tho — Hasn't been around much — has he.

After the service we were standing around talking and Sims, the fellow who sang — said he wanted four children — a soprano, alto, tenor & bass and I told him that we wanted a double quartet. He said I couldn't do much over here and — what could I say ——-

By the way did you hear about Bugs Bunny. He just got married and had a wonderful time on his honeymoon — just he & his wife and an adding machine and Stan got a couple of white mice in London — He calls them Terrify & Tissue — Do you??

Hope you don't darling cause I'm just about to kiss you goodnight & hit the sack. We were standby ship and we didn't have to fly. I wish now we had gone — milk run. Oh well — life's like that.

And now my beloved — I must quit to go to sleep — Darling — I love you so very muchly —
Yours alone —
Jack

Chapter Eighteen
Bad Weather, Worse Weather

MISSION # 15   NOVEMBER 27, 1944
BINGEN = 6:30 HRS

We have been awakened early every day since we got back to the squadron. The days start pretty early whether we fly or not. Wake up, shave (the oxygen mask gives me fits if I don't shave every day), breakfast, briefing, mission scrubbed, and back to the sack. Today we flew even though the weather was lousy. We went and got back. Praise the Lord.

Monday nite 6:10 p.m.
Nov. 27

My darling,
Betcha can't guess where I am. I'm in the sack already. I want to go to sleep early tonight cause for the last three nights I've seen you in my dreams and last night or rather this morning the C.Q. broke in on us — just too soon. So I've got another date for tonight I hope.

I really don't see why or how one man can get so tired. I'm tired enough for two men — I'm sure. But if I get lotsa sleep tonight maybe it won't be so bad tomorrow. We have yet to sleep past 5:00 since being transferred back to this squadron. They are counting up tho darling and that brings me just that much closer to you in person. Holding you in my dreams is nice but can't compare to actually feeling your warm body next to mine and hear you whisper in my ear that you want me to make you mine for always and always. Darling — I miss you so very much — that aching heart of mine just won't be still. It's awfully hard to explain to a heart that a war is necessary. Mine won't convince worth a darn. But let's just hope it will be soon now darling — I want you in my arms so very much. Because I love you darling — always with all my heart —
Your own husband,
Jack

Roy R. Fisher, Jr. with Susan Fisher Anderson

Nov. 28
Tues nite

Darling—

We had a standdown for a change. This makes the first day since we were reassigned to the squadron that we didn't get up early for a mission. Of course we didn't fly every time but we always had to get up. I've got 15 now and before too long we'll be going on Flak leave — for a week.

You suggested in your letter today that I number my letters. That's a good idea if I can remember to do it. You also asked about the crew. Jake is flying ball — He decided that Cole was too large for the ball so he's flying waist. Then if we are attacked by fighters Hume is supposed to go back to the other gun.

The boys in the E.T.O. are sure unhappy about the cigarettes or rather lack of them. Personally it doesn't bother me much. Combat men still get 5 packs a week and so I use them for bones to the guys that are good to me. Just like gold over here.

We just got back from the show. First time in a long while I've gone to a show and I'm fraid I got a little sedimental too darling. We saw "Johnny Eager" and such a show. That and the beautiful moon tonight (oh this is just too good a pun to miss) sure made "Jonny Eager." I'm sorry darling but it just slipped out.

Oh — Joyce — I miss you so very much. You were so much a part of my life that a part of my heart just isn't here. But someday — everything will be ok.

Nite sweetheart. I love you
Jack.

Wednesday night
Nov. 29

Hello my dearest,

Stan took this picture the other day and I thought you might like to see it. It isn't particularly good but it's better than nothing.

The boys are deep in an argument about the building game. Bob & I are just sitting here listening to them & laughing up our sleeves. They're on the subject of heating now and the boys come from all over the country and — gosh what a discussion.

We're alerted tonight and so I'll have to hit the sack pretty early. Stan just proposed that it would be a good idea to sit in front of a glowing fireplace with your arm around a woman. Now that's my idea of a good time. How would you go for a nice evening in front of the fireplace tonight darling — wouldn't that be fun. Remember that Christmas when we spent all one evening in front of the fireplace at home. Nights like that helped so much to give us such a firm foundation for our life together. That has been said so many times before but it really means a lot darling. Gosh — I can't concentrate on this letter with all these guys carrying on —

Better close — but golly I love you so darling. Now g'nite sweet

Jack

MISSION # 16 NOVEMBER 30, 1944
LUTZKENDORF = 7:30 HRS

I'm tired and sick tonight. The MISSION BELLE was out of action due to an engine change, and so we took a ship which had just arrived on the base and had not been modified for combat. The most important thing not modified was the windshield. Unmodified, the windshield was two pieces of 1/4 inch plexiglass with an airspace between and an electrical wire on the edge to prevent icing when the defroster was turned on.

MISSION BELLE's windshield was a solid piece of plexiglass two inches thick. I took one look at the unmodified windshield and had a sinking feeling in the pit of my stomach. The take off and trip to the target were uneventful, but over the target a flak burst directly ahead of the nose sent shrapnel toward the aircraft. One piece of shrapnel penetrated the first piece of plexiglass, and stuck in the second. The impact scared me, but the sight of that piece of flak just at my eye level shook me up. The worst part was looking at that chunk of metal — at eye level — all the way home.

After we got back two planes collided on final approach to the field. It happened just as we began our final approach. The lower plane crashed and burned, but the upper one completed its landing. How would you like to live with that memory the rest of your life. It was bad enough just to watch it. By the time we landed I was a basket case. I was sick, at heart. Several of the guys had bad colds and were grounded for a few days. I hoped they would be back on flight status before we had to fly again. It just wasn't the same without them, any of them. That mission I spent more time praying than I had ever spent before.

I think this was the day when I totally surrendered myself to God's care. That day there was no longer any doubt in my mind, after staring at that piece of flak all the way home, that the hand of The Almighty, of God, was upon me. I don't know whether I knew what it meant to be "born again" but that was my day. It was obvious to me that I didn't have any control over my life or death anymore, so I gave it all God that day. The crew chief dug the chunk of flak out of the windshield and presented it to me. I still have that piece for a souvenir, also. It doesn't look so dangerous, but if it had not been almost spent when it hit the windshield, I could have caught it in my teeth.

Friday morning
Dec. 1
#3

Good morning darling,
It's eleven o'clock now but I've only been up about half an hour. I was so dead tired when we got back last night that I was sick. I went right to bed at six or so and stayed there till just a few minutes ago. We went to that rough target again yesterday and I'm ready to throw in the sponge.
We've all got colds now to a greater or lesser degree. Slim — Stan — and Bob got grounded and Cole should have been. This weather over here doesn't help any and of course Coke is rationed and dry wood is hard to come by so our fires are limited to the barracks at night. The rest of the time we just try to keep warm.
The mail situation is pretty rough again. I've gotten two letters in the past 10 days or so both on one day. But that is to be expected I guess — what with all the bad weather & all.
Yesterday we had quite a tragedy just as we were landing. Two ships collided on the final approach and the lower ship crashed and burned right at the end of the runway. The whole crew was killed with the exception of the tail gunner. They dragged him out but he was so badly cut up that he died before morning. It was Lt. Winter's crew. He

came over with us and has had all sorts of trouble — He landed in Brussels twice — one a crash landing with only one engine. But as long as we fly we'll have accidents I guess. You just have to keep on the ball constantly to stay alive. The thing about that accident is that it could have been prevented. That's why I couldn't write last night darling — I was too upset. You see — I saw the whole thing and it was quite a sight. I turned on the final approach just after the crash and since I was planning to land we were quite low right over the plane as it was burning and it was a sickening sight. I hate that I have to burden your mind with these things darling — but I hope it will help you to understand why I didn't write last night — also — if I tell you these things as I go along you'll be better able to understand my mental condition when I do get home. I'm sure that if you know the reason behind the things I do and say — you'll be able to snap me out of it better than if you do not have that knowledge.

But enough of that —

John Charles Thomas just sang "Thine is my heart." What a lovely song and it expresses my thoughts so exactly. And now — "Through the years." I'll always be with you darling. Side by side — no matter how rough the going is — as long as we're together nothing else will matter and — God Willing — we'll be together again soon darling. I'll hold you in my arms and kiss your sweet lips and run my fingers thru your beautiful hair. Then you can put your head on my shoulder and we'll forget that we have been separated all these long months. These long nights of lonesomeness will fade into the background and we'll be one again my own. Joyce darling — I love you so. So much more than mere words can possibly express. I'm sure you know just what I mean. By for now sweetheart —

All my love — always —

Jack

Roy R. Fisher, Jr. with Susan Fisher Anderson

*Friday nite
Dec. 1
#4*

Joyce darling,
   Just a note to let you know I'm feeling a lot better after a day of doing nothing hard & fast.
   I went to choir practice tonight. We sang a lot of swell Christmas songs and it was so much fun to sing again. I miss that a lot around here. No one ever wants to sing.
   We had some popcorn tonight. Bob got a can of unpopped corn from home and we got some butter & salt at the mess hall & fixed it in our mess kits. Gosh it sure tasted good. It is remarkable what a nice long day like today can do for a person. I feel 100% better than I did this morning. My only trouble now is that I'm oh so lonesome for my sweet wife. I guess I'll never get over that — Must be I love you darling — oh so muchly.
   Now — G'nite sweets — here's a big kiss from yer old man.
   Jack

MISSION # 17   DECEMBER 2, 1944
SOUTHWEST GERMANY = 6:10 HRS

   We are becoming the best-known crew on the line. We're there for every mission, but that way we take the bitter mitt the better. Our approach to England was different, depending on what target we had bombed that day, but we were always relieved to see the white Cliffs of Dover, or the eastern coastline where the frigid North Sea kissed the beach. The return home was always a little bouncier as our ship, relieved of her burden of bombs was more susceptible to air currents. We didn't mind. Instead, we would ease into the landing formation and wait our turn behind the ships damaged in the battle, or worse, carrying wounded men. They didn't have to run the pattern, they could fly straight in.
   By the time we were safely settled in our spot on the flight line, we were anxious to check out the Mission Belle to see how she had survived the battle. As we assessed her battle damage – or lack of any – we were aware of how close we had come to becoming a casualty. We didn't talk about it much, but we were thankful every day that we had returned safely. Others of our group were carrying still human

forms from their ships, dead or badly injured. We knew it was only the grace of God that it wasn't us. It didn't get any easier. No flak house yet, but we did get a 3-day pass from the Flight Surgeon. London, here we come.

Dec 2
Saturday nite
#4

Joyce beloved,

Two lovely letters from you plus a shave and general cleaning up made me feel like a new man — in spite of that mission today. That makes number 17 darling — boy are we picking them up these days. I'm getting to be the best known pilot on the line. The Doc couldn't figure out why we were hurrying so fast unless it was so we could get to the Flak House sooner. Four of the boys were grounded today but they just gave me four subs & sent me up into the blue. But I'm not griping — that's the only way to get finished.

Sounds to me — from the tone of your letter today — like you want a little encouragement as far as outside activities are concerned at school. You're right, darling, you do have the opportunity to get a very broad education as well as just boning up on the subjects at hand. And you know that my attitude toward college is to learn to live a life. Remember — when you leave school you won't have a grade point average to work for. But you do have to live a life and if you can learn something in college which will make that life more full and enjoyable for yourself or those with whom you live — it should be your purpose to avail yourself of those bits of knowledge. In other words darling, don't worry too much about that grade average. But on the other hand — don't forget that you're still the daughter of your father. With those words of wisdom I'll skip that subject.

Now — just a few lines to let you know I love you more than anything else in the world. Your letters today were so sweet darling and so very welcome. Just to have you tell me you love me makes me glow all over & feel like a new man. — In spite of rassling 65,000 lbs around all day — sure sounds big doesn't it — may be —

Now sweetheart — G'nite
I love you
Jack

Roy R. Fisher, Jr. with Susan Fisher Anderson

Dec. 4
Monday nite

My Dearest Wife,

Here I am in London again — It seems only yesterday that I was here before and it was almost two weeks to the day. Yet — here I am — and enjoying my self — more than last time. I went down to see the changing of the guards again this morning and it was the wrong day. When this war is over & everyone else has gone home there will be a poor forlorn figure standing by the gate at Buckingham Palace — still trying to see the changing of the guards. Guess — who.

Well — I'm going to try again tomorrow and then I'm going to give up I think.

This afternoon I took all the enlisted men to see Happy and Glorious. Of course you know how much I enjoyed it the first time so you can perhaps imagine why I went again. Then too I didn't want them to go to some other show and get stung when there was such a good show playing.

Then this evening I went to "Strike it Again" — sequel to "Strike a New Note." The idea is youth on parade and of course a lot of the numbers are imitations (rather poor) of our jitterbug dancing and stuff like that there. They had several good acts but on the whole the show left me rather cold. Perhaps because it is so new, it's only been running a few weeks and the wrinkles aren't ironed out of it as yet.

I think the Flight Surgeon put in his two cents when it came to us getting this pass. You see I've flown six missions since the last pass and a couple were pretty rough. Then of course we got up early every day except one and we were all fagged out. I finally went in to see him yesterday. I had a slight cold and had been having trouble clearing my ears. He fixed my cold & washed my ears out & so I'm practically a new man. I've really felt a 100% better since seeing him. It won't be long now till we're due for the flak House for a week of rest and recuperation. It can't come too soon to suit me. I've been running on nerves alone for quite a while and I can tell that I'm really getting quite excited nervously. Perhaps a nice long rest would fix me up oK. I'm beginning to feel sorta like I'd just finished a year of school and taken my finals — only I haven't taken them yet. Gosh I talk scattered. Maybe I better go to bed.

I really want to get a lot of sleep tonight because when I get back we'll start right in again.

So I'll say — Goodnight — sweetheart till we meet tomorrow — I love you so very very much my darling —

Nite sweets —

Jack

Roy R. Fisher, Jr. with Susan Fisher Anderson

Chapter Nineteen
Halfway Home

MISSION # 18   DECEMBER 6, 1944
MERSEBURG = 7:45 HRS

This makes our FIFTH trip to Merseburg. It doesn't get any easier and when you add our sweating it out, it makes me a basket case. I'm ready for the flak house. The worst part is that we know what to expect on this mission. When we get to pre-flight briefing and they say "Merseburg" the sweating starts and by the time we arrive at the target we're soaking wet, just from the sweat. It doesn't quit till we're on our way home, crossing the channel. The sheer dread of it takes its toll on all the men. We're much more tired after a trip to Merseburg than to any other target.

Thurs Dec 7

Joyce my darling,

When I got back from London the other night there were three sweet letters from you. Dated— the 7-8 & 11 of Oct. And from the tone of them — Life is rough in the States too. I know darling — it must be kinda rough to learn to be absolutely independent and still do things right. The tendency is natural — that of swinging over too far as far as accounts & spending money is concerned. Off & on I have the very same trouble over here. It's so easy to think of a pound as a dollar and to spend them accordingly. It costs me 5 or 6 lbs each time I go to London — More if I buy anything like clothes or presents for someone. Well — that doesn't seem so bad in terms of lbs but each pound is worth about 4 dollars and so that does seem like quite a bit that way. But I'm watching more closely now and it doesn't go so fast now. Perhaps by now you've got things under control too. I was awfully glad to hear all about your shopping spree in C.R. (Cedar Rapids, IA).

There's nothing that builds up morale like a few new clothes. I got a bang out of— "a new lift for things" and — "Life" no less. That — I want to see. How are things anyway — Darling I'm getting so awfully lonesome for you. Instead of getting used to being single again or rather to living like a single man again, I just miss you more

each moment that goes by. But as much as I want you I still can't see going out with anyone else. I'm more yours now darling. You see darling — as each day passes I realize more fully just how much true love means and how important it is to guard this God Given Gift which is so marvelous that we both find it hard to believe it possible. Such a gift must not be taken lightly or we can hardly expect it to be the same when we're together once again. And we must look forward to the time when we are once again darling or we can never survive this separation. But I have no fear darling that our love will be even more beautiful and pure when we're once again together because of the jealousy with which we guard it while we're apart.
   Yours alone always — Jack

Friday nite Dec. 8

Hello Dearest,
   How's the light of my life this evening? Fine I hope cause — considering everything I'm feeling OK. Like the feller says — I'm better than I was but not as well as I have been. I got the package with Christmas presents today and I wrote your folks thanking them. I'm going to wait till Christmas to open them as you suggested. It looks like we'll just about make it to the Flak House for Christmas — Gosh I sure hope so — that will be a good deal.
   We had a big hairy practice mission today. When we came in we couldn't see a fly on the end of our nose. What visability. If they had weather like this in the states — nobody'd ever get any flight pay. We had a big critique afterwards where we all cry in our beer about the poor formation and all resolve to do something about it — next time.
   Now sweetheart — the same old story — it's getting late and we'll have to fly tomorrow so I better quit for tonight. Personally — I want a little double sack time with a cute lovable someone whom I love very very much. In other words — there's slack in my sack. Darling I love you so much and I sure wish I was home.
   Now — Goodnight sweetheart
   Yours alone always
   Jack

The Lucky Bastard Club

Dec. 9
Saturday night

Hello my own,

    As you've said so often — here it is — the time of the day — I most look forward to. And as I put the date on this letter I realize that in a few hours it will be our six month wedding anniversary. Just think darling — we've actually been married for six months. In some ways it seems only yesterday that I waited for the music to start playing and then watched you coming down the aisle to become my bride. You were very beautiful darling. There seemed to be a look of satisfaction on your face. As if you had waited for that moment a long time and now that it had arrived you felt perfectly assured that through those years and months and days of waiting you had guarded your ideals and dreams carefully. And now that they were being realized — they were everything you had dreamed they would be.

    Perhaps I say you had that look on your face because those were the thoughts in my heart. Then you left your father and took my arm and I knew that from that moment on — you would be mine alone darling — just as we'd pledged we would be so many times. You said so too — and so did I — We said that we would always be true to ourselves and to our love and to our God. Then the Chaplain pronounced us Man and Wife — but I knew that we had already become one in spirit. And then you kissed me. Yes — I kissed you too darling but the thing I'll always remember is that you meant it just as much as I did. It was like that the first time I ever kissed you darling and I know it will always be that way.

    Since that night dearest we've become closer and closer together in our thoughts and ideals and body and spirit. And since I left you — nearly three months ago I have an even greater appreciation of all the things which have always meant so much to us. And when we're once again together, darling, our dreams will come true and our love will create and encompass another being. It is for that day I'm waiting and living for darling.

    Now for a few of the incidental things which have happened recently. I've been sending out a few Christmas Cards to some of the boys and to Doc & Twila & Rev & Mrs Perry and folks like that. With the idea that if you send them one too — no harm is done and that perhaps they might like to hear a word or two from the E.T.O.

I mailed a package to Ted today with a book for the Folks — It is a book on Roses. Just happened to find it while I was trying to find "The Prophet" which — incidentally — ain't in the E.T.O. If it gets there in time for Christmas it will be swell but I'm fraid it will be late. Otherwise I'm not sending anything for two reasons — Can't get anything and can send less.

So much for the incidentals. Happy anniversary, my darling, I love you many times more than you'll ever imagine —
Your husband,
Jack

MISSION # 19   DECEMBER 10, 1944
COBLENZ = 6:30 HRS

This mission was pretty much a milk run (easy). But when we got back, you couldn't see a fly on the end of your nose when we landed because of the fog. We tried another approach, and it was KA-BOOM. A really tail-first landing, but it stuck and we got home. Because of the tail wheel, the B-17 was well known for its KA-BOOM landings. We had a lot of them during training. Then, as we got better, there were fewer and fewer. But remember. A successful landing is one that you walk away from. Leaves a lot of room for error, huh?

Sunday nite Dec. 10

My Beloved Wife,
Here it is our anniversary night — what do you know about that?
I didn't go to church tonight. Got home from chow about 4:30 and it's been raining cats & kittens. When we came in this afternoon we couldn't see very much. The visability is really getting sour these last few days. Sure hope it gets better soon. I hate to go around on landing because I can't see the runway and that happened tonight. There we were on the final approach as big as life and couldn't even see the runway. It was over on Stan's side and I tried to go over but we came catywampus and I couldn't kick it straight so I just poured the coal to her and went around. When we finally did land it was one of those Ka-boom landings and it just about scared Slim out of his skin back in the tail but he wouldn't admit it. His sinus has quit bothering him now

and I'm sure glad. He was going thru a lot and yet he wouldn't stay on the ground because he couldn't stand to "sweat us out." That's the kind of boys they are darling. Makes a fellow feel humble to belong to such a swell team. Too bad our endeavors can't be along constructive lines rather than otherwise.

But enough of that. I want to tell you again just how much I really do love you my own sweet wife. –Gee — that sounds so good — My own sweet wife. And you are, darling, mine — and so very sweet. Just to know that you love me and I love you with all my heart and soul, gives me such a warm feeling on these cold nights. Just to remember your warm breast held close to mine makes my heart turn flip flops and my toes turn up. Caus I love you always — and always,
<u>Your</u> husband
Jack

MISSION # 20   DECEMBER 11, 1944
GIESSEN = 8:00 HRS

We flew under the overcast at really low altitude. As we got closer to the target, we got lower and lower. I was flight leader of the low element of the low squadron, and when a church steeple went by we decided to pull up a little. I didn't fly lead very often. But our crew was one of the best and best-trained in the whole Eighth Air Force. That was part of the reason we were selected for lead crew. But there were twice as many spots for wingmen as for leads. By flying wing also, we had a better chance to get home sooner.

Monday Dec. 11

Joyce my dearest,
Another day with no mail from you. I got two packages and a letter from home yesterday and a letter from Uncle Carey and one from Ned today but no letters from you for a month. I know now what you were feeling so low about. Fortunately the only time I have to dwell much on the subject is for an hour or so when I get down on the ground after a mission — before I go to bed. But lately I've been thinking a lot while flying too. I'm not worried — just awfully lonesome. But don't worry darling — I'll be all right. As long as things go as fast as they are now it will all be over and I'll be home. As for starting next semester darling — I believe I would start if I

were you. Bad weather or any one of a number of things might keep me over here till spring. At least if we figure that way we won't be disappointed. However — do as you like. You might rather just stay home and be with the folks than start another semester but don't forget — I promised your dad I'd let you finish your college — Let me know what you think about it and we'll think it over together awhile.

We got caught under some weather coming back today and went down pretty low. Some of the boys got some pictures of those towns in France which have been bombed so often. I hope they turn out OK. One time we were so low that a church steeple went by our wingtip about 15 ft. away. I mean we were on the deck. Most fun I've had in a long time. Oh yes — I flew element lead today — low — low — Oh well — some days you can't make a nickel.

Now sweetheart — it's time to put away my toys and blocks and go to beddybye.

See you in my dreams beloved —
Your loving husband,
Jack

Tues. Dec 12

Joyce my dearest,

I don't know whether this pen is going to make the grade or not. It just keeps dripping and one of these times I'm not going to get the drip off the page before it drips.

What a wonderful day today. We didn't get up till 8:30 and all we had today was a five minute movie this morning and a Typhus booster shot this afternoon. The rest of the day I just sat around like the rock and rested.

Right after dinner I went over to the bath house with a towel — determined to take a bath if it killed me and it nearly did. You see a complete bath is something a little strange around here. In fact when I took all my clothes off I was a little embarrassed to see my bare legs. Imagine that —

We took some pinup pictures this afternoon — I'll send you some if we ever get them developed. Boy — what pinups —

But enough of this idle chatter. I'm sleepy cause it's already after eight o'clock and I should be in bed.

Goodnight sweetheart
I love you very dearly
Your lovin hubsband
Jack

Wed
Dec. 13

Hello my own,

Look –who's in London again. I really didn't expect to be here for a few more days but it seems that our passes are coming more often now and I can't say I mind much.

Actually — I guess it's rather fortunate because as time goes by I find it increasingly difficult to be happy or satisfied or even complacent. I get so fed up with the old routine and particularly do I miss you more. When I come in to London I can see a show or do some sightseeing and — at times even imagine that you can see the same thing — with me. But out at the base — when I climb into that same old sack in the same old hole I get so very lonesome for you I can hardly stand it. I want you to be with me when I brush my teeth and wash up. And when I put on my p j's I remember that night in Rapid when you put on your "purity" nightgown and stood beside the bed a moment before you climbed in. I asked you to stand there and just let me look at you. And my mind photographed a pinup of the most wonderful wife a man ever had — in those few seconds. And now — I can see it so plainly. You were standing there holding my hand with your left hand. Your lovely shoulders were shining because you hadn't turned off the bathroom lights. The cups in your nighty seemed hardly sufficient to support your beautiful, rounded firm young breasts and it clung to your lovely slim waist and full hips — and if I remember I even cautioned you to remember your tummy and you pulled it in like a good girl. Then as my eyes traveled on I could see just the faintest suggestion that there was something else — not concealed yet not shown which awaited for the time when you should actually be completely mine. I often wonder if "she" was and is as

Roy R. Fisher, Jr. with Susan Fisher Anderson

eager as I always seemed to be. Darling — I've never mentioned these things in letters before but I do want you to realize just how very much I do want you and how I miss you. And this — while it leaves much to be desired — can perhaps make up in a very small way for what we cannot show physically. Just to put into concrete words the millions of thoughts & dreams which have been spinning thru my head helps tremendously to relieve some considerable nervous tension. I can almost hear you say — "Darling — please make me yours" and then — "Jack — we're <u>one</u> person," and I realize that — having once been united by that tremendous physical bond and believing as we do in the firm spiritual bond which unites us — we'll always be together — regardless of how long it may be before we are actually together again.

Perhaps — dearest you won't agree that there is any reason for writing such a letter — particularly in view of the fact that it may be censored — but I can't contain these thoughts within me any longer darling. –I'm sure you'll understand. And now sweetheart — my own — Three goodnight kisses from your loving husband — one for your lovely lips and one each for your beautiful breasts — before I go to sleep.

Darling — I love you so —
Jack

Chapter Twenty
Almost Christmas

Sat nite
Dec. 17 (16)

My darling,
This mail situation is really deplorable. I finally got a letter from Mom the other day, but to date — the last letter I've received from you was dated Nov 11 Over a month ago — of course I know that it is just the poor mail service but — nevertheless — I'm getting so low in spirits that I don't know where to turn. I'm just hoping we don't fly in the morning, a good church service would to more than anything to help me to concentrate my thoughts on someone else's troubles. Speaking of other folk's troubles — Cole's brother was shot down over Merseburg on the 30th of last month. All the crew bailed out but he's a P.W. Cole's been down to see him several times and he never made connections and so he has troubles. I can't figure that boy out.

I found out tonight that we won't go to the Rest Home till after Christmas. One of the other boys is going — One who has been here a bit longer than we have. I hope that I will get to hear the "Messiah" this year. It won't seem like Christmas without the "Messiah."

This letter will probably get to you just about Christmas. I'll mail it to our house and the next few the same. I hope you'll be able to spend some time at the Fisher house over vacation — it will mean so much to them.

I've been thinking about you so much today. Wondering just what you'll think when you get that letter I wrote the other night in London. I was feeling awfully awfully lonesome for a little duel sacktime that night and that letter helped me blow off a little steam. You know how important that is and so I hope you will understand. And now my sweetheart — I'll say so long for now —
Your own loving husband,
Jack

Roy R. Fisher, Jr. with Susan Fisher Anderson

Sunday nite
Dec. 17

Joyce my darling,

It finally happened! Yes — today was the day. I got nine letters. Six of them from you. So I'm a happy man again.

Actually things have been happening today to really make things look bright. To begin with — we had a class at 10 this am and we all got up and went to class and he told us that if we had heard the lecture we could leave. So I did and went to Church. It was an excellent service and he used for a text several passages from the Messiah. Of course as he read them I could hear the music in my mind. Then he made a wonderful speech — or rather sermon.

Then when we got the mail this evening I got so many lovely letters. In spite of the fact that we're no longer a Group Lead crew I was thrilled by all the commendations which — I'm afraid were unmerited.

Then tonight Richter came over and told me that he'd been put back on flying status. He's going to become a radar specialist and he will probably be back flying with us again.

But it was your sweet letters which really fixed me up on top of the world. Gosh darling — after not hearing from you at all for two weeks it was just the most marvelous experience you can imagine.

Particularly the one letter where you told me how proud you were that we had gotten Lead Crew — you sure can make a man happy darling. Particularly when that man is me. Gosh — darling — I love you so much and a letter like that one just made chills and thrills run up and down my spine. Well — this place has gotten pretty stirred up. Some of the boys just got back from London & the peace and quiet has gone to H – –. So I'll say goodnight sweetheart

Your own devoted husband,
Jack

The Lucky Bastard Club

MISSION # 21   DECEMBER 18, 1944
MAINZ = 7:00 HRS

Not much to report, except that I was still fighting the war. The Mission Belle was a great ship. Her engines would groan with an almost-deafening roar as she thundered against the wind with her heavy load. Her wings would vibrate and shudder and just as we were sure we couldn't get off the ground, there was a lurch and we were off. With a last little drag of our tail wheel, we were airborne and climbing at 130 mph.

Rising slowly through the clouds, and there were most always several thousand feet of them, we would finally clear into the wild blue yonder where dozens, no hundreds of ships would be waiting for us to fall into formation. Gerry beware, the 8th Air Force is in the air. And each time, in the back of our minds — each of us — was the question, Would we make it back?

Monday night
Dec. 18

My darling,
When we got down your letters #14 & 15 were waiting for me and so in spite of the fact that I'm completely fagged — they really gave me a lift.

They got us up late this morning and we flew without eating breakfast and although it didn't bother us for the first few hours — by the time I got on the ground I felt like I'd been drug thru the proverbial knothole. Feet first no less. The weather today was stinky. We flew in clouds for over half the day and that's for the rabbits. But enough of that. I'm back on the ground safe and sound so who am I to gripe.

Regarding the letters you wrote I was awfully interested in that idea you presented about the sex education of our children. As you know — that is a subject which interests me greatly because as I see the result of my home training and compare it to the results I see around me I'm nothing short of amazed.

I hope none of our boys will ever be up against as rough a situation as we are but if they ever are I want them to have the same background I've had because with it — it is possible for me to just ignore the temptations which constantly arise. In most cases I'm quite sure that it is just a lack of respect for the opposite sex. I'm beginning to be convinced that a proper respect is about the most important single item in the whole problem. But enough of that for now.

I'm so tired I can't see straight and so I think I'll go wash & shave and hit the old sack. As you said darling — another 24 hours have gone by and I'm just one day and one mission closer to your arms and you to mine. It won't be long dearest till we'll be together and this painful separation will be at an end. I do miss you so very much darling because as each moment passes my love for you grows greater and more important in my life.

And now sweetheart — goodnight and sweet dreams —
Husband
Jack

Wed nite
Dec. 19

Hello sweetheart,

Hows my little cuddle kitten this fine evening? Personally I'm doing OK considering I'm here & you're there. I've been re-reading a couple those wonderful letters I got the day before yesterday and listening to Dianah Shore. Quensecontly I'm feeling sedimental. But I get to feeling that way often these days.

So you "borrowed" my shirt did you — well — I can't think of any reason why you shouldn't get some good out of it. I was going to give it to you when I was home but forgot to — <u>How does it fit?</u>

Just another day of doing little or nothing. Got lotsa sacktime today. Nothing but pp weather — socked in but good — Stan had his fingers crossed.

So you see sweetheart — I've got no news — I'm just sounding off so I guess I'd better quit & go to bed. Stan says we're going to fly tomorrow

Your loving husband,
Jack

The Lucky Bastard Club

Wednesday nite
December 20

My own sweet wife,

Here it is just five days before Christmas and I have yet to feel at all Christmasy. I began to get the spirit tonight at choir rehearsal, but the spirit of giving is tragically absent. Tomorrow night we're going to sing at the Red Cross officer's Club in town and there are supposed to be a bunch of little kids there. I hope there are because that is what really gives me the spirit. Perhaps my letter tomorrow night will be in a totally different mood.

As you can see our plans for Flak House for Christmas have been dispelled. One of the other crews who has been here longer beat us to it. However — we'll be there within the next week or so. And I'm of the opinion we need a nice long rest pretty bad. Particularly now that we have so much spare time. When we were flying every day we developed a sort of daze in which we worked & flew and thought. We were so dead tired most of the time that nothing bothered us. Now — however we get P Oed at our roommates and at each other and at ourselves and we can't seem to get over it. Nor do we try particularly. It is a trial at times to keep smiling at Stan & Ott. They are such boys about so many things. Bob and I sort of try to keep things on an even keel. There seems to be the tendency for them to rebel against all authority and to be incooperative as far as the squadron is concerned and it takes a lot of psycology to keep them going. But if it weren't for trials like that to worry with I would have absolutely nothing to occupy my time. But I'm not griping darling — They're really good boys — it's just that they are tired and don't realize it. I just wish we could all go home tomorrow.

Here comes Bob Hope on the radio — I'm sure he'll help my spirits out considerably. He's out in the California desert and that's the only place where the soldiers <u>could serve their country & eat it too</u>. (speaking of wedding cake and you did in your letter of the 16th). So you went to a wedding? I'm awfully glad you told me all about it. It sounded like a beautiful wedding but why did everyone stand up — or do they at those kind of weddings. Poor people — don't see what's going on. But I love you darling — even tho you are not quite tall enough to see from the back row. You see — sweetheart — love is no respecter of size. Anyway I'm not very big myself.

Roy R. Fisher, Jr. with Susan Fisher Anderson

I'm awfully glad you're getting along so well with your piano playing. I'm sure you'll get a lot out of that little skill. And when I get home I'll sure do my best to keep you in practice.

I've been thinking a lot about just what I want to do during that thirty day leave I'll have when I do come home and I think it would be fun to rent an apartment for a month. We could stay at the homes (yours or mine) for part of the time but I'm 'fraid we'll need nearly all that time — a lot of it by ourselves — to find ourselves again after this Hell of separation. Let me know what you think about the idea Joyce — if it is a real problem. I don't want our folks to feel neglected and yet I'm 'fraid I wouldn't want to go thru another week like the one just before we went to Lincoln. I just can't see that. I've got enough trouble trying to figure out my own mind without trying to fathom everyone else's. Or at least — that's the way the problem as it is appears to me. That's the main reason why I want your help.

Now my sweet — as the radio sez. "Have you tried on Oh my achin back sack, Mac?" It's a program over the A.F.N. (America Forces Network.) He's a character that comes on wed nite at 10 and plays records for the abovementioned sack corporation. Personally — I'm only interested in the duel models. With my own sweet little wife. Gosh darling I love you — G'nite hon,
Jack

MISSION # 22   DECEMBER 23, 1944
KAISERLAUTERN = 7:45 HRS

This was about two weeks after the start of the BATTLE OF THE BULGE. Our troops were fighting — and losing — to the overpowering drive of the Germans' last real offensive of the war. The Air Corps' fighters and bombers had been grounded off and on for two weeks due to weather. We just couldn't get off the ground and we were terribly frustrated. We were briefed nearly every day, and then the mission was scrubbed. Either our base was fogged in so we couldn't get off the ground, or the target area was, or the base at time of return was, so we couldn't land when we got home, or all of the above.

We had heard about the problems; the Allies were having a hard time breaking through the enemy lines. How we wished we could go help them. But the weather is so unpredictable in the winter. Down on the continent, the battle lines were so close that it was hard to tell who was who. Unless we could clearly see what — and who — we were bombing, we might be more trouble than help. Today they sent us to another target. At least we could do some good somewhere.

MISSION # 23   DECEMBER 24, 1944
BABENHAUSEN = 8:00 HRS
CHRISTMAS EVE

Christmas Eve Day the weather finally cleared. Everything that could fly was ordered into the air on a MAXIMUM EFFORT. We were to bomb every target we could positively identify. We bombed bridges, railroads, support columns, and any other likely target that we could hit. We could see the rolling hills and the countryside. Below us we could also see the effect of our efforts as the forest turned black and red as fires were ignited by our bombs. It was hard for me, a Forestry major, to watch the trees ablaze due to my labor. But I was fighting a different war today. I was helping to clear a path. Now our tanks and foot soldiers can get through for front line support. We really felt a part of the BATTLE OF THE BULGE that day.

We did a lot of good, and I'm sure were instrumental in the final victory of General Patton's troops. We found out later, that just our presence was a powerful morale factor. The troops on the ground knew they were not alone. Someone on their side was helping. I am also sure that we probably bombed some of our own troops, although we were never told so. The battle lines were so indistinct that we could not always identify our own. We did, however, bomb at low altitude, and got plenty shot up in the process, and lost a lot of ships to ack ack; including General Castle. The German 88's were very effective when we were under 10,000 ft.

The problem of the mission was our return to base. When we got back to England, our base was open. As the weather moved in, more and more bases closed; socked in so tight the planes couldn't land. After we were on the ground, other groups were diverted to our field, one of the only ones still open.

As they stacked up, waiting to land, the planes in the landing pattern turned on their red and green clearance lights — red light on left wing, green light on right wing — for protection against each other. Each group of thirty-six ships flew in a vertical column. Lead squadron slightly in front, High squadron above the lead, and Low squadron below. From our vantage point on the ground, the sight was amazing. At one time I counted six groups circling the base with over 70 red and green lights on each group. They looked like six real live Christmas trees.

MERRY CHRISTMAS FROM THE EIGHTH AIR FORCE.

December 25
Christmas nite (late)

Hello my sweet,
Merry Christmas darling. As you can see — we're in London again. Things were awfully confused today. We didn't get up early for one thing — first time in several days and so of course the mission was scrubbed. They just can't fly without us.

I got up about 9:30 and took a nice hot shower and went to church. We had the most beautiful Christmas morning. It was — believe it or not a real white — Christmas. Not snow — but hoar frost and just as beautiful as a soft snow without being nearly so inconvenient. The trees were simply gorgeous (never could spell) anyway — we had an awfully nice service and then a wonderful turkey dinner. We had a bunch of extra men on the field but they managed to feed them all without too much trouble. We had white tablecloths and <u>service</u> and ice cream for desert. So you see it was really a fine Christmas. I was almost sure I would fly on Christmas so I opened your package on Christmas eve. I was so greatful for the shorts & shirts — there's nothing I needed more at the time. I'll try to acknowledge all the gifts when we get to the flak house and if I don't make it then I'll let them all know when I get back home.

Then this afternoon we got our pass so we took off like a herd of turtles & when we got here we found that all the subways were on strike. Well — the Tail Transportation office fixed us up with a truck and so although it is awfully late — we did get here — anyway. Fortunately we had made our reservations ahead of time so they were expecting us.

Well darling — I've had a lovely warm bath and so I'm all sweet & clean just for you. But as you said — I'd better not get started on that or there'll be no stopping me. I think I'll make a copy of a part of this letter & send it to the folks so they'll know how I spent Christmas. It was really enjoyable because we had the spirit and that's all that really matters.

Nite my darling —
Jack

Dec 27
Wednesday noon

Joyce Darling,
Here it is the 27th already and just about time for us to go back to the base again. I really can't figure out just where the time goes.
Yesterday I got up about 10 and went right to work trying to get a ticket to the Messiah. Finally worked it and so yesterday afternoon I went down to Royal Albert Hall for that. Gosh — what a tremendous place. It seats better than 8,000 people and the soloists didn't need to use a microphone. I've never seen such a large hall with such marvelous acoustics. When I got back to the club there was a big Children's party in progress. Santa Claus had just arrived and you never in your life saw so many sparkling eyes and expectant faces. Various schools in the states had sent packages of Christmas toys and S. Claus distributed them. The boys — Stan, Ott and Bob were having just as much fun as the kids — or more so.
Last night Bob and I went to a play. Not too bad — not too good. Then home & drank coffee for a couple hours before we hit the sack. This morning we got some pictures that we'd had made. I'll enclose some of them. You might find flak if you look — by for now sweets —
Jack

MISSION # 24   DECEMBER 28, 1944
KOBLENZ = 7:15 HRS

We lost two engines just before the bomb run and couldn't keep up with our squadron, so we tacked on to another squadron, and dropped our load with theirs. With some help from a little "friend," a P-51 who flew with us to coast out, we made it safely out of enemy territory. However, the trip across the channel got a little hairy as well. Having lost two engines and still losing altitude, we were afraid we might have to ditch in the North Sea.

Roy R. Fisher, Jr. with Susan Fisher Anderson

It was mighty cold to have to ditch — our life expectancy was only about 15 minutes in the frigid water, if we didn't get wet. As we flew lower and lower, I was kept pretty busy keeping the plane aloft while the men began throwing over everything that could move: guns, parachutes, ammo, radio equipment, even extra fuel. Since we had just crossed the enemy coast Jacobs was still in his position, cranked down in the ball turret. From there, Bob could see, better than any of the rest of us, how low we really were.

If you are familiar with the ocean, you may know that the ninth wave is usually bigger than the others, and that the ninth of the ninths is the biggest of all. Bob learned that interesting bit of trivia in a particularly traumatic way. He was still in the ball, our having just hit coast-out, when the ninth ninth wave splashed all over the ball turret. Cole got him out, and they didn't tell me about it until 50 years later. I guess they figured the "old man" had enough to worry about that day. It still gives me goose bumps thinking about it. We managed to maintain our altitude, able to take advantage of the Venturi effects created by the pressure difference between the water and the air; and were even able to climb a little as the ship got lighter. We were able to make it to the emergency field, and then back to Bury — home.

Thursday night
Dec. 28th

Hello my darling,
Here I am — back at work again. Yes — we flew another one today. We're really racking them up. Sorta thought we'd get to the Flak House this week but I'm 'fraid we'll not make it till next week. It was sorta rough today. The squadron is working hard to get a citation and every abortion counts against us so I didn't abort although I guess it would have been much better. Instead I kicked her over the target on two engines at 130 miles an hour. Of course I lost the formation but when we got near the target I found another group and we bombed where they did. There were lots of friendly fighters so I guess we weren't in much danger, but I sure felt conspicuous up there all by myself about 5 thousand feet lower than everyone else and crawling along at 130 — trying to keep from stalling out. Well — anyway it's just one more mission counted up and the squadron record is still clean. Our C.O. has been working pretty hard and the

The Lucky Bastard Club

whole outfit will be able to wear the ribbon — even the ground crew so that will make it worthwhile – but gosh I'm tired. I'll probably feel better about the whole business tomorrow morning after a good nights sleep.

No mail again today. I understand that the only mail that is coming by air is V-mail. But — I'd much rather get mail a little late than to get V-mail. I think you can see what I mean. Your letters — in your own handwriting are what it takes to make your little hubsband happy. I did get a package from the folks today and a box of caramels from you. Just those few words written in that "familiar scrawl" helped a whole lot. Mom sent me some shirts & shorts too, honey, so I'm really well outfitted now.

The ground is still covered with snow — believe it or not. I guess it is still that real heavy frost but in some places it has drifted slightly and the ground is frozen and there is <u>no mud.</u> Yes — it's cold — all the <u>crappers</u> are froze up and things are not quite as convenient as might be but my sack is warm (if lonesome) and there is a good fire in the barracks and I know that if I fly every day it won't be too long now till I can hold you in my arms again. You may not get much more than started in spring semester darling — perhaps you had better just skip it. You might go and look us up an apartment to live in while I'm home and set up housekeeping. No — that would be entirely too lonesome but you might keep it in mind.

My eyes are getting heavy dear — perhaps I should go wash & shave and sack up. As you can see — I'm using some of the stationary Mother & Father Day sent. I like it so much — I'm going to write them awful soon,

But not tonight — too tired.
No somphin — loves — ya muchly —
Yes I doo —
Nite darlingest,
Jack

Roy R. Fisher, Jr. with Susan Fisher Anderson

Dec. 29
Friday night

Joyce my own — my own,

Four wonderfully marvelous letters from you today. Numbers — 16 -17-18 & 19 — believe it or not. Four consecutive letters and — the last you mentioned getting some mail and I'm so glad.

Darlingest — who knows any better than I just what agony it is to go for several weeks without getting any mail. It is just a necessity for even the barest peace of mind that is needed to keep us from going entirely bats —.

And in the last letter when you told me about that night when we were together for the first time — well darling — you've no idea just what a thrill I got out of reading that part of your letter. I could just see you as you revealed to me for the first time the most beautiful body in the world. You were so sweet and lovely and patient that night too dearest. I know what you must have endured darling and it only makes me more awed by the wonderful experience which our love is and as I look back over the months we've been separated and see how clearly I can recollect all those moments we spent together I realize just what a powerful force holds us together. There is so much more than the mere physical attraction which we felt so strongly that first night and yet that physical attraction and bodily oneness is very important too dear. Particularly now that we're so far apart we must guard that attraction because as our separation becomes longer that physical desire is stronger and we must keep it focused rather than let it wander. Yes — my sweet — I miss the caress of your hands on my body and I miss the touch of your soft breast and yet with each recalling — you seem nearer to me. Sometimes I can even see you darling — day or night — makes little difference. You just appear to me all of a sudden — like an angel — and so beautiful. Gosh — I'm such a lucky guy to have such a marvelous girl for my wife — Now darling I must hit the old sack.

Goodnight my own —
Your loving husband,
Jack

The Lucky Bastard Club

MISSION # 25   DECEMBER 30, 1944
MANNHEIM = 7:30 HRS

We flew high element lead. We had a tail wind so we kept overrunning the lead ship. They had the same wind, but it got stronger with altitude (jet stream? Probably). When flying above the lead ship, I had to keep my eye on the leader, keeping his plane in view below and between my engine nacelle and the wing root, and the left side of the aircraft. When Stan flew it was the opposite. Man, it was a rough day, but it counts as one more.

Saturday night
Dec. 30

Hi sweetheart,

Here's your hubby for a short chat. I'm pretty tired again tonight darling and as soon as I let you know what's on my mind I'm going to hit the sack. I got three packages today — one from Joyce Fisher — wonder who she is? Bunches of candy bars — thanks so much dear — they sure taste good on these long missions. I also got a package of cookies & candy (fudge) from Don & Issie and a box of divinity from the Ways. Unfortunately the latter has melted in all the damp weather so I had to throw it out. Issies' cookies were good — they're already gone.

As I told you we flew another one today so I'm closer to you tonight than I was last night. It wasn't particularly rough except that it was a long haul and we were flying high element lead. In that spot you fly above and behind the lead ship and it is sorta hard to keep in position 'cause if you get over on top of the lead ship you can't see a thing. But we didn't give our wingmen a rough time so I guess it wasn't bad.

There's a good possibility darling, that I'll be back in the states by my birthday or so — so perhaps you had better forget about going to school. I hate to think of wasting all that time and money if you'll only be there a month or so and I'm sure you won't want to be in school after I get home. What do you think?

I had a wonderful dream about you last night — sweets — all about you. In fact the sheets were a little stiff in spots this morning. That's one place where I have the advantage. I can still dream — and oh — what a wonderful dream you are —
Darling — I love you so — nite sweetheart
Your loving husband,
Jack

MISSION # 26   DECEMBER 31, 1944
HAMBURG = 8:00 HRS

We had a really strong headwind over the target. It seemed at times that our ground speed was zero. At one point we had the city framed between the #2 engine nacelle and the fuselage for what seemed like hours (actually, it was only about 20 minutes) until, finally, the command pilot decided to lose a little altitude so we could pick up some airspeed and get home.

New Years Eve

Beloved,

Here's that man again — Remember me. I'm the guy you spend New Year's Eve with. Usually. Gee what a beautiful New Years Eve this is darling. Wonderful full moon and everything. By the way am I to understand that you're back on that old schedule again. Each time there's a full moon I remember all those full moon-lolipop parties we used to have. They were fun too — weren't they darling — Funny how you remember little things like that so well. Just the old story of things we do together being more fun than anything else that ever happens — even if it's nothing more than sweating out the moon — together.

Well — we chalked up another one today darling and I'm awfully tired. We really sweat it out today. It was a particularly rough target and it was visual. On top of that we had a strong headwind and it seemed like we were standing still. But we're back and that's all that counts.

I just wrote your dad a short note, thanking him for his letter and the folks for the box.

And now darling — I think I'll hit the sack and welcome in the New Year dreaming of you — What a wonderful New Years.

G'nite my own — I love you —
Jack

The Lucky Bastard Club

Chapter Twenty-One
The Flak House

Jan 2 1945

Happy New Year Darling,

Here it is 1945 already! I really don't feel much different than I did two days ago and yet the New year does hold so many things in store for you and I and indeed for the whole world.

As you can see — I'm in London. This time only for a night while enroute to the rest home for a week. We're traveling on orders but they authorize a night in London so here we are at the Duchess Club again. The rooms were all filled but we have a lot of good friends here and so they found room for us. That's one of the advantages of always coming here. It is really like a home because we know everyone and they all know us and are so glad to see us.

Last night they had a tea dance out at the base and since we weren't flying for a change and I knew we wouldn't fly today I went to it. There were about three nurses there and the rest were "limey" girls. I never got so disgusted at anything in my life. I'll tell you more about it when I see you but rest assured I'll avoid those parties in the future.

Right now I'm sitting in the music room listening to a Senior Pilot play the piano. He is a Chezk and he is playing a lot of his own music as well as a general international program. It wouldn't surprise me if we start singing before long. Sure hope so — I haven't been in on a good Jam session lately. Right now — Beethoven's Moonlight Sonata. Lovely — I got your letter just the other day where you mentioned that letters mailed from here get to you so much more quickly than the others so perhaps with all our recent excursions you've been able to keep up with your husband to a certain extent. The one thing you may or may not have noticed is that at the present your hubby is awfully — awfully lonesome. Why? Because I have the most wonderful wife in the whole wide world waiting for me and it's been so long since I left her. Guess you can't blame me for feeling that way and as the days go by that aching lonliness just gets worse and worse. (He played "Together") That is sorta our theme isn't it darling. No matter what

147

happens, we'll be able to take it on the chin — as long as we're together.
  Nite my dearest wife,
  I love you so,
  Jack

The FLAK HOUSE was a very real place where crews were assigned to help them regain their perspective, and get some R & R — rest and recuperation. Somewhere in the middle of the tour all crews got burned out, and a three-day pass was not enough recovery time. They tried to get most crews to the Flak House about halfway through — right around the 20th mission, we were almost 2/3 done before we got to go. We waited unduly long, but finally it was our turn.

Physically, it was one of the many gorgeous estates that the owners turned over to the war effort. For our purpose it was a total change of scene that reminded us why we were fighting this war. Breakfast was available when you got up, even at noon; real "high tea" in the afternoon; real eggs and real meat, and all sorts of pastries and goodies — all served by motherly types who were good listeners. Tennis, riding, hiking, or just reading or lying abed — take your choice. The girls were always scheming to try to get us involved in one activity or another.

The enlisted men had their own and the officers all went together to another. The Flak House was run by the Red Cross in cooperation with the Army Medics. The Medics provided the booze. Some guys just like to get harmlessly drunk. Everybody relaxes in his own way. I don't remember much, but the week went by really fast. Oh, and games of bridge! Such were the trials of combat flying in the E.T.O. Then back to the war.

The Lucky Bastard Club

Wednesday nite
Jan. 3, 1945

My Darling wife,

    A few moments ago I was so sleepy I was afraid I'd never be able to find my way to bed but I stumbled upstairs and undressed — yes (even my long underwear) and put on my nice clean blue pajamas and did twentyfive situps and now I'm quite wide awake. That's a good formula — you might remember it for future reference —

    But to get up to the present.

    We left London at 9:57 this morning and arrived here shortly after noon. This rest Home resembles nothing as much as it does a large fraternity house. It is set on a large estate — just how large I don't know cause I've spent all afternoon in the house — but I'll tell you tomorrow.

    Downstairs there are three large rooms — one a living room — one a library (and at present the office) and the other the dining room. In the large central hallway is one of these English oversize billiard or snooker tables and in the wing are the kitchen, pantry and servant's quarters. Upstairs are about 8 or 10 bedrooms with room for about four people each and with a bath adjoining each room. The army & Red Cross personel live upstairs over the servants quarters. The adjutant is the boss — they all call him "Pop" and he sorta runs the show. He's a pilot who's finished flying for some reason and has this job for a while. The rest of the personel I'll wait till later to describe.

    As I said, there are four to a room and of course Stan Bob Ott and I are here together. Bob is already in bed and I'm sitting in bed with the covers pulled up and a pillow propping me up to write this. Most of this afternoon I spent just resting. I find as I relax I become increasingly tired and will probably be well worn out within a day or so. Then I can start building up my strength and resistance again. I could only do twentyfive situps a little while ago. But my back would get sore too —

    Well darling — I must close for tonight. Goodnight my love
Your husband
Jack

Roy R. Fisher, Jr. with Susan Fisher Anderson

Thursday nite
Jan 4 —

My darling wife,

Thursday nite already. My the day has gone quickly. Nothing to do but have a good time and rest. Got up about 9:30 — just in time for breakfast, and went for a long walk around the estate with one of the other fellows. It was a beautiful sunshiny day but there was a frosty wind blowing and it was bitterly cold. After lunch we went horseback riding and I'm fraid I'm going to be awfully stiff tomorrow. I had a big horse that rode somewhat like a tank. The rest of the horses were not nearly so big and so we could walk nearly as fast as they could trot. And when "Patch" broke into a gallop it was like hitchhiking on a V-2.

Tonight — after dinner, Becky, (Red Cross Girl from <u>Lincoln</u> — was she ever tickled when I told her we were married in Lincoln. She wanted to know all about it so I told her. I love to tell people about marrying you because it makes me glow all over to relive — even for a few moments those wonderful hours when we became husband & wife) Anyway — Becky suggested that we all go in to town to the dance. Well — that was ok by me — so off we went. It was a pretty sad affair and I wanted to leave on the first truck back but I missed it and so I stayed. We started a big crap game in the middle of the floor during intermission and I think we shocked some of the local residents. Tough —

But — as you can easily guess — it's after 1:00 now and I'm pretty tired so I guess I'll close for now.

Darling — I do love you so —
Jack

Friday nite
Jan. 5

My beloved,

The days seem to hurry by so fast when I'm busy. Today went so quickly I hardly realize it's gone. Of course — to begin with — I stood in bed till nearly noon. After that big day yesterday I could hardly pull myself out of the sack at all — Gosh am I stiff. And is my back sore. For that reason I sort of took it easy all afternoon — just sorta rested. Just before dinner we played two rubbers of bridge and made two slams — one big — one little.

This evening we had a movie. "You can't ration love." Remember when we saw it — I believe it was at Rapid. Remember — all about a college that had too many girls or too few men and how this one girl made 2 point Simpson into a really slick number and in the process fell in love with him. Well when they got married at the end of the film and he kissed her. Well believe me I had a little trouble keeping the tears back. I remember that kiss so well and in those few seconds I relived the joy of kissing <u>my wife</u> for the first time.

Gee — I'm sure a lucky guy. But also a little sleepy — Better sign off for tonight hon,

I love you my darling,
Jack

Saturday nite
Jan. 6

Darling,

It sure is drunk out tonight!! It is already after 1:30 but the boys downstairs are still going strong. We had quite a party here tonight. It was awfully nice except that one or two guys had too much to drink. Naturally you know how that irritates me. That's why I'm here in bed instead of down there. Need I say more. But as long as they're having a good time I can't object. After all — that's why they're here. To forget combat for a while.

I wrote several duty letters this morning. Finally managed to tear myself away from the snooker table to get them off. After dinner I shot skeet for a while — shot about 75 rounds or so and I'll bet my shoulder is sore tomorrow. If it isn't–I'll sure be surprised.

I took a nap this afternoon too and I'm planning to take one tomorrow. I sure am enjoying this rest. Some of the fellows can't find enough to do but I have trouble keeping from doing too much. Just imagine — Butler wakes us up at about 8:30 with a glass of tomatoe juice or something and we don't have breakfast till 9:30 and only a handful of guys get up for that.

This is the way I want to spend that 30 day leave darling — Just you and I together — doing everything or nothing as we please.

Roy R. Fisher, Jr. with Susan Fisher Anderson

That's really the only way to get one's feet back on the ground and I want mine there. How about it?
  Now I better sign off —
  Nite sweet — I sure love you —
  Jack

Sunday nite
Jan. 7

Hi sweetheart,
  It's awfully cold here in the room but I'm waiting for Bob to finish taking a bath and then I'm going to take one. In the meantime I'll catch you up on the happenings at the Flak House. Boy oh Boy did they ever have a party last night. Some of the boys were still reeling this morning and as soon as the Pubs opened they began tieing on another one.
  Tonight I went into town to a show — Very poor one and coming home — Lisa — little blond Red Cross girl that runs this place held my hand to keep it warm cause somebody stole my good gloves the other night. Are you jealous? You needn't be but I'll sure be mad if you aren't.
  I never saw such a lazy crew as this outfit around here is. This afternoon there were nearly twenty guys spread all over the living room on chairs — sofas and even on the floor. Some of them were reading but most of them were just peacefully sleeping. Then Lisa came in and woke them all up and we had to go out and play volleyball with her. Gosh what ambition!! But we soon got cold so we all hiked back into the house and resumed our many & varied Restful Positions. I began "The Exile" by Pearl Buck and it is really a wonderful book. I enjoy her so much.
  Now — time out to get all sweet & clean —
  Monday morning.
  I stayed in the tub about an hour just resting and reveling in the nice hot water and in the fact that there was really no hurry in getting out. As a consequence, when I finally did pull myself out I was so sleepy I couldn't keep my eyes open, so I promptly hit the sack.
  Darling — I've missed you so very much these past few days. Just lounging around with nothing particular to occupy my thoughts I spend most of the time thinking of you. It seems that no matter what I

do — it always reminds me of something we did together. Last night when I was lying in the tub I thought about the Harney Hotel. Remember what a nice big tub they had. I love to have you wash my back and I love to wash your back (?) too. Funny how I always got carried away when I was doing that isn't it? But I don't think you really minded.

Then too — when I get up early around here and Becky tries to get me to go play tennis I think about the fun we used to have together. Member the day those three boys wanted to play with us. I think we learned something that day.

And then I think about getting home and what the first thing I'm going to do when I do get there. And I wonder if things will be the same and if I'll have to avoid too much contact with people until I get back into the swing of things and then I quit worrying because I know that as soon as I see you and hold you in my arms and we are one again the rest of the world will just fade away. I love you my darling with all my heart

Jack

Roy R. Fisher, Jr. with Susan Fisher Anderson

Chapter Twenty-Two
Back to the War

*Tues nite
in London
January 9*

Joyce my dearest,
Tonight your husband finds himself in quite a muddle of emotions. To explain myself — we're back in London for a couple of days before we go back to the old grind. One of the boys at the base collected all my mail and brought it down with him so I got 12 letters and a post card today. — When we arrived in London and — for that matter — from the time we left the Rest Home it had been snowing and there were several inches of snow on the streets. It was the soft fluffy sticky kind and it nearly tied up traffic. I went out for a while this afternoon and got in three snowball fights. Big ones — and I haven't lost my touch. I could make & throw 3 balls to any one englishman I found. Then — tonight I went to see Spencer Tracy in "Thirty seconds over Tokio."

Perhaps you can see from all those incidents why I sit down with mingled emotions to write the most wonderful little wife any man ever could have. First of all darling — your letters, I never cease to wonder at the marvelous peace of mind your letters bring to me. Nor do I cease to wonder, yes even marvel, at your magnificent command of words and thoughts. Darling — in just those seven letters from you — there is so much food for thought that it will take many days for me to realize the full beauty of your words. I've in mind particularly the anniversary letter — which you wrote on the 10th of December. Our thoughts certainly spanned the broad expanse of space which separates us physically for that night I felt you so near me, just as I do tonight — and always. Before I read your letters, I read those beautiful poems and marveled at the wise words that were contained therein. Yes — darling — ours is perhaps the pain of too much tenderness and yet as I revel in that pain I wonder if there can be too much. As each day passes and your love becomes more of a pillar the pain seems to

Roy R. Fisher, Jr. with Susan Fisher Anderson

My beautiful
Coed wife

become more sharp. And yet I would have it no other way, because always in my heart there is the awareness that although times are difficult we are only being convinced more completely that our love is more than a mere physical attraction which would vanish when our bodies are far apart. Yes — I realize that this separation is building our love and our understanding to a point which conceivably might never be attained thru constant association together.

Now for the papers on parenthood. At first glance they seem to me quite deep and vague but before I say more I shall think deeply on the subject in all its ramifications. You see — dear — without considerable time & energy I can not understand those things because — of necessity my mind is geared to much more concrete thoughts. It is really awfully hard for me to get the full value out of something like that and so when I get home we'll really talk it all out.

The picture of me in a battle jacket — I'll try to have it made tomorrow — We did manage to get a couple at the rest home.

As for that movie I saw tonight I'd advise you not to see it unless you want to get so lonely that you'll cry your heart out. Yes — I cried and my fingernails took an awful beating and my heart is aching although this long chat with you is doing a lot to ease that ache. Each time he took his wife in his arms darling I closed my eyes and you were there and I kissed you and tried to tell you how much I do love you — I only hope you could know just what you do to a lonely heart like mine. And yet — it's not lonely because you're always there Joyce — always — always with me — Wherever I go & whatever I do — Goodnight my darling wife
    I love you
    Jack

Thurs nite
Jan. 11, 1945

Joyce darling,
    Back at the base again and greeted by all sorts of mail and three lovely letters from you, and most important of all, three of the most beautiful pictures I've ever seen. They're all lovely pictures and the fact that they're of you just makes them perfect. Gosh what a beautiful wife I've got. And she's just every bit as sweet as she is goodlooking. Gee — I'm sure a lucky guy. Whoever took the pictures did a

wonderful job. As for being expensive — I would say that they were probably worth at least a million times what you paid for them. I can't think of a better investment than that, can you dear. Anyway — your hubsband is sure a happy man now. All I really need is to finish my tour imegiately if not sooner and get home to that beautiful subject in these pictures. I'm enclosing a cartoon that came out of Stars & Stripes today. I got a big bang out of it. Particularly the first picture. Personally I'm really looking forward to seeing "the same ole things day in, day out," <u>Oh my yes.</u> Now — must sign off Joyce,
 Your everloving husband
 Jack

Friday nite
Jan 12

Joyce darling,
 Lots of letters again today. The most recent is Dec 28-also-18, 22, 23, 24, 25, 26, so you see — I really got caught up on all the news and you've no idea how much your Christmas letters meant. It was more like the real thing just reading your letters tonight than at Christmas because we were so busy at the time. I'm so awfully glad that you could be with my folks for Christmas eve. I got a letter from Mom today too and she told me how much it helped to have you there. Just to know that you're helping to ease the burden on them relieves my mind a lot. I know that they worry about me and I wish they wouldn't. After all — we're just doing a job — like hundreds of other guys and there's no percentage in worrying. We don't and so why should they — I know — it's just like talking to the wind.
 I was also awfully glad to get the letter in answer to all the "things I'd had on my mind for a long time." It certainly helps my morale a lot to know that you miss me as much as I do you. Each night as I hit this old solo sack I go to sleep thinking about you and how nice it would be if you were there beside me. That one sentence in your letter seems to me a most beautiful and wonderful expression of our sexual relationship. "All of our being seemed to be culminated in that act of mutual consecration of our souls and bodies to one another." Darling — that statement is so beautiful. It expresses so exactly my feelings in the matter. As for the frequency adjustment which you mentioned darling, that — I believe should be determined

only by our desires. If there is a mutual desire for union it should never be denied as long as it is physically possible to fulfill that desire. It is so much a part of our lives and we should only strive to make it always more beautiful and satisfying. As for <u>our</u> strong desires — yes darling — mine are as strong as yours, I see no reason to make any excuses for them. I love you — darling — and my love for you doesn't seem complete till you are wholly and always mine. Your letter made you seem so very close my dearest and I'm sure that you can see what I mean. As for what you can do to help me — Just keep writing such sweet letters sweetheart. Let me know your thoughts and innermost desires — even perhaps at the expense of current news, for it is on a common ground of thought that we are closest. Actually your doings are so far removed from mine that I can little more than imagine them. But your thoughts — Those are the same whether you're with me or a million miles away.

As for what I've been doing. We moved again today. Back up to the 331st area. Until now they didn't have room for us but they sent another crew to the 33rd so we moved bag & baggage. What a job! But we're settled now for a while and I hope the next move will be to you.

And now my dearest — I simply must get to bed cause I wouldn't be surprised if we fly tomorrow — I hope.

A big hug and kiss from your
Ever loving husband
Your very own
Jack

MISSION # 27   JANUARY 13, 1945
MAINZ = 7:30 HRS

Our first mission back after the Flak House. After sleeping late, eating too much rich food, and no exercise except bridge, it was really hard to keep up, but we made it. Nothing special, just same old, same old.

Roy R. Fisher, Jr. with Susan Fisher Anderson

~~Friday~~ Saturday
Jan. 13

Joyce my darling,

We flew another one today. Had a little trouble keeping up with everyone because we hadn't flown for a while but after we got settled down it wasn't too bad.

When we got back to the base it was socked in pretty badly — gosh what an understatement, but we landed anyway. This weather sure gets stinko at times.

Got another letter from you today and it helped like everything cause I'm really tired tonight. Also I'm pretty P.O.'d again. They've got a new system of groundschool now where they ground a crew for three days and they do nothing but go to groundschool. Of course we drew that. The fact that we've been doing nothing but sitting on our big fat rusty dusty's for the past week seems to have no bearing on the case. Oh well — maybe someday we'll get finished up and then we can go home and this group can go to —

As I said darling, I'm fagged so I think I'll hit the old sack.
All my love — always,
Jack

Sunday night
Jan. 14

Hi sweetie,

Here's that man again. How's the light of me life tonight? I feel swell considering I've spent all day listening to a bunch of paddlefeet tell me how to fly an airplane and I told them what I thought about it and so it was an unsatisfactory day for all of us.

The weather foot had his say today. He read a speech that he must have copied verbatim from some weather book. It was full of high sounding words and I could hardly keep from laughing. I was reading the "Thin Man."

This new barracks we're in is sure a lot quieter than the last one. The boys are nearly all in the sack or else sitting around the fire reading. A fire is sure a luxury these days. I had to climb an old dead tree & break off some branches for wood. Things are really getting rough.

Jake just came in with Richter with a flock of letters to be censored so I had to leave you for a while — dja get lonesome? Well I am — constantly. I think these guys around here are going to get the idea after while that I'm lonesome and I want to go home to my wife — sure hope it's soon. Gosh darling I miss you so. Guess its cause I love you so much,

Night sweetheart, Jack
P.S.
Wrote to Grandma tonight —
Told her to look for us when I come home OK?
Jack

Jan 15
Monday night

Joyce darling,
 I love you. Didja know that? Well — I do anyway. I wonder how I got on that subject so early in this letter but things are like that. Guess I just can't keep my mind off such a lovely subject.
 Well — we had groundschool again today. One or two lectures by our engineering officer sorta made me mad. One in particular when he started riding some pilots for aborting with no reason so I told him he was crazy as hell and I don't think he liked it very much. Well — it burns me up when all the paddlefeet tell us how to fly and I told him so. Then this afternoon one of the lead pilots who has finished his tour and is now Group training officer gave us a couple of lectures on what it takes to be a lead crew. He got pretty well started on "the burning desire to hit the target & hit it hard with no regard for flak" and I'm afraid I laughed out loud. He was sorta unhappy too. I'm sure a bad boy darling but I'm having fun and it really doesn't hurt anything.
 One more day of groundschool and then we'll start flying again. Boy I'm sure anxious to get started again so I can get finished and get home to you. I really don't want anything much when I get home except a chance to live with you and love you like we always dreamed of. All I really want is just the same sweet wife waiting for me in our own room — if not our own house and no one to bother us with insignificant details. Sound ok to you honey. Well — must close for now.
 Your everloving husband,
 Jack

Roy R. Fisher, Jr. with Susan Fisher Anderson

Tuesday nite
Jan. 16

Sweetheart,
    I just finished reading over several of your last letters and I'm going to catch up on a few things as I go along.
    The Christmas letter is awfully nice isn't it? And did we ever make the news. Confidentially when your Dad made that remark in the one last year — well I couldn't just let it go by unnoticed. I really had to do something about it. You didn't know that was one reason why I married you did you? Course — there were other reasons too. I love you — and life without you is only half a life and reasons like that but I think you really should know the whole story.
    All kidding aside — your Dad did a swell job on the letter. I'll write him if I get around to it but you tell him I said so.
    Again — your lovely letter of the twenty second where you told me just how much our dreams and memories help you and indeed they help me too. I too feel that dissatisfied and restless feeling you mentioned darling. I can sympathize with you wholeheartedly and I think that only thru letters can we hope to achieve a satisfactory evasion of those feelings. If we can just put them aside for a while — perhaps it won't be too many months till we can be together once more and then all this stored up emotion can find full and complete expression. Darling — there's not a day that passes that I don't thank God we're married and not just engaged. Just being married to you has made my life so full and beautiful. Even when we're so far apart it still makes me feel all glowey inside when I think how sweet you are and how much I love you.
    And now beloved, I must say goodnight.
    Your own husband,
    Jack

The Lucky Bastard Club

Chapter Twenty-Three
Belgium

MISSION # 28   JANUARY 18, 1945
KAISERLAUTEN = 7:30 HRS

We lost two engines after leaving the target, and couldn't keep up with the formation on only two engines. Flak continued to be bad, and we looked for a place to set her down. We probably could have made it home, but didn't know how much real damage to the aircraft had occurred. We found a strip, but at the last minute spotted a crashed B-17 on the strip, blocking the runway. Almost immediately we spotted another and slipped into a quick landing. I thought it was France, but Bob tells me it was really Belgium. We were not the only ones to have seen this strip, however, and soon the field was full of ships that couldn't make it home. A field portable kitchen showed up and we got some chow. Bob Miller, my bombardier went in a jeep with a young corporal to get blankets and returned with enough so we wouldn't freeze.

What a night we spent. It snowed and rained and blew and raised particular Ned all night and we were mighty cold with only an army cot and one blanket. There was more mud than anything else. Personally, I decided that if the rest of France (or Belgium – the borders don't show up very well) was like that, they really should have quit fighting for it. It's not worth the trouble. We spotted a JU-88 (German fighter) nearby and scrounged a gas tank cover for a souvenir. Sam looked over the plane and got one engine running again. Since we could take off and fly home on three, we did. We sure didn't want to spend another night here. We were too close to the real war. The Air War was so different.

Friday night (coins enclosed)
January 19

Hello Mommie,
   Yes — *that was one of the letters today. One of three of the sweetest letters from you and a letter each from Mom and Pop as well as a couple Christmas cards and the newsletter from Ways. Normally you'd think that was enough for a day but better than anything else I*

got another lovely picture of my beautiful wife. I'm sitting here looking at you now darling and I can't keep my mind on my work. Gee — you're beautiful. I can't get over it. How I ever managed to get such a wonderful wife I'll never know.

Now a little hot poop on why I didn't write last night. It's a long story but the point of the whole thing is that we landed in France last night. The weather over here was more stinko than usual so the whole outfit landed over there. Gosh what a God forsaken place. We landed at a base that was quite near the front and they didn't have any place to put us so we stayed awake nearly all night. I was just too cold to sleep. I'll tell you more of the details when I see you because much of it is not for publication. I had my first taxi accident last night. We were taxiing on a narrow strip with ships parked on both sides and I clipped a P-51 prop with my right wing tip. Tore a couple small holes in the wing but they may have to replace the wing tip. We were just lucky that it was no worse. We patched up the holes with some fabric & dope and it flew ok.

The letter you wrote the night of the 28th when you stayed in our bed at "622." You sure set the memories buzzing darling and with those thoughts in my mind — with your permission — I'll hit the old sack and make up for last night —

Your own husband,
Jack

Chapter Twenty-Four
Heading Down the Home Stretch

Sunday night
Jan. 21 1944 (1945)

Joyce Darling,

   Tomorrow is the beginning of your second semester and I'm anxious to know whether or not you're going to stay in school. At present it looks like I'll be home before too long but you never can tell. Some of the boys have been pulling a tour of flying with the Air Service Command for 90 days after their tour is finished but I'm hoping they won't need me. I want to go home.

   I was awfully interested in what you said in your Dec 30 letter. You know — the day after the fall and while you were still unhappy about things in general. I think, darling, that unconsciously you stumbled onto one of the biggest reasons why I'm always so uncomfortable over at your house. It is the absence of those common courtesies to which you have become accustomed and on which our relationships have always been based. And as long as there is that attitude I will never be able to feel at home there. I always have the feeling that the house is divided against itself and it scares me. Darling I never want to see the day that you don't welcome me home with open arms and I never want to leave without kissing you goodbye. I want you to feel that you deserve the little courtesies of life as much or more now that we're married as you did before. Nevertheless darling, these things should have no real bearing on how you feel toward your home or me either for that matter. I know you love your parents very much and you musn't let little things like that influence your love for them. If — however — we can learn something about how to make our life more full and happy — so much the better. As for not being able to understand why the family doesn't change as we do — that's just one of the funny things about life. I guess if it weren't for that feeling nobody'd ever want to leave home and start a home of their own. I really don't know how I got onto this subject of a home of my own but somehow I feel that I'd rather come home to a small apartment and you than to either my home or yours. The ties have been broken and although I want to see both the families because I do love them and I know they want to see me —

Roy R. Fisher, Jr. with Susan Fisher Anderson

nevertheless — it will be just a visit until we can have a home of our own. Maybe you don't feel that way but I just can't help it.

We had a meeting with the Colonel the other night and he told us all about the wonderful job the 8th had done last year and then the next day this handbill came out and I thought maybe you'd like to read it. It is a pretty good example of the "paper" war they're fighting now. I got a new leather jacket the other day and we've been painting a picture on the backs of all our jackets so last night I started on that one. It will be about the only thing I can bring home so you'll be able to see it.

Last night they had another big brawl up at the club but I couldn't see it. I stayed home as did most of the other boys.

Well darling — I guess that just about says it for now. I sure got windy but I feel much better.

Goodnight sweetheart, I love you.
Yours alone — always,
Jack

London
Wed nite
Ja 23 or so (Jan. 24)

Hello my darling,

How's the light of my life tonight? I just got home from "Wilson." Pretty good show but just a little long & drawn out. Here I sit in the writing room at the Duchess Club. I really don't have a thing in the world to say except that I love you and I could spend all night telling you that and how much I miss you but perhaps I'd better not get started. I bought you a little present today. About two yards of some lovely scotch plaid material. It is the real McCoy & I'm sure you'll like it. I thought perhaps you could make a skirt while you're resting. I wanted to get enough so you could make me a shirt too but couldn't manage it. I also got some pieces of parachute silk the other day and I'll send them along in the same package. It feels so nice and soft and silky — I got a scarf made from it and although it is non regulation — I still like it.

The silk reminds me of things like those white silk panties you wore to get married and your purity nightgown and things like that. Then there is that little blue ribbon that I carry in my billfold. So many little memories darling to bring you closer to me and to help me *through the rough spots. It sure makes me feel humble to have such a wonderful wife and such a marvelous store of experiences to look back on and point to with pride. These memories darling mean so very much when we're so far apart. Oh — how I wish you were here with me tonight. We could sit here in one of these cozy chairs and just smooch for a while — would'ja like that honey? But there I go again.*

I'm so sleepy I can't write darling so I better quit for tonight. Sweet dreams —
Always,
Jack

(enclosed in box)
Jan. 26
Friday

Happy Birthday Darling,
I had hoped that I might be with you on your birthday but I'm fraid that will be impossible. I hunted all over London to find something nice for a present & I think this wool is as nice as anything I saw. It is straight from the Scottish Highlands and should make a lovely skirt. The pieces of nylon are from a parachute that was condemned and I got a scarf from it too.

Now — Happy Birthday and all my love from your own husband.
Jack

Jan. 26
Friday night (pictures enclosed)

Hello Sweetheart,
Here we are back at the old hole again. Just before we left yesterday I picked up these pictures and so I'm sending them. I hoped I could mail them from London and then you'd get them sooner but they weren't back until just before we left.
I got your V-mail about the new semester today the 26th. That made sixteen days for V-mail which isn't too bad but to get to the subject. By the time you get a cable it will be time to start anyway so there's little reason for cableing. It is just up to you darling as you see that end of the picture. If you do start school I may be home before the first of March or if you don't I may get sucked in over here & stick around till June or so. As soon as I finish my missions & do

know the score — of course I'll let you know. As yet I'm still pretty much up in the air cause we haven't flown much recently.

As for coming home as soon as possible you can bet your life there's nothing I want more than to come home to you as soon as possible. Sure hope it's soon.

All my love — always,
Jack

Jan. 27
Sat nite.

Hello my darling,

I'm going to attempt to write a letter in the midst of all this bedlam around here — just what will happen I can't fortell.

They got us up early this morning but things didn't work out so we got back into the sack till noon. The orderly came in twice this morning to tell us that the major would be around to inspect the barracks and we didn't even move till about 20 till 1 and we had to get up then & go to chow.

We had one class this afternoon and then Stan & Sam & Jake & I went up to the bomb dump to get some crates etc to burn. It was a nice long cold ride but we've got a nice warm fire tonight so I guess it was worth it. First time I've been warm for days. I sure needed a hot water bottle last night. Gee whiz that sack was cold. Of course I'm particular about who I take to bed with me for a hot water bottle. Fact of the matter is — there's not but one person in the world who can fill the bill. Wonder if you could guess who I mean. You can't? Well — I tell you — I've got the sweetest little girl waiting for me at home. Yes — she's my wife and the most wonderful wife a guy ever had.

Boy — I wish we could get up in the air one of these days soon. We're sure not getting home very fast this way. Besides that — we're getting just like that other crew we were living with — always haggling over nothing and knocking ourselves out over less.

D'ya know what I did just now. I sat for about a minute and just stared at your picture. Hope you didn't mind but you're so beautiful I just can't resist. Especially in that new picture you just step right out and tell me you love me. And I love you too darling — with all my heart,

night sweet —
Jack

The Lucky Bastard Club

Chapter Twenty-Five
Thank You, Mr. Lundgren

MISSION # 29   JANUARY 28, 1945
KOHENBUDBERG = 5:45 HRS

No problems on the mission, a relief after taking off in a snow storm. Taxiing was a little tricky when we left, but once we got up to speed, the big bird took over. By the time we got back, however, there were about six inches of new snow on everything. When we touched our brakes for the first time on landing, the wheels locked and skidded. At that instant we got a call from the Tower, "Agmer H Howe *(our call sign)*, EXPIDITE YOUR TAXIING," which — translated — meant, "Get the hell off the runway, boy, somebody is landing on your tail!" We had already cut our inboard engines, but I gave full power to the outboards and when we got to the end of the runway, I cut back on #4 engine and we made as nice a right turn as you ever saw. Thank You, Lord, and thank you Mr. Lundgren! That lesson under the wing in 100° heat had born fruit, and probably saved our tail, if not our lives.

Jan 28
Sunday nite.

Joyce my darling,
I'm really in no mood to write to you or anyone else tonight because I'm so darn tired and worn out. Tired physically and worn out mentally. Gosh — what a day. But enough of that — by the time you get this letter I'll feel swell — in fact I feel some better already — just knowing that you're listening to my troubles.
The weather here is still showing off for our benefit. For nearly a week now it has snowed nearly every day and when it isn't snowing it gets foggy and the fog condenses just like snow. As a result — England is really under a white blanket and under the glow from the lovely full moon it is a fairyland to behold. We're pretty well supplied with fuel now and will be for a while to all appearances, the cold weather isn't really too bad. Of course the runways & everything is are am slick as glass and that does nothing but add to the general discomfort of everyone concerned. You know how much fun it is to

feel yourself skidding in a car — well — you can imagine what it feels like in a B-17. But there I go again telling you my troubles. Hell — you've got troubles of your own.

Darling — I'd like to talk to you a long time but I simply must got to sleep. I hope that one of these days soon I'll be able to write you a real letter instead of just one of these rambly pambly ones —

Be that as it may — one thing you can be sure of darling and that is that your love for me and my love for you mean more to me than anything else in the whole wide world and eventually we'll be together to help God create living images of that beautiful love — Your own husband
Jack

Monday nite
Jan 29

Dearest Joyce,

Here's your lonesome hubby for a little chat before I go to sleep. I spent most of the day in the sack resting. Got up about noon for chow and then went over and signed the payroll. Then I hit the sack for a couple of hours — got up and got a haircut — not before I needed it and had chow. Went to see "Fannie by Gaslight" tonight. A limey film — banned in the states but it wasn't particularly good. Now I'm back in the sack.

Right now we're getting ready for a big inspection. The general is due to come around to give us a stand by inspection one of these days. I just hope I'm not here but I'm fraid I'm not going to be able to get out of it.

I reread some of your letters this afternoon. In one you mentioned that you'd seen Frenchman's creek. I saw it the last day we were in London. I enjoyed it a lot but I got oh so lonesome for you. When he took her in his arms that night by the campfire — I thought about our picnic up in Rapid when we went out to Dakota Lake. You sure got your pants dirty that night. As I remember — there was a beautiful full moon that night. But we had a wonderful time that night — and every night for that matter. Each night with you was a beautiful new adventure. Just to hold you close to me was heaven itself and then to make you my very own — well it was just too marvelous for description. To know that from that first moment in Lincoln you would

always be mine and mine alone meant the world to me darling and I consider it one of my greatest accomplishments that I was and am yours alone also. Such beauty can never be defaced darling — We'll always be made for one another and for no one else.
Your devoted husband,
Jack

Wednesday nite
Jan 31

My darling,
I haven't gotten any letters for so long. The mail situation this past week has been absolutely nil. Not that I'm griping — I know it isn't your fault and for that matter I haven't quite held up my end but things are getting so stale here — me included that I can hardly concentrate on a letter for more than a couple of minutes at a time.

With this big inspection coming up we're all so PO'ed at the general in particular and everyone else in general that we spend most of our time moaning about our misfortune. We don't mind taking all our lights down and getting rid of all our unauthorized equipment but when we have to paint everything and wash our walls — that's going too far. Oh well — this can't last forever — maybe the war'll be over soon and all these wheels will be civilians again and then I can tell them just what I think about their damn army.

Right now the whole barracks smells like fresh paint and although that is a satisfying smell at times, under these circumstances it is nothing short of annoying. Now — here comes Richter with a bunch of letters for me to censor — see you later.

Hi babe —
Back again — it didn't take too long. I have to sew a couple of patches on tonight — sure wish you were here to help me. I never was particularly sharp at needlework. Then maybe after you get all the busy work done — we might find some more enjoyable pastime. Ok —

But you know — darling — what will happen to me tonight if I let my mind dwell too long on such extremely pleasant subjects so I better quit. Anyway — you aren't here — (damn the war) and I still have to sew those patches on. So for tonight — A goodnight kiss to

my dearest wife — and all my love — always — to the most wonderful girl in the whole wide world.
   Your loving husband,
   Jack

MISSION # 30   FEBRUARY 1, 1945
KREFELD-VERDINGEN = 6:15 HRS

It's almost Joyce's Birthday. We've been married eight months and together only three. I don't like those numbers. It wasn't a very long mission, not like some we've had, but I'm beat. I'm almost too tired to write. The end isn't very far, but still it seems like forever. Oh well, racked up another one.

~~Jan~~
February 1
Thurs. night

Joyce my darling,
   We had one today. Consequently I'm pretty tired and this will be a pretty short letter but that's the way it goes. One of the boys in the barracks has gotten pretty well drunk tonight and he's sure talking a leg off everyone else. He just stepped outside for a minute so I'll try & get this started before he gets back. He's in the sack now and he'll be asleep before two minutes —
   I hope —
   I'm still trying to get "Red" shipped home. It's sure a hell of a job. There are more people to write and more red tape to cut than you can shake a stick at.
   Well — dearest — it's only six days till your birthday. Only a few more days in your teens and then you'll be twenty years old. What do you know — twenty and already married nearly eight months. And only three months with your husband. Gee — honey — that's sorta tough on both of us isn't it? But the only way to think about it is that those wonderful three months are only a sample of what our life together will be. And what a wonderful sample it was darling. When we were together, I for one, experienced the happiest days of my life, and I'm sure that you feel the same way. Just to live each day with you is the most wonderful thing that I can possibly imagine. From the time you wake me up in the morning until I go to sleep at night I can't

imagine a more marvelous series of events. And it won't be long darling till we'll be in each others arms again. For good I hope.

Now sweetheart — I simply must go to sleep — nite — sweet dreams,
Jack

Friday
Feb. 2

My darling,

I love you — very, very muchly — though this may be a little early in the letter to start on such a pleasant subject. Tonight is such a beautiful night that it makes me romantic. I haven't seen the stars so bright since the night we climbed the hill behind our house at Rapid City. Remember how close the stars seemed to us that night. And just lying up there on that hill and watching the base lights was so much fun cause we were together.

And remember — after we walked home again and got in bed — the moon shone right in our window. But I had to get way over close to you or I couldn't see it at all. Darling — it was so much fun — I hope we'll always have such good times together. I'm sure we will. It just couldn't be otherwise with such a sweet wife as I've got.

Now sweets — gotta go to sleep —
I love you, —
Jack

Roy R. Fisher, Jr. with Susan Fisher Anderson

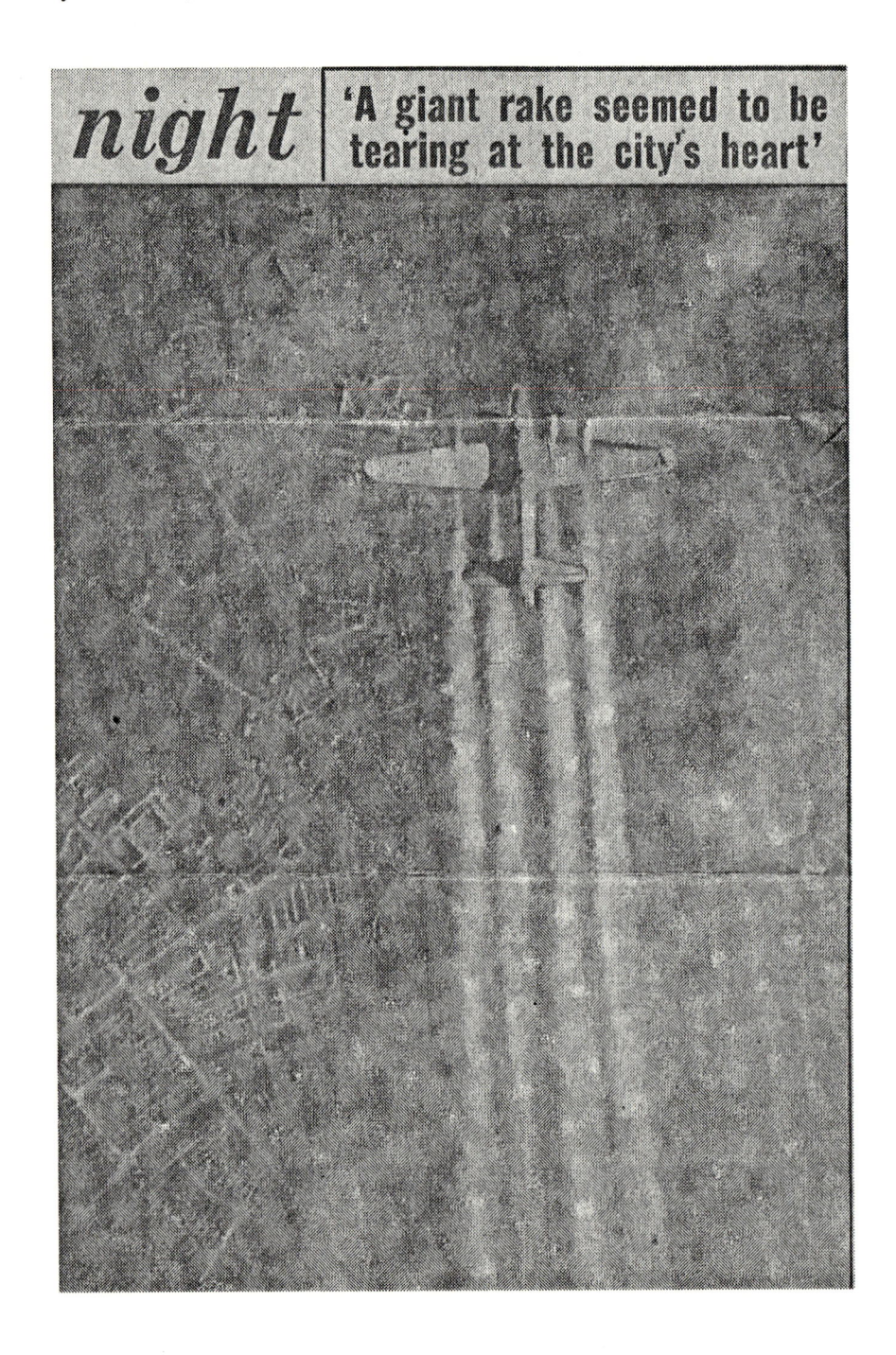

night | 'A giant rake seemed to be tearing at the city's heart'

Chapter Twenty-Six
Berlin

MISSION # 31   FEBRUARY 3, 1945
BERLIN = 9:00 HRS

Our first trip to Big "B" made us really feel like the end of the war might be getting close, when we bomb the capitol. Can we dare hope that maybe it's not too far from over? A few days later, <u>Stars and Stripes</u> ran this picture of a B-17 with four white contrails over the city of Berlin. I sent it to Joyce.

Slim Schanze was finally grounded by his sinus problems. We had no idea the pain he was enduring — so severe that when we were at altitude he almost went crazy. It probably had a lot to do with the cold conditions in his position — the tail. Poor Guy, He just didn't want to quit.

As the missions added up and the time grew shorter, they were trying to figure out what they could do with pilots like me to keep us a little longer, without us having to fly any more combat missions. The war in the Pacific Theater was far from over and there was some discussion about shipping us over there–to C.B.I. (China, Burma, India). There was also talk of making us paddlefeet, or assigning us to Ferry Command. Me? I just wanted to go home to my wife.

Saturday night
February 3

Joyce my darling,

We racked up another one today. Pretty big one as you will be able to tell from the papers. Gosh am I tired — so is Stan — we worked pretty hard.

Well — Slim is all finished with combat flying I think. That sinus of his is aggravated by the weather over here and he can't get the necessary operation over here that is needed to clear it up. Naturally flying at altitude is so painful he nearly goes crazy and so he finally decided to give it up. He's still listed on the crew and so he'll go home when I finish — as will all the other enlisted men. The officers will have to finish up thirty-five. There's a shortage of bombardiers now and so Bob only flies in deputy lead ships so he's getting a little behind.

I've been wondering a lot about whether or not you started the second semester. If I get stuck over here in the ferry command for three months you'll wish you'd started and if I get sent right home then you will want to be with me and so I'm way up in the air. Then too — we've been sweating out the possibility of getting a second tour over in C.B.I. Of course I don't like that idea a dambed bit and I'm going to pull every string I can to stay in the states with you. Darling, just the thought of leaving you breaks my heart and I can't bear it. So we'll both think real hard and figure out how I can stay with you forever. Joyce — my dearest — don't ever let me get out of your sight again — please — I love you and miss you and want you with me for ever & ever —

Amen!!
Jack

Monday nite
Feb. 5

Dearest-my own,

So many sweet letters from you I don't know what to say or do. Except just thanks darling — Thanks for being so sweet and so thoughtful and so understanding and beautiful and most of all — Thanks for being my wife. Thanks for loving me and letting me love you. Cause you see darling — you're my ideal too. My ideal of the perfect wife and mother and the best friend a guy ever had — all rolled into one. My ideal of the things I'm fighting for. My ideal of the way to live a life. You just fit dear — and no one can ever take your place. Yes — darling our love has been satisfying to the utmost. It has been and is and will continue to be so beautiful that it is almost beyond belief. And I know it will always be so — Free and unrestrained yet pure and free from stain. Such a love makes a fellow realize just what a wonderful Creator is behind the universe of ours. And as long as we keep faith with each other and with Him our love will be a source of beauty & strength not only for ourselves but for all with whom we come in contact.

What have I been doing — Well yesterday I had link at 8:00 am and I was so mad because they got me up so early that I just *disappeared for the rest of the day. Well — it seems that my ship needed slow timing — new engine (#4) and so when they couldn't find me — instead of just sending up someone else they just waited till I showed up for chow. I flew from 8 to 12 last night. Any further questions. Then had to get up this morning after only three hours sleep. But they scrubbed it so I sacked up and stayed there till afternoon. Cleaned up the shack a little this p.m. That big inspection is still coming and by now I just don't care what the old coot thinks. (Hope this isn't censored)*

I'm in an awful quandry about whether you're in school or at home. Your last six letters were about evenly split — Yes I guess I will — no I guess I won't. It looks now like when I'm finished I'll be home but quick so I hope you haven't started but that's up to you. You see — all your letters get here too late for me to cable you anyway — I don't know nuttin. Well — dear that's just about it. Tomorrow is Sam's birthday and yours the next day & Ott's the next so we'll probably celebrate by flying like mad. With that in mind I better quit & log some time in this lonesome old sack. Darling — you don't need to ever argue with me about double beds.

Your coldfooted husband,
Jack

MISSION # 32   FEBRUARY 6, 1945
CHEMNITZ = 10:00 HRS

This was the longest mission of our tour. Wow, were we beat. It was Sam's birthday and we couldn't think of a better present for him than to deliver our presents to the Fuhrer. I really missed Joyce, her twentieth birthday was the next day — it had been two years since I gave her my fraternity pin. As the war dragged on, sometimes it seemed like it would never end. Still, the memories and our commitment to each other sustained me. The end — for me — was growing so close, yet the closer it got, as the missions accumulated, sometimes it seemed so far away still. I couldn't quite imagine being finished and going home. One day, one mission at a time.

Roy R. Fisher, Jr. with Susan Fisher Anderson

Wed nite
Feb 7

My darling,
　Happy birthday — and I hope it has been cause I want you always to be happy.
　As for me — it's been rather hectic. The general came — per schedule — and although we managed to dodge him when he inspected our barracks we still had to parade all afternoon. We marched all the way out to the line and down the longest runway to line up for the personal inspection. He came by us at quite a brisk walk — In fact Col. Dougher had to almost run to keep up with him. So we didn't get much of a look at him — but at least he did show up and that is something. At least all our preparations weren't for naught.
　We got our pass about 5:30 tonight and although we hurried like mad we still missed the early train so we didn't get here in London till after 12:00. We just finished getting squared away and everything and I'm oh — so tired and I do want a nice long hot bath. How about coming in and washing my back for me. I really have an awful time trying to keep it clean. You will — darling you're so sweet. But now I simply must close.
　Darling — I love you so —
　nite dear
　Jack

Thurs nite
Feb. 8

Dearest, my own,
　Today has been a rather busy day and on top of that one yesterday which I told you about last night — I'm worn out. In fact I can just push this pen & that's all. I'm really getting awfully tired darling. Physically and mentally I'm just about shot. I just hope I can finish up real soon and come home to the most wonderful woman in the world — my own sweet wife. Darling I need you so much right now — tonight I need to have you say — It's all right Jack — the war won't last forever. Just hold my head in your lap and run your fingers through my hair and kiss me and tell me you love me. That's all that really matters darling — Just you and me and love and dreams and a life that will be the most wonderful ever. A family that

we can be proud of — Children and grandchildren to exemplify our love for each other. Such a beautiful experience. Here I am — hundreds of miles from you and yet just this little chat makes you feel so near. Just as if my own heart were saying these things and comforting my soul. For my heart is really yours darling and when I need a little help — all I have to do is just give it a chance.

Now darling — I must sack up. It is hard & cold & <u>lonesome</u> but I need <u>sleep</u> lotsa <u>sleep.</u>

G'nite my own sweet wife — Your husband luves ya tu. Can't spel neether —
Jack

Saturday nite
Feb. 10

Darling,

"Our House" sounds wonderful. I had been hoping that some such arrangement might be made so that we could just be ourselves — man and wife — instead of sombody's daughter & somebody's son. Not that I don't want to see our folks and visit with them — but that's all it can ever be. For the longer we hang around the more apt we are to become offended and to offend. I guess I've spent as much time thinking about that as I have about the fact that soon we'll be together once again. I don't want to hurt anyone — particularly your folks — because they have been so sweet to me. But in spite of all that they will always have difficulty in understanding just why I can't feel at home for very long — why I must be on the move. No, darling — the cottage is the best idea. We can spend at least two weeks there and if folks want to see us — well they can come on over. I'd love to entertain both parents & friends in "Our" home with the most wonderful hostess in the world presiding. Course — that's just my opinion. But I warn you — these first pilots aren't to be trifled with.

Gee — what fun it will be darling for me to cut wood & keep a nice fire going in our fireplace so we can sit & hold hands. Subtle — aren't you? Well — I'll be a real good boy & maybe — then I can kiss you twice. Huh.

I've been trying to get "Red" shipped back home but I'm afraid it is going to be nearly impossible unless I fly home & bring him with me. There seems to be only about one skipper in the whole Atlantic *fleet that will condecend to take a dog over. So if I can't get him home myself I think I'll leave him to some Flak House. The boys sure enjoy the company of a dog at the flak House and I think Red would be tickled.*

Just before we left London Bob & I went to see "Since You went Away." Oh darling — what a tear jerker that was. Remember the scene when they went for a walk in the country and became engaged. It reminded me so much of Feb. 7 — two years ago when we first knew we loved each other and when the realization of love was just revealed to us. Like opening the pearly gates & seeing Heaven for the first time. And it's been Heaven ever since darling, loving you & having that love returned is too wonderful for any words. But it won't be long till we can make up for the insufficiency of writing.

Now dearest — I must close. I sent $100 extra this month too so we should have a pretty nice backlog by now.

Good nite my darling —
Your
Jack

Sunday nite
Feb. 11

Darling,

An anniversary slipped by yesterday and I didn't even know it. Hmmm eight months — and only three together. Yet as I look back over the past eight months — those three far overshadow the other five when it comes to beautiful memories of exciting experiences. The most marvelous of which — to me — is the experience of being in love with you. Somehow I can't imagine being in love with anyone else. It just wouldn't be right. And as for sharing those privileges and experiences which we found so beautiful and satisfying — darling, I just can't even imagine it. Not that there is a particular absence of any desire in me — on the contrary — You know me well enough to know that my desires and appetites are strong — too strong at times for my own good but when I get to feeling that way I try to direct that energy toward more creative lines. Writing or reading or even chopping wood and try to work it out of my system. Especially now as the time grows nearer when we will be together again, I find it increasingly difficult to keep calm & take things easy. Naturally these last few missions weigh pretty heavily too and as if that isn't enough — we're on ground school for three days starting tomorrow. Nevertheless darling, I'm tryinin every way I know to keep myself physically strong — mentally awake — and — by far the most important morally straight. And I'm keeping on top. With a few sweet words from you now and then to remind me that I'm not fighting the fight by myself. When I know that you miss me and need me as much as I need you, dear, it helps me to keep my head above water. Now dearest — I must close for tonight cause I want to go to church and stuff.

   I love you, darling,
   Jack

(Berlin clipping enclosed) *Monday*
Feb. 12

My darling my own,
   Seven (7) lovely letters from you, including the one mailed on Jan 23 in which you really boosted my morale. Whoever it was that said "don't tell him how much you miss him" was crazy, Darling — a letter like that just sends chills up and down my spine. I know I miss you — sometimes I get so lonesome that my heart swells up in my throat and I can't talk. Of course I realize that you feel the same way but I love to have you tell me anyway. Certainly it would be strange if we didn't want each other so very very much. When two people love each other as much as we do and have had so little time to express that love it is certainly no wonder that we both get so lonesome. I also realize that those certain times are a lot rougher now that you're all alone. But let's hope it won't be too long till I can be there to love you through the rough places. What you said about my uniform was very pretty dear and it goes double for me. Cause when we are together in natures uniform we can feel completely natural and uninhibited. Joyce my darling — as I read over those sweet words — tears come into my eyes. You make our love so beautiful and meaningful. I too await with eagerness and I'm afraid impatience the first act —
   I'm enclosing this picture for our album because it is so expressive. Just a reminder of the beginning of the end — I hope.

Roy R. Fisher, Jr. with Susan Fisher Anderson

To get back to your letter. You've no idea how close you are to me tonight as a result of that letter. As we review those thoughts & desires we become one in thought cause — try as I might — I can think of little else. Darling — I want you so.

I love you-I love you-I love you
Jack

Tuesday nite
Feb 13

Hi Honey,

How dja like this new stationery? Pretty slick huh? This is some of my Christmas present and this is my first chance to use it.

Nothing much happened today. Groundschool all day — you know — same old stuff. If only they'd get on the ball & get some new stuff now & then. I wouldn't mind so much if there was a ghost of a chance of learning anything but — Our last two classes were cancelled — The instructor didn't show up so we came home & hit the sack. Been reading a book that has been pretty dull till just now and all of a sudden it got on the ball. Sort of a funny story about a family before — during, & after the last war.

No mail today but I got seven yesterday and so I'm still feeling — so very nice —. You write such sweet letters darling — sure make me feel good when I read them. Gosh dear — "How come you're so cute?" I just ran thru my billfold & looked at all your pictures. I'm sure a lucky fellow. Incidentally — I'm sorry I interrupted you so often when you were boning up for all those exams but you know — it's just cause I love you so.

Yes — more than anything else in the world.
Always — your own
Jack

The Lucky Bastard Club

Wednesday nite
February 14 - ♥

Happy Valentines Day Darling,
I love you very much and Please Mrs. Fisher — Will you be my Valentine. For always & always — cause you see I love you — oh — you know that! Oh — that's why you married me — oh —
Yes — today was the last day of groundschool for a while. And it was such a lovely day too. No clouds in the sky — Lovely day for a picnic or a picnick or however you want to spell it. I cut two classes & went up flying this afternoon. Someone else flew my ship this morning & had a flat tire. They pulled "Belle" off the runway and got her quite firmly stuck in the mud so I had to go out & help the boys get her out. Then I went up and shot four or five landings. Worked pretty hard. Had the Operations officer for a Copilot & we didn't get along too well. He's a command pilot but he can't fly copilot for my money. Stan didn't want to fly or I wouldn't have taken him.
Well — tomorrow we'll be back on operations and so perhaps we'll get home sometime soon. Sure hope so. Gosh dear — I miss you more & more each minute. I do so want to see you & talk to you & tell you my troubles. Would ya hold my head & tell me everything's ok. I'd sure love that. You're so sweet darling — and I love you so.
Now — I must shave & hit the sack.
Goodnight sweetheart,
Jack

MISSION # 33   FEBRUARY 15, 1945
COTTBUS = 9:00 HRS

This was another long mission. That made two back to back, but, thankfully, only two more to go. While Stan flew, I thought of Joyce, it sure made the time go fast. These long missions really wear me out. Sometimes I'd find myself thinking back to my flight instructor and agree with him that I was too little to fly this airplane.

Roy R. Fisher, Jr. with Susan Fisher Anderson

Thursday nite
February 15

Dearest, my own,

Here's your devoted husband for a short chat before I go to sleep. I spent about half the day today dreaming of you. We chalked up another one and as each one is knocked off you seem closer and closer. When Stan was flying I just sat and thought & dreamed and I could see you so plainly.

I could see you in our little room on Smith Street in Lincoln. I remember how hot the nights were — and how terribly short. And do you remember the night we had a picnic all by ourselves. Gosh that was so much fun. We could just lie there & love to our hearts content and know that there could be the beautiful culmination of that love when we got home. So different from the times when we used to have to be so careful lest we get carried away. I'm so glad we both waited till our wedding night.

Then I saw you in that hotel at Allience Nebr — Remember that night — We were both so tired but so much in love and so happy to be together. And then that first night at the Harney when the maid walked in on me as I was getting ready to take a bath. And then you came in & we washed each other's backs. Remember what a time I had — I couldn't figure out where your back stopped and I just kept right on washing. You have such a beautiful body darling. It seems more remarkable each time I think about you. I can see you so very clearly. By the way — have you been doing your situps. Remember what I told you. But I suppose, you need me there to urge you a little. I need some myself right now after all this high altitude flying. Besides — they keep me awake.

Oh yes — I was going to tell you the favorite gag for returning husbands to write their wives. "Take a good look at the <u>floor</u> these next few weeks darling. ——————— "Cause when I get home" —— —— I'll just let you figure that one out.

Gee darling — I can hardly wait to come home to our little cottage. What a wonderful idea that is.

Oh and darling — please tell Mom that it isn't that I don't love them that I'm not writing as often. It just that I've only so much time and I just can't think of things to write them I guess. You keep them posted and I'll try to drop them a line soon. It's so hard to write to anyone but you. With you I just write as I think — You're so much a part of me that what I think is what I write but I've lost that feeling or perhaps it never was the same with the folks. Can you see what I mean? Darling — I must go to sleep now.

Always your very own,
Jack

MISSION # 34   FEBRUARY 16, 1945
HAMM = 6:30 HRS

It's kind of the same old thing, day after day. But only one more. We're so very close now. I can't wait to get home. I hate the poor excuse for toothpaste they have over here. It tastes like Listerine smells. Yuck.

Friday nite
Feb. 16

Joyce darling,

It won't be long now. I got a letter from you today & you asked why I haven't been telling you what number mission I'd flown on a particular day. Well — today I flew #34. It won't be long now beloved.

Richter just came in and until now it was pretty quiet but now things are getting noisy. He always has that effect on his surroundings. He's flying now with a regular crew. The boys are a little behind me now. Stan needs 4 more and Bob & Ott both need 5 or 6. The rest of the boys will all be finished when I finish. They don't have to fly thirty five.

Guess that about tells the news. But I do want to tell you that as the time to see you and be with you again draws nearer I realize just how true those words were. The time you said that as the time for our reunion draws nearer the physical consumation of that union seems to press all other thoughts into the background. Perhaps that is only natural. Certainly it would be hard to imagine how it could be otherwise in view of the fact that for the short interval of three months we were able to partake — rather freely — of the priviledges which marriage allows. And then after having whetted our appetites to a fine point we have become total abstainers for over five months. Hardly a wonder that we can visualize each other so easily in "natures uniform" and that that picture often predominates the picture.

Well — dearest — I must hit the sack now with the hope that I can fly #35 tomorrow & then come home to you. I'm waiting too darling — and I always will — just for you. Because now & always I'm your loving husband

Jack

Saturday nite
Feb. 17

Hello Darling,

I only got one letter in my box today and that was the one I wrote you last night. I forgot to put a stamp on it. I'm sure getting absentminded in my old age.

Well, Ott went to London tonight on a three day pass. He's been having a devil of a time with a couple of teeth and they finally had to operate on him to drain an absess. Of course that meant he had to take quantities of Sulfa and that grounded him for several days. My crew has been split up pretty badly lately what with Bob flying only when we carry a bombsight and Slim being grounded for his nose & then Ott. I sometimes wonder why it's never me and then I realize that there must be some guiding force that is taking me thru these trials of the moment and then back to your arms.

I got into a very interesting discussion last night with Chambers — a bombardier who did one tour last year and is back now doing another one — about the difference between combat crews that are coming over now & the ones here a year or two ago. The question I asked particularly was whether or not the boys who really went thru "when it was rough" (see footnote) drank as much as the fellows do now. In a lot of cases it seems to me the boys are perpetually on the lookout for a good excuse to get well lit. He pointed to the age factor as far as the crews are concerned and I can see how that might have quite a bearing on the matter. These boys react to a rough mission just as they would to a rough math test (which they probably flunked miserably) — they just get drunk & forget it. It isn't that I was worrying about it at all — I just was wondering how the boys reacted under circumstances far more trying than anything we endure.

I hope I fly tomorrow cause I want to get finished up. I'd like to get down to see Cousin Robert before I leave England and I'll undoubtedly have several days before all my air medals get cleared up before I can clear the post. Yes — we get a cluster for each sixth mission & one for completing a tour. What a lot of ribbons to signify nothing —. If we were actually fighting the war it would be different but so much of it is just on paper. I still don't know what I'm going to do with "Red". I can't arrange to have him shipped home for at least a year or so because of lack of shipping space so if I can't take him with me I'll just have to leave him over here with a Rest Home or something or have him destroyed. That's what I should have done when I first came over but it seems such a shame.

Well dear — my thoughts haven't been too pleasant on a whole but I feel so much better for having talked them over with my darling wife. You've no idea how I love the sound of those words just as I do,
Your husband,
Jack

That expression grows from the fact that all the old combat men use it so often we resent it because fundamentally it is quite true.

Sunday nite
February 18

Joyce darling,
Tonight I have a problem on my mind which is going to be as hard for me to think through as was your problem of whether or not to remain in school. In fact your decision in that matter will no doubt have quite considerable bearing on the answer to my problem.

First of all it should be said that neither I nor any one else over here knows exactly what the setup is back in the states but the rumors have it that returning combat men are held in the states from 4 to six months & then shipped out to C.B.I. Whether or not this is at all true I've no idea but the fact remains that it is certainly a possibility. Now that is apt to be particularly true of men who have completed their tour in less than six months & have no more overseas time.

Now I'm very definite in my desires to get home — and stay there. Atlantic Sub patrol I wouldn't mind but I'm not going to leave you again. However I'm wondering if it might be wise to just stay over here & be a foot for a while so to speak and thus perhaps increase my chances for staying home.

Roy R. Fisher, Jr. with Susan Fisher Anderson

But there are these overbalancing questions. First — you're back at home. That is nice for your folks & mine but hard on you & me. Hard because each day you will lose a bit of what we found together and become again the daughter of your father. As each day passes it is unconceivable that you will not become more dependent on your folks & they on you and the break that was once made will have to be made again. That's one reason why I address your letters to my home because I'm hoping that you can divide your time or perhaps even stay at "622." Of course — I know deep in my heart that that will never be as long as I'm overseas & your father remains unchanged. Yes darling — fundamentally I'm jealous. That independence which we found together or perhaps interdependence would be a better word, was one of the things which helped us to sail along so smoothly last summer and I don't want them to become so used to having you around to help with the work that they can't get along without you. Ye— I know this is all silly chatter and I'm really worrying my head over nothing — but I'm nervous now darling and those things worry me.

Then — the most important reason of all is that when my job is finished here — there is no power on earth that could make me volunteer to remain separated from you. Nothing under the sun do I want more that to be with you once again.

And — I'm just enough of an optomist to believe that the Good Lord that has guided my steps this far along the rugged trail of life surely has some plans in mind for you and I and our family to be — so darling — when I finish up — I'm coming home imejiately. You see — you talked me into it didn't you. Well darling — there's one other argument in our favor. Suppose I did stay over here with the group and the group moved for some parts unknown — I'm sure not anxious to stay with this outfit. There are too many guys who care much less for the job that gets done than for their own chances of advancement and believe me — I don't like it. Such selfishness & greed is one of the things I'm fighting in this war & if I can't fight for it here then I might rather be home with the sweetest little wife a man ever had. My darling this has helped so much — thanks for listening. I'll try to be more pleasant in the future.

I do love you so dear —
Yours alone — always
Jack

Chapter Twenty-Seven
Final Mission

MISSION # 35   FEBRUARY 19, 1945
WESEL = 6:00 HRS

They put us on a milk run and we made it. We buzzed the field as per custom. Contrary to orders, of course, but what the hell, the enlisted men and I are done. All the months of waiting, worrying, wrestling with the emotions and the fears, are over. We survived. And, reflecting on the number of men who didn't, that in itself is a miracle. I survived and so did the men over whom I was given charge.

FeB || *19* ||
1945

My Darling
There is cause for exceeding happiness and great joy tonight for on the above date I finished my tour of 35 combat missions over Germany. And so now — my beloved — tho it still may be several weeks till I'm actually with you & can hold you in my arms again — you need worry no more about my coming to a violent or sudden end. Boy am I a happy man. And also a very tired man darling — and getting more so by the minute. You see dear — as I start unlaxing I get tireder & tireder. So I'll just let it go at that for now.
Nite my darling,
Jack

Roy R. Fisher, Jr. with Susan Fisher Anderson

The Lucky Bastard Club

From the time I first began my flight training at Hemet, each time I flew was carefully recorded in my Pilot's Log Book. Each entry included the date, type of aircraft, origination and destination points, duration of flight, how much time was logged and whether it was day, night or instrument time – and how much of each. When I started flying my combat missions, the destination was listed as "COMBAT" with the name of target in the "remarks" section, both written in red ink. This is my last red entry in the logbook. I was too tired to even sign the page. I just wanted to go home.

Now I Am A Member Of The Lucky Bastard Club

Roy R. Fisher, Jr. with Susan Fisher Anderson

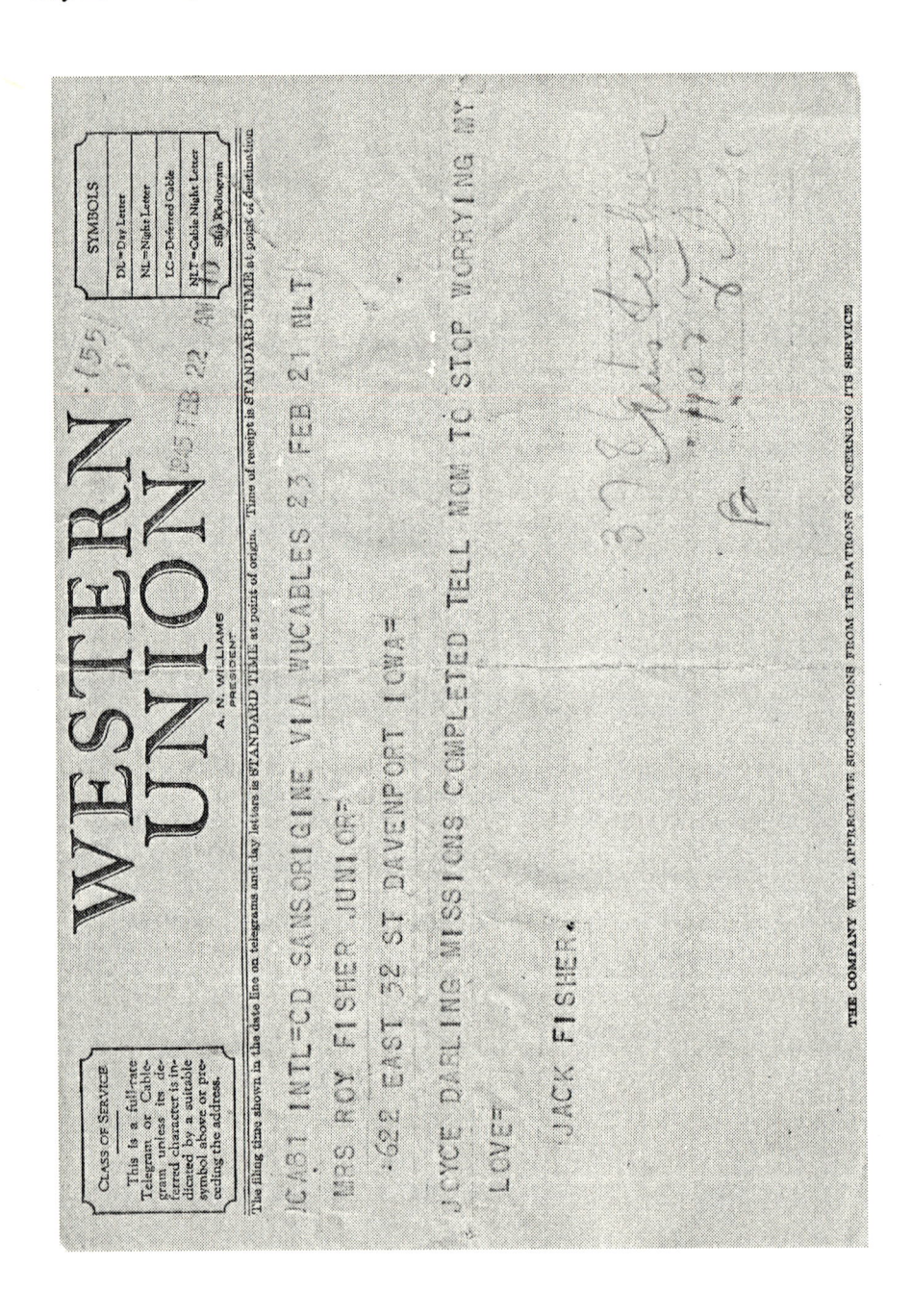

```
WESTERN UNION

1945 FEB 22 AM

JCAB1 INTL=CD SANSORIGINE VIA WUCABLES 23 FEB 21 NLT

MRS ROY FISHER JUNIOR=
:622 EAST 32 ST DAVENPORT IOWA=

JOYCE DARLING MISSIONS COMPLETED TELL MOM TO STOP WORRYING MY
LOVE=
    JACK FISHER.
```

What a relief. I still can't quite believe that I'm really finished. It feels like a lifetime, but it has only been a few months. Today I'm taking perhaps the first deep breaths in a long, long time. I only wish Joyce was here to celebrate with me. And, I can't bear to have her worrying a minute longer than necessary, so a cable is in order, as it will be several weeks before she gets my letter. Then, I think it's got to be London for a few days.

Friday Afternoon
London

Joyce my darling,
Just a note to let you have some idea of just what I've been doing the past few days. I spent a couple of days down at Southhampton trying to catch up with that cousin of mine — all to no avail. I haven't been back to the base yet so I don't know whether my orders are in or not. When they do come in — I'm going to try to make another trip down south to catch up with Bob. The Navy is sure an undependable outfit.

Speaking of undependable, that Rundell has got me and most of the Duchess Club going around in circles. He's been going quite steadily with a girl here at the club & the other night he left here in the middle of the evening without so much as an Aye yes or no & nobody's seen him since. So I had a big long talk with Scotty (the girl) to try to make her feel a little better, but I'm 'fraid I didn't help much. I imagine Stan just got scared as several others that I might mention here in the course of experience but I'm not sure. He's sure a funny guy, to try to figure out — I've about given up trying.

I'm going back to the base tonight. I sure hope I'll be home soon. I've had about all I can take. And it's so darn hard to take when you aren't with me. Darling I need you so and just this little chat has helped a lot.

Bye now my darling,
Jack

Roy R. Fisher, Jr. with Susan Fisher Anderson

(Cartoons enclosed)
Saturday nite
Feb. 24. 1945

Hello Darling,

How's the light of my life this fine evening? I'm in pretty good humor as you can see by the enclosures. I got a bang out of them — thought you might like them too.

Well — I got my orders today and I'm going to come home. How long it will take me depends a lot on how I come home but anyway I'm on my way home to you, darling. .

Coming back from London on the train yesterday, I was in a compartment with a lady & a 14 month old little boy. He was so cute and of course the train ride was just about too much for him. I took him for a while just to rest his mother — and did I have myself a time. He was so cute and had the prettiest big brown eyes. Mommie — can I have one — please. I know — I must be patient but I do want one of our own so very much. Also — even moreso I want you in my arms again. Darling this waiting is getting on my nerves. I sure wish I could get all my clusters & finish clearing the post and get home. But I guess that feeling is mutual.

Darling — I started this early in the evening but it's late now so I better quit & hit the sack. I'm going to try to get in to London tomorrow to see Bob — my cousin. While I'm sweating out those awards I might as well do some of those things.

Gnite now my sweet —
I loves you so muchly —
Your husband Jack

Feb. 28

Joyce Darling,

Here I am — London again. Bob called me up night before last and told me to meet him here and as I was just marking time — waiting for those awards to come back I got another pass & came down to London again. We've been having quite a time running around to all the shops and trying to find some things for me to bring home. I think I've got just about everyone taken care of now. Of course — in the meantime we have had ample opportunity to discuss the many events which have shaped our lives during the past few

194

years. And of course the most important of all — He wanted to know all about you and about the wedding and did I recommend it as the thing to do etc. Of course I put him on the right track — but definitely.

But best of all — you can't guess who I met yesterday at the Grovsner House officers mess. Roger Krakow. There he was just as big as life and twice as natural and so he ate dinner with us and we spent yesterday afternoon & evening together and he's sitting here with me right now writing a letter. Now — what do you know about that. Of course he wanted to know all about you too so you see, darling, all your boy friends are still interested. Just remember — I'm pretty jealous. Cause you see darling — I love you so very much. Dya mind? I've been sorta hanging back on this letter writing hoping that I would have some definite news or dates to give you but I guess I won't know anything till I get to my next stop. Then perhaps I can help you make some definite plans. Gosh darling — I'm getting so doggone lonesome I just don't know what to do.

Now dearest I must close & write Mom a note —
Yours alone —
Jack

March 1 –

Joyce Darling,

Back at the base for a day or so to finish everything up and then head for home. That's my schedule right now. I got nearly everything wound up. My last three clusters finally came thru and so I was able to clear the post this morning and then I flew 4 hours this afternoon so I could get my flying pay for this month. I also talked Spencer into flying me to my next station tomorrow so I won't have to go into London again and sweat out all those train rides. Hope we can get a plane. Of course the enlisted men will go with me. Stan & Art are all finished now and so we have only Bob to sweat out. Of course Richter's only got 13 missions but he doesn't seem like one of the crew at all.

Oh — so many lovely letters today. Five from you and one from Harvy & Pezzy & two from the folks. I'm really getting quite enthused about that little cottage too darling. But any place in the world is heaven so long as you're there. It really doesn't take much any more

Roy R. Fisher, Jr. with Susan Fisher Anderson

to make me the happiest man on earth. Just to have you by my side to talk to and to dream with. A goodnight kiss and a smile when I wake up. I'm really not a hard guy to please — I just want my wife & I don't want to be overseas. Dya mind if I just come home & never leave my darling wife again? I sure hope not cause I don't ever want to let you out of my sight.

Now my dearest — I must go to sleep —
All my love — always,
Jack

Chapter Twenty-Eight
Heading Home

Saturday nite
March 3

My darling wife,
    Well — here's your wandering hubby for a little chat before I go to bed. I just got back from a show. Deana Durbin in "Little Nellie Kelly" — such a sweet show and I do love to hear her sing. On the way home to the barracks I stopped in to watch the boys in a big blackjack game. They don't shoot craps here like they did before. Just little friendly blackjack games — yes — I'm kiddin. Anyway — I'm going to stay out — Never could win any money at cards.
    Well I didn't have that long train ride after all — Spence and a couple of his boys flew me over here yesterday. It sure does beat going by train all to pieces. Then of course I flew all the way over and I had a good time. I believe I told you about flying four hours the first day of the month so I'll get flying pay this month. It's the skotch in me lass — So here I am and will be till I can prevail on the powers that be to get in gear & send me home to me lovin wife. I'm still trying to make my birthday darlin and I can think of no better present than you in my arms once again.
    In the meantime there'll be days and nights of longin & waitin but my darling — I'd wait the rest of my life for you Sweetheart. I love you so very much.
    Now sweet — I've got to go shave & brush my teeth so I can go to sleep & dream of you.
    Now goodnight Joyce — I love you so.
    Your own husband,
    Jack

March 4th
Nite again

Hello darling,
    First and foremost — before I forget again — Congratulations on those marvelous grades, darling. Guess that prooves my theory. All kidding aside dear — I think that is marvelous — especially

Roy R. Fisher, Jr. with Susan Fisher Anderson

considering the circumstances under which you studied. I don't see how in the world you could manage to get such swell grades. I'm sure proud of my wife — she's not only the most wonderful wife a fellow ever had — She gets straight A's too — Gosh you're wonderful.

Today was not particularly nice — sorta rainy & wet & generally miserable. I got up for breakfast cause we had fresh eggs & then went to church this morning. The sermon was fair I guess but I couldn't keep my mind on the sermon darling – couldja guess why? Yes — that pretty little wife of mine keeps intruding on my thoughts when I should be concentrating on religion. I guess the Good Lord knows just how much I miss you darling and I wouldn't be surprised if He understands why my mind is wandering so.

My roommates here are a couple of A-20 pilots from France & they've been telling me about their experiences and vice versa — then you know me — I've had fun getting to know them — I love to meet people.

Well — that's about all the poop from the group so I guess I'll sign off — Here's a goodnight kiss from
Your lovin husband
Jack

March 5, 1945
Monday nite

My Darling,

I love you. Now what do you know about that? I love you with my heart & soul & body and as the time for our reunion draws closer my thoughts center more & more around you and how beautiful you are and how much I do love you.

I just had a nice warm bath and so I'm all sweet in clean and ready for love. As I lay there in the tub I got to thinking about those times in Rapid when we used to take our showers together and how much fun it was just to be together and do those little things and as the thoughts ran thru my mind — junior got all excited & puffed up with his own importance You know how that goes. He's sure been getting eager lately darling but he'll wait for you — just as he always has. I'm even more sure darling, now that it's almost time to come home to you — that complete continance is the only solution to the *problem of sex. Because — like any appetite — it can be curbed and under the circumstances no other policy could possibly work. You see darling — in spite of the fact that we were together as one for three months, I had developed quite a habit of avoiding all comprimising circumstances long before we were married and I just fell back on those ideals & morals — with the added strength of knowing that you were mine and mine alone and I yours.*

I spent an hour or two last night rereading a lot of your letters which I had assembled in order and darling — you seemed so close. It was almost as if you were right here in bed with me — talking in my ear.

Now sweetheart I must sign off for tonight and go to sleep. You know how sleepy I get after I've had a bath.

Goodnight my darling wife —
I love you so
Jack

March 6 th
Tuesday nite

Dearest,

It has been such a long long day. Nothing to do all day long except wait & wait & wait. Nothing is as hard as that and I know that it's just as hard for you now as it is for me — perhaps more so. We didn't get up till about ten — and wouldn't have gotten up that early except that we were alerted for an inspection and so we had to clean the place up a bit. We had just finished when it was time for chow but the afternoon was interminable. We had seen the show and there just wasn't a thing to do. I tried to read but it was too cold in the room and the club lounge is always too full & too noisy. In other words darling — I'm not happy here — I'm nervous in the service.

Gosh I'm a long way behind on my letters. I owe practically everyone — especially your folks & mine but I just can't settle down to write to anyone but you darling. I hope they'll understand cause if they don't well — that's gonna be rough. You take care of them all till I can get there & explain — will you darling. Make them understand that it's not because I don't love them — it's just that I can't find anything to say and I get so disappointed with myself when I write letter after letter and say practically nothing.

Roy R. Fisher, Jr. with Susan Fisher Anderson

And I'm 'fraid that's the way this letter will end if I don't say — I love you and make it mean something. I do love you darling and I hope that soon I'll be able to show you in a much more concrete form just how much —
Your hubby
Jack

Sunday nite
March 11 —

Joyce Darling,
I haven't written for two nites cause I ran out of stamps and I know you won't get these till I get home anyway. But I miss these nitely chats so much that I'm gonna write you anyway and just save the letters till I get home & then if you want to read them then — I'm sweating out orders now. My two room mates got on orders today and I got here when they did so it shouldn't be too long now.
I had quite an interesting day today darling. It all started out by my going to chapel like a good boy. Tex went with me and when we got started back to the barracks we got to cussing & discussing the sermon. He had said that the time had come for us to place our faith in God rather than in physical tangeable things. We should love our neighbors and look toward Christ and his teachings to help us in the peace that follows this war. We should get out of the rocking boat and walk on the water. Of course that isn't possible without tremendous faith and so he really had a point. Well we got started on the love your neighbor idea and we really had it out.
Then we went to see This is the Army this afternoon and while we were waiting for the show to start we got to talking to a fellow who had just come back from Sweden. He got to talking about the girls over there and the kind of deal they had. He said that he got a girl to keep house for him and cook his meals & so on. It seems that they take a very liberal view on couples living together — sort of trial marriage idea —. Well — when we got back to the sack we got on the subject of sex, fidelity and how different it is over here in these older countries than it is at home. Then of course that brought up the old argument about the double standard. How the wife should be a virgin regardless but that it really makes no difference as far as the man is

concerned. Well — darling — you know I don't believe that and I know you don't. At any rate it was quite a discussion.

But to get back to the show. Remember the scene where the girl finally prevailed upon him to get married and they were joined by an army chaplain in the wings of the theater. I closed my eyes when they started saying the vows and I saw the prettiest bride in the world. Dressed in a white linen suit she stood there beside me as the service went along and then she turned to me and looked me straight in the eye and said she'd be mine forever. I could look right into your heart that day my darling. I could read your heart more clearly than I ever did before and I knew that you meant it with all your heart and soul and I hoped that you could read my heart too. I wanted you to know that my heart and soul reflected & radiated the same truth & sincerity which yours revealed to me. Yes — darling — I cried this afternoon tears of Joy filled my eyes as I remembered that kiss that made you my wife forever. And then I wanted you beside me more than anything else in the world. I wanted to have your hand in mine so we could repeat those vows to each other and reaffirm them in each others hearts & souls. And I wanted to hold you in my arms darling and feel your breast pressed close to mine.

Dearest — I want you so very much. Because I love you so very muchly —

Nite sweetheart,
Jack

St. Pat's Day

Joyce Darling,

I haven't written for the past few days because I thought I'd be getting in gear but it looks like I'll be here forever so I just want you to know I'm still alive and well & as happy as can be considering I'm just about crazy with this eternal waiting. I thought that by now we'd be together again but things are a little slow. Guess I'm not very important darling—I just want to get home so badly but this army doesn't seem to understand.

Tell Newell & Beeber howdy & also M.A and the boys.
So long for now darling—I love you so
Jack

Roy R. Fisher, Jr. with Susan Fisher Anderson

Friday March 21

Hello darling,

Looks like I'm not going to make it home by my birthday. I hoped for a while I might catch an air shipment and get home in a hurry but I'm on a boat list now so that's out of the question.

I'm sorry now that I didn't keep writing to you after I got here but we thought we'd be here about a week at the most but it just seemed to stretch on & on and now I've been here 20 days — nearly a month — just waiting — waiting. As it is you can't possibly get this letter before I get home so I'll just bring it along. I can get along for a few days without writing you but then I just get to feeling so dogone low that I've gotta have a little chat with ma sweetie to pick me up.

I did another big washing today. I've been trying to get things washed up so that you & mom won't have so much to do when I get home. I washed two sheets today — That's quite a job by hand isn't it.

They had a stage show here last night. A limey show but it wasn't too bad. Lotsa funny stories. Not too nice perhaps — but funny. We're in a funny state of mind now. It takes very little to amuse us and we laugh uproarously at the most inane things. Guess that's just another form of "nerves."

I got to thinking last night about my state of mind toward our parents & came to the conclusion that it was a rather adolecent attitude. I started figuring just how long it will be before we'll have a home of our own where we can take all our junk and really make the break away from home and I came to the conclusion that it will be several years at least before we can possibly hope for a home of our own and complete independence. I guess it is a personal natural reaction after all I've put up with from your dad — from the time I first started going with you — that I should want you to myself and no longer responsible to him. Particularly in view of the attitude he has taken a couple of times toward you. I was thinking particularly of that time a year ago when he had it out with you about late hours. I was so mad that day that if I'd seen him I think he probably would have had a fight on his hands. In spite of all that — he was probably right. That's one reason probably why I was so mad. Naturally when a thing like that happens I want to do all I can to shield you from such a thing and so my attitude is isolation. Isolation — I'm afraid — is no more likely to work in our attitude toward our parents than in the world situation and I guess this is probably the first time I've really tried to think it all thru. Perhaps I was just afraid of what thinking it thru might lead to.

At any rate I'm of the opinion that from now on my attitude is going to continue to be one of patience & understanding because no matter what our age or what our mode of living — unless we adopt hermitage — we will constantly have to make allowances for the thoughts and feelings and desires and wishes of those who surround us. Not always easy particularly after being away from people for a long time but I'm sure that with the proper attitude of mind on my part and with a little moral support from you everything ought to be much better and our adolecent viewpoint will soon be forgotten or outgrown.

Gosh I didn't mean to get so windy on the subject but that's the way it goes. I've got some other things to say but they can wait till later. Some of these thoughts I want to get in concrete form so I wont forget them.

By sweets —
I love you so
Jack

March 23
Friday—

Dear,

Three weeks in this place now. You've probably gotten the letters I mailed when I first got here by now and have been sweating me out all this time. But you know the army darling, we have no way of knowing what the big picture is or why there is all this delay but no day lasts forever darling, and if I'm not with you for my birthday or to show you off in the Easter Parade — well then I'll be home in time for Tommy's birthday (April 17) or to celebrate our anniversary (June 10). The days seem to never end darling and now — the nights are almost the same. I've caught up on most of my sleep and I lie awake a lot — thinking and dreaming. And you're always there with me my darling. As you said in your letter (Jan 22) at the time of day or rather nite when that consummation was realized — those thoughts crowd out all others. Yes my darling — you're always there. Maybe taking a shower with your hair all up in that ungodly bathing cap, washing my back for me and letting me wash yours. And not minding if I get a little sidetracked and wash your beautiful breasts or your tummy. And looking up at me out of the corner of your eye and saying "yes darling — I'm all yours — always." And giggling a little when I kiss the curls at the back of your neck — the ones that didn't get tucked in. And then when we're out of the shower and still all wet and you just seem to melt into my arms and kiss me with your whole soul. No wonder I get a little excited. Even now as I write this Junior begins to assert himself and I imagine when we're sitting in our own little house and we read these letters together — he might assert himself more purposely.

And then as we get ready for bed and tumble in together and just lie there in each others arms for a minute I know that all my life I'd waited to do that — with you. It somehow seems so right and natural that I have never had a feeling of selfconscienceness with you. Which is unusual considering my lack of experience in bedside etiquette. But with you there has never been any pretending or false modesty or shame. We understand each others' physical makeup and respect it as natural and perfect. We love each other so completely and so wholly that it seems right and natural that we should be lying there in each others arms. And when our little love play is over and we're both a little spent but so completely satisfied and so much more in love than before and when you lean over and kiss me goodnight it's always the face of an angel who tells me she loves me — just before I drop off to sleep. Darling — Our Heavenly Father has been awfully kind to loan you to me for a while — I only hope I can live up to your expectations and to His — and with a little boost from Him now & then and a lot of help from you I think we'll make Him proud of us.

Goodnight now my darling
I love you so.
Jack

This is the Army, Mr. Fisher. We spent days and weeks just waiting for something to happen. I guess probably the worst part of it was the fact that the Army knew we were going home, so they were sending all our mail back. So there we sat, not only bored out of our minds because we had nothing to do, but also without any contact from home — without the precious letters which had kept me going no matter how tired I was or how terrible the things we saw and did became. So we waited. And waited. And waited. And without any work to do, all I had to do was think about Joyce and about home, which made the waiting all that much worse to endure.

March 24
Saturday nite
just before supper

Darling,
I'm so low tonight. I don't know of any reason in particular except that I'm getting so unbearably lonesome for you I can't think of anything else day or night except getting home to you — and we still aren't alerted. I was pretty sure we'd be alerted today and so it was really quite a blow. I know I shouldn't worry about it because I know that although you are a little impatient probably — by now — you'll always be waiting for me but darling — I'm so lonesome.
You see no matter what I do these last few days my thoughts are constantly with you. I'll be standing in a mess line — looking at nothing in particular and seeing your sweet face & the guy behind me will give me a gentle shove to remind me that he wants something to eat — even if I don't. It's embarrassing — that's what it is. I can't keep my mind on a bridge game for more than about 1 rubber and from then on I'm entirely lost with you somewhere. Sometimes doing something in particular like necking on a mexican blanket while Buck & Barb chase each other around the bushes, or maybe being close to each other in a hayloft out at Gatewood's or walking by the creek at Mt Vernon & sitting on a log or necking in your parlor after a picnic and cautioning you that if you leave your shirttail out my hands will wander. Funny isn't it — the things a fellow remembers when he's lonesome and blue.
Every picture is oh so realistic my darling — each incident is so vivid in my mind as though you were right here in the room. I can see you in A.J. hotel in Rapid City. Lying there with your legs all wrapped up and so mad you couldn't talk because of that rash. I guess you didn't see how I could possibly love you like that but maybe someday I can make you understand that no matter what the minor inconvenience may be — whether rash — or a full moon or no matter

what — I love you just as much. In fact I don't really know how deeply I do love you until some time like that when I can find myself completely unaware of whatever it is that's wrong. It's just that I love you so very much darling that little difficulties just help to intensify that love.

Darling — I'll never forget that afternoon. You couldn't take a shower because of the rash and so we helped each other take a sponge bath and then when we were all sweet and clean we climbed back into bed and kissed each other all over. I remember how you held me ever so tenderly and said "Darling — isn't it marvelous — that's where all our babies will come from. Our babies that we've always wanted." You have the most wonderful light in your eyes darling when you say something like that. It is as though you have just made a remarkable discovery which shall change the course of the world. I guess maybe I'm just sentimental but those things make a tremendous impression on me darling. Guess it's because I love you so doggone much.

Your own husband —
Jack

Sunday nite
March 25

Hello my darling,

Here's the luckiest man in the world to tell you how he spent his 22nd birthday. I'm no longer — just barely a man —, darling — but well started in my twenties and what a beautiful life I see ahead of me with you by my side.

It rained nearly all night last night — especially along towards morning. A nice soft spring rain that made everything look so clean and nice. It was still raining when I got up at 7:30 for breakfast but stopped soon afterwards and began to clear up. I went to church this morning — Palm Sunday — and we had a rather nice service. The music wasn't all that could be desired but we had a pretty good sermon and that redeemed it. Otherwise it was a rather usual day. We had a nice dinner — baked ham and mashed potatoes. This afternoon I went to the show "Each Dawn I die" with Jimmy Cagney. Pretty good but not nearly as nice and warm as "Eve of St Mark" that I saw yesterday.

I read a couple of books tonight and now I'm just about ready to hit the old sack. Of course it wasn't a perfect birthday darling. How could it be without you to make it so — but somehow just the knowledge that you are there waiting for me eases that pain a little. Cause I know, darling, that you're mine and mine alone and nothing — not even a couple thousand miles of ocean can change that deep abiding love which makes our union such a comfort to us both.

> *Oh I got trials*
> *And I got woes*
> *And I got heartaches*
> *Here below*
> *And while God leads me*
> *I'll never fear*
> *For I am sheltered*
> *By all his care*

I don't know why I wrote that — it just sorta popped into my head just then & I almost sang it out loud.

Yes dearest — I'm a lucky man to have such a beautiful wife who loves me so much and to whom I can return that love.

What more could a man possibly want.
Your 22 yr old husband
Jack

Finally it was my turn to board the troop ship which would take me home. Because of the war, many fancy cruise liners were commandeered by the government to aid in the war effort. We had been waiting so long because the ship had to deliver the load of soldiers ahead of us to New York and then come back across for our group. But, finally, she arrived and we boarded the ship, then waited for the proper tide to get us underway. After over a month of waiting, I was finally on my way home.

April 2nd
Monday nite

Dearest —
I missed you so terribly yesterday. I had wanted to be with you on our first Easter so very much but that's the way it goes. I spent most of the day going to church. In the morning we had a regular Easter

service with a sermon & everything and then last night we had a band concert by the USAAF band. It was a very nice concert with mostly religious music and a few hymns & afterwards there was a communion service. The first time I've ever held communion in the middle of the Atlantic Ocean.

    I've been so terribly lonesome the last few days I hardly know what to do. We left port last Thursday nite. We had been on board since Wednesday morning so we were pretty anxious to move. As I said we got under way in the evening and we went to bed pretty early. The next morning it was awfully rough and although your hubby didn't get sick — he didn't feel too sharp. So — I kept pretty well to my sack all day & by Saturday I was feeling pretty swell. Not as well as I would on good dry land — but well-enough.

    Since then I've been spending most my days & nights on or near the sack — catching up on my sleep ya know——

    I've been reading two or three books a day. This afternoon I read Flood of Spring — by the same author as Kings Row. Not a bad book and not nearly as sordid as Kings Row but rather stimulating sexually. Gosh darling — If I don't get home to you pretty soon I don't know what I'll do. I hope this separation hasn't been as hard for you to bear as it has for me because if it has I feel very sorry for you. As I look back now I can see how I always had the strength of moral purpose to keep on the beaten track and not wander off on some enticing bypath but I know that it was you and you alone who's kept me clean. It has always been you darling. My training at home or in scouts would have failed me many times had it not been for you —

    Just got back from another concert by the band. They're really good and it helped a lot to settle my nerves & ease off some steam. Boy I've sure been building it up lately. I'm fraid if I don't get home pretty soon I'll burst.

    Darling I've been thinking of so many things that I'd like to do when I get home. When we go up to Cornell — I'd kinda like to go on up to Ames for a few hours & see some of the boys and how the school is getting along. I want to take you out for a drive some pretty night up to Riverside Park and wouldn't it be fun to have a real old necking party like we used to. And if the cops came along we could say — go away & leave my wife and I alone — we're reminiscing.

The Lucky Bastard Club

    Joyce my own today is Monday and by Sunday you should be in my arms. I guess this is probably the last letter I'll have time to write but before I close I want you to know dear that thru this medium of letters I've been able to keep so close to you that in times of stress when I think I can't go on — a few lines to you about my troubles always seems to help out. It's just like a goodnite kiss before we go to sleep. Regardless of little differences or troubles during the day — that goodnight kiss reminds us both that our love is big enough to overlook such trifles. And now my own sweet wife,
    Goodnight — Sweet dreams —
I love you
Your husband
Jack

Roy R. Fisher, Jr. with Susan Fisher Anderson

Spring, 1945
Reunited at last

Finally honeymooning
with my beautiful
bride, 1946
Mexico, left
Texas, below

Epilogue

You've heard about a "slow boat to China," well, the boat we took home from England in March of 1945 seemed much slower. We traveled in style, on the Queen Elizabeth, and since it only took us five days, I'm sure our crossing of the Atlantic was not the slowest in history. But to a lonely boy on his way home to his loving wife, it sure seemed that way. I hopped the train to Davenport, and when I first laid my eyes on Joyce's sparkly blues, it only reinforced my vow to never let her out of my sight again. And I haven't for 59 years.

The war in Europe ended the month after I got home, and I spent the remainder of my tour in Memphis checking in B-17's and ferrying them around the country to their final resting places. Many of them ended up carrying fire retardant to fight forest fires for the Forestry Service or in the private sector, since they were such sturdy birds and so versatile. Joyce and I finished college at Iowa State. She wanted to try out for the cheerleading squad so I went along to watch. Since they needed a man to be the head cheerleader, I was drafted (again) and we became the first married cheerleaders at Iowa State.

After graduation, we traveled around the country a little and soon settled down back in Davenport, where I joined my dad in the Real Estate business. Joy, our first of seven daughters was born in February, 1948, to be followed by a brother, Roy Robert Fisher III — who died of leukemia at the age of seven — and six more girls, Susan, Carol, Rebecca, Molly, Lucy and Anne. They live all over the United States, New York, Wisconsin, Indiana and Texas, and have blessed us with 24 grandchildren and 8 great-grandchildren.

Young people are full of dreams and goals, and probably the most wonderful thing about our life together — Joyce's and mine — is seeing those dreams come to pass and those goals realized. Especially now, as we see our children having children and grandchildren; and we see the values and standards we tried so hard to maintain repeated in our progeny, and in theirs. We didn't do everything right — we'd be the first to admit it. But the heritage of our parents and grandparents, the faith and love we inherited, the freedom we sacrificed so much to preserve is reflected in the lives of

Roy R. Fisher, Jr. with Susan Fisher Anderson

Jack's 80th birthday party with all the girls, March, 2003
From left, Molly, Rebecca, Joyce, Jack, Anne, Lucy.
Back row: Carol, Susie, Joy.
(Photo by Penny Rathbun, *The Celina Record*)

The Lucky Bastard Club

our children. And there is no greater joy than to watch them teach these things to the next generation.

Today, a new millennium has come and we are old and gray. We don't get around so fast as we used to, but we still hold on to the unshakable truths we learned at home as children: God, family, country. The life we planted with love on June 10, 1944 has grown into a mighty tree and, even after almost 60 years of marriage, we still hold hands when we walk down the street — and not because we need the support! Joyce's eyes still sparkle like they did when she was 16, and my heart swelled with pride when she processed with her class to receive her second master's degree — at the tender age of 65.

I didn't talk much about the war when the girls were growing up. They knew I had been a pilot and flown 35 missions in a B-17, but not much detail. I think it is hard for lots of guys to talk about the horrible things they had to see and do during wartime. War is a living hell that makes boys into men — often against their will and without their knowledge or consent. We kept in touch as a crew through the years, even with the spouses of those crew members who were no longer with us. We had our most recent reunion in 2001. In fact, it was in preparation for one of those reunions that led me to write down my recollections of our tour, mission by mission, often referring to the letters Joyce had saved for all these years.

When we moved to Celina in 1996, we got involved in substitute teaching in all levels from grade school to senior high. I began to share some of my recollections with the students — what do you do in French Class when you don't speak a word of French? The rapt attention and enthusiastic response of the students encouraged me to compile a written record of my experiences. After all, "Those who fail to remember the past are doomed to repeat it." I also found my children — and especially my grandsons were fascinated by my life as a pilot. And so the story grew, with help from my crewmembers, who remembered things I had forgotten, and related stories I had never heard — like the ninth wave.

Though some of the fellows have gone on, we still try to keep in touch with those who remain. The bonds forged in the furnace of war are strong.

Roy R. Fisher, Jr. with Susan Fisher Anderson

Author/Editor's Note

When I first received my copy of "the book" from my dad, the note attached said, "Here it is, 19 pages, I don't know if there will be more." As I read through his brief outline of his experiences during the war, I told myself, yes there would be more. Much more.

Dad didn't talk much about the war as we were growing up. It was past and he had moved on with his life. I think, though, that as much as he tried to put it behind him, it was always there. What he went through as a young man, slightly more than a teenager, had done much to shape his character and his life. As we grew and began to have children of our own, my sons began to ask him questions about life in the war. He told a few stories, but nothing of this magnitude. In fact, until I got that first book in 1999, I didn't even know that Mom had saved all his letters. It was with those letters that my journey and this project began.

As a baby boomer, the only war I knew personally was Viet Nam, an unpopular, undeclared conflict which did more to divide this nation than bring us together. Then, in the television series M.A.S.H., many of us got our first glimpse of war, its personal impact on normal people, and the patriotism necessary to survive it. As I read about WWII and the state of the world during the decade of the 40's, I began to wonder what my own father had experienced and how it had affected him. I was determined to write a book about his life and times in the war, and how it had shaped him as a man. I had no idea the changes it would make in me.

My daughter, now grown with a baby of her own, made copies of all the letters and I started to write the book. I soon realized that this book was not mine to write, Dad had written it already. Every day— almost— in a letter to his young bride, Dad, nicknamed Jack before he was born, had painted a picture of a lonely husband doing his duty, far from home. It would only need a little explanation here, a little fleshing out there—in addition to the letters—to tell the story. So I began. I soon realized that the letters themselves were so powerful that I decided to weave the rest of the story around Dad's first-hand account.

From Jack's Senior Pilot log book, pre-combat – Above.
Below – the next page, after his first mission

As I read the letters and transcribed them, often unable to put them down, I found myself captivated by their story—their love, which had begun in high school and blossomed in the hot house of world war. I saw my dad—dark wavy hair, sharp and confident, and totally swept off his feet by the new girl in town. As I investigated the story, grilling them to fill in the details of their life before the letters started, I saw him woo her and win her. Then I saw my parents as young newlyweds torn apart, but remaining true to each other and to the faith and standards they held dear.

I also saw the cost of war and the magnitude of its effects on one young man. Putting the letters together with his missions, I spent many hours poring over his pilot's logbook. What I saw surprised me. As each page of the logbook was filled, he had to sign his name. That wasn't surprising in itself, until I really looked at the signatures. His early signatures were written in a manner which, though not worthy of an A in penmanship, were still legible. Beginning with the first page after he began combat, the signature was the same as it is today: three vertical lines with a loop on each end – indecipherable – the impatient scrawl of a man with work to do, and a lot on his mind. I felt both sad and proud.

What emerged as I typed in letter after letter — verbatim, including spelling errors, intentional and otherwise — was a vivid portrait of a fellow, barely more than a kid, who was ordered to do a man's job. His tools were not only his airplane and training, but also his faith, his character, his sense of humor, and—most of all—his deep and abiding love for a cute little, blue-eyed brunette—his wife, my mother, Joyce. As I typed, I learned more and more about my father, and much to my surprise, about my mother. I had originally thought that this book would be about him, my dad, 1st Lt. Roy R. Fisher, Jr. But, as the pages came together, I realized that this book isn't just about him. It's about them, and especially her, my mother.

In my training for the theatre one of the skills of character development they teach is to learn about your character, not just by reading his lines, but also by studying what the other characters say about and to him. I never really knew my mom very well. What child really does? After all, our whole lives are defined as a step by step separation from our mothers. Birth, weaning, potty training, school, dating, driving, moving out — they all define the level of our maturity by the level of separation from our mothers. All my life I was, and I think many or most of us were, more concerned about separating from her than in getting to know her.

What a tragedy that would have been. I only knew Joyce as my mother: making rules, asking me to baby-sit my little sisters—I was the second of seven, driving 60 miles to college (when I was in high school) and running my car out of oil; and now at 78 moving slower, taking medication and spending a lot of time going to the doctor. I never knew her as she really is, bright, pretty, funny and smarter than anybody my dad ever met, and he's met a lot of folks in his 80 years. It took seeing her through his eyes for me to open mine and see this woman whom I resemble so much. Only a few months ago I was embarrassed to see her looking back at me from my mirror, or to see her hands at the ends of my arms. Now I am so very proud, of her, of what she has accomplished, of who she is and who she has raised and encouraged me to be.

Their lives have not been without tragedy; my brother died suddenly of cancer when I was only five. But, still, the unshakable character of my parents held true. We never had a lot of money, but we were always loved, and always called to a higher standard of conduct and character than many of our friends in the 60's and 70's. We had curfews, we had rules, we even had chores — with a family the size of ours, we had to help out. But we also learned to laugh, to sing together, and to rely on each other for support and encouragement.

When I moved to Celina a few months ago it was, originally, to help my sister care for them as they grew older. We, the seven of us, were determined to keep them together instead of putting them in a nursing home — as their doctor was recommending. Yes, they depend on each other. Yes, there are things they can no longer do for themselves. But what most people don't know about them is that they truly are one: spirit, soul and body; inseparable, devoted, and deeply in love. They are best friends — still, after nearly 60 years of marriage. I have begun to realize, finally comprehend, the depth of their love and, more than that, their unwavering commitment to each other. And, that is what marriage is all about. I can only hope to pass on such a legacy to my children. Yes, they are my parents, but in the last few months they also have become, more than ever before, my role models, my mentors, my confidants and my dear friends.

This book was created as an attempt to get it all down before the stories were gone forever. It is my hope that our readers will be inspired to learn their own histories first hand, from parents and grandparents who still live. Do it now, today, because, after the funeral — and it will come sooner or later — it will be too late.

Finally, I want to say, Thanks, Mom and Dad for who you are and for giving yourselves so unselfishly for us.

Susan Fisher Anderson

Roy R. Fisher, Jr. with Susan Fisher Anderson

To Our Readers

War is fought by young men, often interrupting the prime of their lives. In that sense, every war is similar. The thoughts, emotions and effects are the same, no matter which war. In every generation those who believe in the right are called to defend it, sometimes at great cost to themselves. Freedom isn't free, and it doesn't come cheap. Take every opportunity to express your gratitude to the ones who go into harm's way in defense of your liberty. And to all you who are veterans or current military, Thank you for serving. Your effort and sacrifices are not unnoticed. May God richly bless you for your devotion to duty.

We know many of you have stories of your own, or have parents or grandparents whose stories you may not know. We encourage you to talk about the past and learn from it as if the future depended on it, because it does.

We hope you have enjoyed this book, and would love to hear from you. You may write to us at:

Roy R. Fisher, Jr.
P.O. Box 1207
Celina, Texas 75009

Or email:SFA77@earthlink.net
(Please put "Lucky Bastard Club" in the subject box)

Printed in the United States
28719LVS00005B/64-147